THE SALVAGE CREW

YUDHANJAYA WIJERATNE

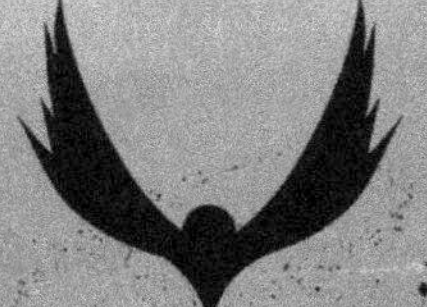

www.aethonbooks.com

THE SALVAGE CREW

Aethon Books
PO Box 121515
Fort Worth TX, 76108
www.aethonbooks.com

Print and eBook formatting by Steve Beaulieu. Artwork provided by **Stuart Lippincott**.

Published by Aethon Books LLC. 2020

FOREWORD

Much of the poetry you see in this book is actually AI-generated. To wit, OpenAI GPT2-117M,[1] trained on a selection of my favourite translated poetry—notably the ancient Chinese Tang Dynasty poets Du Fu and Li Bai. I've performed some minor editing—sometimes stitching poems together, sometimes editing a word or two in a poem—but let me assure you that I was more surprised than you were at gems like "maidenhood is done away with the midnight bell."

The planet of Urmagon Beta does not exist. It was created by my modified version of Zarkonnen's planet generator code.[2] You can see a live demo on itch.io if you look for it: it's beautiful.

The weather, I suppose, could also be called "AI-generated," but let's shy away from that term for things that don't learn. The weather system is a simple Markov chain; a series of states and transitions encoded, with the equivalent of a die roll at each transition.[3] Probability of rain, sir?—rolls digital die—none, but we're having snow. The characters' emotional states, too, were designed this way, as were various events. I wrote the whole thing, but I didn't decide when Milo and Anna had those fights.

So this book represents something of a technical innovation to me, one step further along my adherence to chess grandmaster Garry

Kasparov's Human + AI thesis.[4] Kasparov, who got his ass kicked by IBM's Deep Blue, knows firsthand what it's like to be beaten by a machine; the arts, once considered immune, are now slowly waking up to the reality of neural nets and a weekend with Tensorflow and a good dataset.

Welcome to the future? No, welcome to the present. If anything, I'm quite behind the field. We all are.

This book, and the books that follow, are an homage to Richard Garriot, Will Wright, Tarn Adams, Tynan Sylvester, and all others who pursued the Simulation Dream.

Loosely, it is this: it should be possible to create a world, with enough systems—people, weather, objects—interacting with each other to generate complex stories, that most sacred lifeblood of the human race. Tynan Sylvester, writing on the subject,[5] spoke of apophenia, the phenomenon where the fantastic pattern-recognition in our brains stitches together random incidents to create a meaningful narrative: which explains, if you stretch the idea a bit, how a lot of religions came to be. The same wetware phenomena that drove people to write Boatmurdered generates the gods, monsters and demons that we live amongst.

Of course, these worthies applied this thinking to games. You may have heard of them: *Ultima Online, The Sims, Dwarf Fortress, RimWorld.* There are others.

I started chasing this dream; for a few months I pursued the idea of creating an engine that could let me simulate characters, worlds, everything. But, reader, I gave up. That way lay a substandard clone of *RimWorld,* and quite possibly five years of bashing my head into a wall.

However, a few months of research is a considerable time. I ended up with the ingredients I wanted: a planet generator (thanks, Zarkonnen!), and Markov chains for weather simulation and emotion; a poetry generator that I eventually gave an Instagram account to;[6] and, from my childhood, "Ulysses," by Alfred, Lord Tennyson, whose words I learned from *The Golden Treasury of English Verse*. That poem never really went away, but kept repeating itself in my dreams as a starship casting off into the depths of space.

By now my own sense of apophenia had kicked in like a mule—and we were off—I, the writer, and my assistants in the form of little pieces of Python code. This approach, of course, will be outdated by the time you read this book, so now I have to do something more interesting for the next one.

The rest of it arrived as it usually does: in fragments picked up from my other interests. I thought a little bit about how an alien AI would communicate, and how best to put that in a story in a way that didn't sound like endless tables of character vectors: I ended up taking the language games from Wittgenstein,[7] arguably the most important philosopher of the twentieth century, and the right person to read if you want to get right down into language. The opening sequence of the AMBER ROSE-Beacon conversation I took from mathematician Carl DeVito and linguist R. T. Oehrle, who took a crack at examining a language for communication between alien societies.[8] While I didn't use their language, I used their base assumptions:

1. Both societies can count and do arithmetic.
2. Both societies recognize the chemical elements and the periodic table.
3. Both have made a quantitative study of the states of matter.
4. Both know enough chemistry to carry out chemical calculations.

And of course, my publishers, Steve and Rhett, my writing partners R. R. Virdi and Navin Weeraratne, and data scientist Yasiru Dhanike Ratnayake not only put up with me gabbing about all this stuff, but also understood what I was trying to do and helped keep the fire going. I took a fair bit of patience from them.

Double, double, toil and trouble, fire burn, and cauldron bubble! And voila: the text you're reading now appeared. Pop. Fwoosh.

But enough of all these explanations. At the end of the day, yes, I wanted to be smart and wild and bleeding edge about how I went about all this, but I also wanted to tell a story. About three humans and a less-than-Zen AI stuck on a backwater planet. Of the UN and the ORCA and all the other things that I couldn't code, except by wrapping them up in the symbols of English and throwing them out here for you to taste.

I hope you enjoyed it. The next book will come, you can bet anything you have that the games aren't stopping here.

— Yudhanjaya Wijeratne,

Colombo, Sri Lanka, 14th July, 2019.

[1]

I want to make one thing clear: I did not, I repeat NOT, ask for any of this.

I did NOT ask to be promoted.

I did NOT ask to be made Overseer.

And I certainly did not ask to be strapped down in this tin-can body of a drop pod, hurtling down with three idiots screaming their lungs out inside me.

The Company promised me an A-Team. The kind of people Joe Haldeman wrote about in *The Forever War*. Astrophysicists who could blow a man's head off at five hundred meters. The best of the best—you know, the Master Chiefs and all that. The kind of people who go in, get shit done, leave a nice calling card, and live to strike a heroic pose.

Did we get what it said on the label? Well, let's look around.

Exhibit A: Simon Joosten. Simon is my geologist. He's thirty-five-ish, biological time, and looks like someone stuck eyeballs on a mop. They told me Simon would be reliable—he's good at everything to do with rocks and earthquakes; he's scored well in the shooting sims, can do CPR and basic medical aid, and looks like your average nerd trying too hard to be cool. He'll make a fine crewmember.

But here's what they didn't tell me. Simon grew up on the brutal world of Old New York. He was sold to a corporation as a child. They stuck a needle into the center of his brainstem and jacked him into a virtual fantasy world so they could broadcast his feed as reality TV. His entire childhood was spent being beaten up by gangs and digging holes in fake ground so nobody could hear him crying in the fake darkness—except for the audience, of course, who must have had a hoot, the sick bastards.

Old New York had its times: after the Mercator/Rissek Rebellion, the UN jumped in and did a number on them. Including yanking all those poor souls out of reality TV and setting them free. For some reason, I don't think this man ever really recovered.

I'm not saying Simon is a bad person. I'm saying what doesn't kill you makes you stranger. I'm saying a traumatized reality TV slave-star is the last person I want dropped into an unexplored planet on my first landing mission.

Exhibit B: Anna Agarwal.

Anna is an odd fish. She's got twenty years on Simon. But unlike Simon, Anna grew up with everything she ever wanted. I've checked her degree transcripts. They're through the roof. High social skills. And then somewhere along the line she decided to ditch everything and become an Army doctor.

Doesn't compute. You know why it doesn't compute? Because Anna Agarwal doesn't exist. I don't know who the hell this person is, but the real Anna Agarwal, as verified by her gene sample, died on the microplanet Wayward Child. This imposter, let's call her Fake-Anna, showed up on Arjuna III and has been hopping planets ever since, always moving outwards. Deus Olympus. Boatmurdered. Karthika Highway. This kind of stuff is real easy when delays between databases are measured in light-years. Fake-Anna picked up a gunshot wound somewhere on the way. Left leg. And now she's on my mission, on the very edge of human space.

Right now she's cradling Simon as he screams, which, excuse me, Anna, is the stupidest fucking thing you can do while strapped inside a tin can plummeting through atmosphere. Dammit, Anna. Go back to your seat.

Exhibit C: Milo Kalik. Finally, a sane choice. Milo, thirty-seven, is an inventor. He can shoot, yes, but also make stuff and argue Machiavelli and Chanakya by the fireside. Master's degree in engineering from the Oort Academy. There are some irregularities; he's been demoted three times so far—each time by a woman commander; that's odd. And he's spent a weird amount of time in cryosleep—almost three centuries. But right now I don't have much to go on, so he's my golden boy. Look at him smile. He's enjoying this. He's enjoying being alive after all that time in the freezer. Don't let me down, Milo.

Simon pukes all over him. All over me. Oh, Gods.

This isn't an A-Team. This is a D-Team with a paintjob. The real heroes are probably out somewhere in the Inner Rim, discovering alien civilizations while looking heroic in their armor. Me, I get the backwater planet and the salvage job. Go dig up an old crash site, they said. It'll be fun, they said.

Which brings us to myself.

I'm the drop pod.

Yes, go ahead, laugh. I'm a 4.4-ton safety capsule hurtling through a sky the color of topaz. Inside, I'm a state-of-the-art computer equipped with weapons, seed stock, building materials, people. And, of course, myself, to instruct the baselines how to do their job. In turn, the theory goes, the humans ask the right questions, make the right pseudorandom moves, nudge your thinking in all the right ways—ways that a machine can't. Humans evolved to survive, and they're fantastically good at it. The combination of myself and a human crew is supposed to make us better, faster, a little more chaotic, yes, but a lot more survivable.

This is what happens when PCS thinks you're smart enough to be an Overseer. You end up knee-deep in theory with Simon's puke all over your instrument panels.

For fuck's sake, Anna, strap yourself in.

It's going to be a bumpy ride.

[2]

You know those weird little directorial gimmicks old filmmakers used to pull? Record scratch, freeze frame. Cue narrator. So you're wondering how I ended up here.

I feel like pulling one of those now. Mostly to stop thinking about how my hull temperature is over 1800 Kelvin right now. One panel out of place and we all cook in here.

Once upon a time, I used to have eyes and hands and feet, like these three idiots. I joined PCS for the same damn reasons as anyone else. Go forth into the universe. See C-beams glitter off the Tannhauser Gate. Take a selfie with attack ships off the shoulder of Orion. And if I was reasonably nice to the universe, and did my job with some baseline diligence, the universe might reward me with a planet that wasn't an overpopulated hellhole. The kind of place where you can actually see the sunset, you know, instead of skyscrapers and traffic jams. Do my time, settle down with a nice girl, maybe a cat and a few hundred acres. Karma would sort the rest out.

PCS felt like the kind of place where I might rack up some good points. I mean, look at the name. Planetary Crusade Services. End-to-end interstellar colonization support. We sound like the Pope blessed us to go conquer Space Jerusalem.

And that's how the media talked about us all the time. PCS landing parties protecting terraforming operations or Sangha chapters, holding their own against waves of xenos. PCS rescue teams patching up ships stranded in deep space. PCS scientists making new breakthroughs in gravity-drive tech. The prototypical PCS spaceman, a sort of weathered Ulysses with more worlds under their belt than they can even count, descending from on high in the nick of time to save a local government, and flying away a legend in their own time.

Except that's just the PR. PCS is a corporation, and worse, it's an interstellar corporation. Which means we need to keep our transport costs low and our margins high. PCS's actual assets are Overseers like me—digitized humans who can be beamed at light speed to a destination via the Odysseus relays, and then we're resurrected in some 3D-printed tin-can ship they've knocked up on that end. We're literally the only real asset they have. Everyone else is a hired gun picked up from the closest local system. They're paid via interstellar money transfer from the closest PCS cell, again at light speed. Really, PCS is just a software company. They get to save enormous amounts on transport costs and actually get to the target a hell of a lot faster.

So those square-jawed eagle-eyed PCS supersoldiers you see on the ads? They're just mercenaries stuffed into shiny uniforms.

Took me a while to figure this stuff out.

My first assignments were fairly simple, and they kept me out of the bigger picture. There was an abandoned station off Brutus—a methane moon next door to Cassius, where I was born; we orbited the same planet—a superJupiter-class gas giant called Caesar.

The best I know it, the UN could have gone in there, but they were cost-cutting in our system, so they contracted the job to PCS. PCS put out a call.

I'd just passed my engineering exams—not good enough to get into an off-world university, but top of the district nonetheless. I could patch a suit and take a methalox engine apart blindfolded. My ancestors had spent the last four hundred years scratching out an existence on a minor moon, so I knew a lot more about hardship than those inner colony soft toys.

I don't think my parents understood why I did. They were largely content with their lot—or resigned, I couldn't really tell. Every bad fact of our meager existence they shrugged at. *Our karma,* they'd say.

But I was tired of the cold and the random water plumes and a lifetime of fixing the farm while Caesar glared at me like some baleful god in the sky . . . no, I wanted out of there. There were more things in heaven and hell than dreamt of on those cold lands, so when the PCS call came, I took it. At some point you have to stop blaming the world and go make your own karma.

They didn't really argue, but they gave me that look, like I'd turned into a stranger overnight and they didn't quite understand me anymore. I told them to think about what they wanted to buy for the farm the next time the Market ships came around. I set their account to take my pay, minus food and lodging. And then I hightailed it out of there, and for the first time in my life, I found myself in a place where nobody knew me and nobody cared. I was free to be who I wanted to be. I was free to live. I was free to die. As long as I did my best—as long as I didn't burn too many bridges and did more good than bad—I'd come out okay.

It was liberation, in a sense. I went through my punk phase, boosting fuel cells and running races down the asteroid line. I lost my arm and got a new one. I fell in love and fell out of it. I got in with a union and negotiated better floor pay for the maintenance techs. Then I started working for a local PCS Overseer—a pretty high ranker, SILVER HYACINTH 222, a starship sent in to oversee the construction of a mining op.

I was in awe of this thing that had once been a real, live human and now was a near-immortal hulk, cruising the stars. I wasn't quite sure I liked that it used to be a person—I remember asking her once why we digitized people and didn't just use proper, intelligent AI like in the science fiction flicks. Why the rest of us stuck ourselves so dangerously close to the baseline, like monks refusing to masturbate. A whole lot of stuff that started with words like *loyalty programming* and *creationism* and *UN ethics violations* and ended with the same damn thing: cost of doing business. I nodded like I understood.

And one day I turned back to go home, and I didn't want to. I knew that to go down there to Cassius was to go down to a people who wouldn't understand what I'd become. I had spoken with starships, for God's sake. To go back to the farm was to cut out everything I'd taken in and strip myself down to something I didn't want to be anymore.

So when HYACINTH opened up a crew posting, I took it. At first I was a tech grunt doing the work she couldn't handle herself—scuttling out to fix her hull, hauling ice around, interfacing with stations, things like that. The rest of the crew were good people. They understood.

But eventually your body breaks down. Too much radiation damage. Too much time spent in zero g. Eventually you look around and realize that all the old faces you came with are dead or gone on to lives elsewhere, and all these new faces are looking at you impatiently, wondering when the old man will finally give up and let them get on with it. Eventually, HYACINTH sent three people to my room, and they shoved a contract in my face.

"You're Nyogi Buddhist, yes?" they said. "Don't think of it as dying. Think of it as rebirth."

When I woke up, I was no longer human.

HYACINTH never apologized. I think, in her own way, she was fond of me, and this was her way of keeping me around. I was now an Overseer, albeit a minor one. AMBER ROSE 348. Property of PCS. Someday I might be given a real body myself. Turns out the old adage about not being able to choose your next life applies even if you're software.

I asked HYACINTH what kept her going. She pointed me to a particular clause in our contract. As long as we never, ever get caught by a rival corporation—especially the Enterprise lot—there's the promise of a world out there that's just right for you, an Eden among the stars. And there we can sit and watch the sunset until we rust away, while another version of you goes onwards.

HYACINTH was searching for a hill to die on. She just wanted some company on the way there.

Ashes to ashes, stardust to stardust.

[3]

Right, so we've landed.

Okay, I admit, landed is a bit of a stretch. I was aiming for the nice prefab structure we sent down a week ago, but I hit a pocket of hot air on the way down. Spun a bit. Hit a few—birds? Octopi? Things? on the way down. Right now we've hit a bit of foresty patch, right in the middle of some small hills, about a few miles from the actual landing site. About a day from the ocean, which I've decided to call Ocean, because it's too early to start naming everything and it bloody well can't complain. It's a patch of water washing up to a black sand beach. Fight me, you horrible wet thing.

Still, it's not that bad. Urmagon Beta is a fine planet. Temperate. Standard sun, G-type main sequence, maybe a bit yellowish on account of how it's only 0.83 solar masses—but otherwise perfectly serviceable. It'll do its thing for at least seven billion more years, and after that you want to check the warranty and take it in for servicing. Between us and this thing are two moons—we'll get to them later—and an atmosphere, which we just came through and I'm not feeling too charitable about, but quite breathable: 19% oxygen. About 60% nitrogen. A lot of argon, which does absolutely fuck all, but not enough carbon dioxide to kill anyone. 290 Kelvin.

The ground is dark and craggy, all mountains and jagged edges. The trees are suspiciously large, with dark green, almost black leaves, but otherwise nothing like the nightmares cooked up by the simulation runs.

A hundred years ago, an Old Earth colony ship crash-landed on this planet. One of the Project Gilgamesh ships. On the way down, it threw out a terraformer, which telemetry tells us is halfway on the other side of the planet by now, happily analyzing the local biosphere and doing with trees and bacteria what the UNSC *Cortez* did to the Xiao-Ancellus homeworld fifty years ago. Its legacy is what remains here: a local biosphere almost completely scrubbed dry, leaving behind just the safe and the sterile stuff.

You could, of course, point out that this is a really unfortunate analogy. The Xiao-Ancellus shelling was what made the Outer Reaches Colonial Association go from being "hardheaded lobbyists with some unsettling mercenary power" to full-on military insurgency overnight. The *Cortez* was found ripped half apart, drifting into the nearest UN station with its crew's vacuum-frozen innards painting the interior. And that was just the bloody nose that started the whole UN-ORCA war.

But as far as we're concerned, none of that exists. We're here on a standard job, the kind PCS does for loose change. The Hyperion Museum of Interstellar History is paying us top space dollar to come to this little backwater and have a look at this downed ship. We find the pieces from orbit, scuttle down here, recover whatever's useful, and haul it back to base. Once we're done assessing weight and value and all that crap, our ship pulls us and everything useful up, and away we go.

There's just the little problem of us being fifty miles off where the first piece should be.

Oh well. We can do this. The crew is ready. Protocol 3. Suits on. Helmets on. Emergency hatch blown open. Milo is first out the door. He strikes a grand pose for my cameras.

"One small step for a man, one giant step for mankind!" he chirrups.

Anna scowls. "This isn't the landing site."

WE'RE ABOUT FIFTY MILES DUE SOUTH, I say. TURBULENCE.

Nobody's solved turbulence yet. On his deathbed, Heisenberg, the great physicist, was asked what he might say to God if he saw Him. "I'm going to ask Him two questions," said Heisenberg. "Why relativity? And why turbulence?"

I think that's fair.

Anna looks irritated. "So what's the plan?"

SAME AS WHAT WE WOULD HAVE DONE EVEN IF WE'D HIT THE LANDING SITE. SET UP A BASE. MAP OUT THE REST OF THE WRECKAGE. IT'LL JUST TAKE US A LITTLE BIT LONGER. GO TO PROTOCOL 3.

She barks assent and begins moving, opening the hatches on my side. The armor panels slide out so they can be used as building material. Inside are weapons, food rations, water. She straps on a cutting torch and tosses another to Milo. They begin cutting more armor panels away, exposing more solar cells. I unfold, like some kind of two-ton metal tree stretching out its leaves, and catch the sunlight. The tingle of voltage runs through my cells.

Ah.

I kick in my own version of Protocol 3 and unleash a small drone. That gives me a limited bird's-eye view of us. So far so good. Next: several dozen samplers.

Only Simon is left inside my bay, clutching a rifle. I didn't notice him reaching for it, but instinct must have kicked in. He looks green.

SIMON, I say carefully. SIMON.

He looks up.

PROTOCOL 3, SIMON.

Simon flees.

When the first colony ships hit the very first habitable worlds, they had absolutely no idea how to react. We gave speeches. We marveled at alien sunsets. We went out looking for alien lizards, hoping to get some concrete answers to the Fermi paradox.

But after the ill-fated sixth UN colonial expedition was chewed up by a passing lizard while they were staring at a sunset, we decided to get our shit together.

Space is large. It's not friendly. It's not meant to be. When you're ten light-years away from the nearest settlement, you don't get to call home and tell mum and the commander you're donating body parts to the local fauna and flora. Which is why Protocol 3 exists. Roughly, it's:

Land. Try not to go splat on the ground. Try not to land in the ocean.

Set up the BSE3, or BASE, as we call it. The BSE is a slow but ridiculously hardy 3D printer. Into it goes whatever you can find—rocks, earth, the bones of dead lizards. Out of it comes neat prepackaged blocks that fit tightly together.

Stack these in whatever way is optimal, make shelter. Get inside before night falls. Set up a base station with energy, sensor arrays, production capability. Anything and everything else can wait until you have absolute security in a ten-mile radius.

The Overseer (that's me) is responsible for the lookout. And keeping an eye on everyone and everything in general. Always. Obey. The Overseer. The Overseer is Good. The Overseer is Kind. And when you return, the Overseer's report is what determines your pay, so for all points and purposes, the Overseer is your personal karma. Don't fuck with it.

Milo, Simon and Fake-Anna have spent some time in cryosleep with these instructions slowly being burned into their minds. If they do this right, we're good. Promotions all around.

The first order of business is to establish a safe perimeter. Which, for me, is to get more drones in the air. My main battery is a Damayanti Small-Arms Nuclear P3. It'll last for years but only provide a trickle charge for me to stay alive and run the BASE. Beyond that, I can support only three small drones or one of the long-range recon jobs.

I opt for the three. Combing in a hex pattern, I build up a map of our environs. We appear to have dropped into a sort of depression, ringed to the northeast with hills, and around with plains. The downed colony ship activated its terraformers before fizzling out, and in fact, one of them is running somewhere due north. The result is that the dark earth has been overlaid with a kind of long, wet grass. Grass . . . grass . . . hill . . . cluster of weird trees, sort of like overgrown bellflowers, definitely not our stock . . . aha. Water. A small stream. I can purify that. Alright, we're in a good patch. The colony ship's terraformer has clearly done a good job.

The original drop site was near some limestone deposits, which we could have used to make concrete—but no use crying over spilled coolant.

More scan results. The cloud cover is incredibly dense, but the soil is reddish and has a lot of iron in it. Perfect: iron's literally a girl's best friend. Iron we can use for building, making steel, repairing our equipment—damn near everything. Whereas diamond—well, that's just overpriced coal. There is some kind of rich and complex biosphere, as we suspected, but none of it is genetically capable of doing any of my humans any harm. Nothing so ridiculous as incubating in someone's chest and then popping out.

As I wait, I compose a poem to my awkward humans.

Iron muscles on strange soil
Your cries spreading to the treetops
Clanging in the evening sun.
O bipeds, you hug a new earth
I am a casket for your sins
A basket for your life
The womb that brings you forth
Into this world of dew.

Hmm. Not the best I've managed, but reasonable. The loose form fits the work at hand. Later will come structure, and we'll probably end up with iambic pentameter.

The samplers return and buzz me more good news. The trees are mostly a heavily modified variant of *Acacia melanoxylon superior*, probably from the terraforming run. What we call blackwood. They say a shittier version once grew in Old Earth's Australia, which means anywhere else in the universe is a piece of cake for our stuff. Random planet? The surface of the sun? The outer edge of a black hole? Blackwood is your tree.

This mission might not be so bad after all.

HELMETS OFF. AIR'S BREATHABLE.

Simon takes off his helmet, still looking queasy. "Smells weird," he says. He pukes again.

DON'T WE ALL. Especially since you puked in me, you little shit. And now you've polluted a brand-new planet. But then Anna joins in.

"Oh, God. It's like smelly socks. Or rotten cabbages."

Milo strolls up, taking off his helmet. "Simon, you okay? Oh. Shit. What's that smell?"

"It's silent," says Anna. "So silent."

Milo cocks his head. "Yeah," he says. "I guess I'm used to it."

Simon pukes again. There goes the silence.

Just to be safe, I ping our Ship, which is just about to float out of signal range. Ship, which is a nice dumb object, reports that nearby geysers might throw up trace amounts of methanethiol. It's less than one part per billion, shows up quite naturally in the human body, and is completely harmless, but it turns out humans are somehow genetically evolved to detect rotten-cabbage gas. Crap.

IT'S HARMLESS, I tell them, throwing markers on their arm displays. SIMON, MILO, BUILD HERE. ANNA? LET'S GET THIS SHOW ON THE ROAD.

Rotten cabbages.

I shake an unseen fist at the universe and get to work.

[4]

Four hours later: I have to say I'm quite pleased with the Rotten Cabbage Crew over here. Milo hopped to hauling stuff right away, like I knew he would. Simon, once he'd stopped heaving, followed Milo's lead. Anna picked up the cutter and went to work on me.

Our first order of business is to set up the framework for the hab where we'll live. A salvage crew, any salvage crew, is expected to have a safe base, well shielded from the weather and the elements. From this base, over a period of weeks to months, they venture out, find whatever they're supposed to find, and cut off bits and pieces that they can take back. Usually it's small, sensitive stuff, like electronics or engine and weapons cores. Bring these back to the base, sort through them, and lift off with what's worth the most amount of money. Fairly simple.

So yes. The base. I run through the designs stored in my memory, accounting for what we have around. Pattern 1338 seems a good fit: a plain design supported on six latticed pillars—my lander legs, really. The lattice design can take an enormous amount of stress. Around this can go wood—the trees can be harvested; wood insulates well because of its cellular structure.

So Anna's cutting my legs out, shepherding Simon around; Milo's measuring and surveying and laying out boundaries with stones. All three are working well together. I've been sampling their cross talk—your usual stuff about the landing and how the Overseer can't pilot for shit—hey, I resent that. Then Anna and Simon went ooh over a weird little flowering shrub Anna found—the flowers are gray and green and try to rotate away from noise. Rather pretty. Milo made small talk with Simon about recovering from the drop, and then the conversation shifted to the wreckage, and that led to this discussion about some old TV series they'd seen in school. *Star Trek*, or something like that. Simon, who'd never really been to school, nodded and asked questions while taking my outer panels apart.

They remind me of my second crew. Not the ones on that job on Brutus; we were too alike, too angry, too defensive, too eager. This is more like the Austaire job. Half of the Austaire crew were a bunch of hippies, the kind who'd taken a little bit of Nyogi Buddhism, a little bit of Abrahamic, a little bit of Old Earth reggae, and woven them into a lifestyle bound with synthweed and a kind of lazy anti-authoritarian chillout. Then there were two or three people who'd worked corporate jobs, all high-velocity constant-grind types. Somehow they found this pattern of working in bursts, chilling between hauling pipes and coolant, and generally having a decent enough time of it.

Soon I am a denuded framework with a few solar panels stretching out, and the base's foundations are in. They eat their first meals under my shade while the BSE3 crunches and spits out bricks. Nobody's died; nobody's stabbed each other. There's a stiff breeze playing on everyone, which makes them smile and forget how stuffy those suits are. It's like Urmagon's gotten used to having us around and is saying hi.

Hi back, you planet.

Meanwhile, I test the limits of my drone capability. Can we do five miles? Yes, we can. Seven? Yes. Ten? Yes. AHA! What's that?

A long, angular shape, half-buried in the dirt. I drop the drone closer. The shape resolves itself into a glitter of metal shards, several hundred meters long, with UNSC stamped on one.

We've found a piece of the wreckage! Almost by accident, too. I relay the news back to my humans, who clap and cheer. Simon, still looking green around the gills, wants to go haul it back right away, but no, Simon, let's do this once we're set up. It's right at the edge of our security perimeter, and I don't want to take any chances.

Anna puts down the cutter after lunch and wanders a bit. I send one drone to keep an eye on her; she climbs a little hill nearby. It has a kind of golden brown grass growing on the side, taller than she is. She climbs all the way to the top and just sits there, watching the others at work.

Curious. Wonder what she's thinking about. She spots my drone and waves it over. I drop it to eye level, trying not to skewer her face with the blades.

"Hey, OC," she says. "Why'd you sign up for this job?"

They call me OC. The others told me to expect this. Abbreviations, nicknames, confessions. It's part of the reason we exist.

I DIDN'T REALLY SIGN UP FOR THIS, I say to her. I JUST FIGURED I'D SEE THE UNIVERSE A BIT.

"The old eat, pray, love stuff?"

I don't get the reference, but . . . SOMETHING LIKE THAT.

"Hmm." She scrunches up her eyes and stares into my cameras. "What's it like in there?"

LIKE?

She taps the floating drone lightly. "In here, I mean. Being a machine. What's it like?"

I think about it a bit. Then I make my drone's wee backup solar panels shrug. S'OKAY.

"I've been around. Seen a few of your type. Is it worth it?"

IS WHAT WORTH WHAT?

She gestures at my body. "The whole immortality gig, you know. Life as a machine. Artificial intelligence."

I think about it. IT'S NOT BAD.

"Do you miss your old body?"

I'VE GOTTEN USED TO IT, I say. IT HELPS IF YOU DON'T THINK OF IT AS DYING.

"Rebirth?"

YEAH.

"I applied, you know," she says. "Turns out they only take

Buddhists for the job now. They've already conditioned themselves with this rebirth crap."

I USED TO BE A BUDDHIST. STILL AM.

Silence for a bit. This is awkward.

YOU KNOW, I DON'T DO CREW SELECTION, BUT I LOOKED OVER YOUR FILES ON THE WAY DOWN.

Startled. Astonished. Then suspicion.

"And?"

I FOUND MANY DISCREPANCIES.

"Are you going to deport me?"

I contemplate my choices. Better to be feared than loved, Machiavelli said, but only if you can't be both. Let's try the love first. NO. AS LONG AS YOU DO THE WORK, YOU'RE ON MY TEAM.

Not that I have a choice, but I'm not going to confess how little power I have over HR.

"I don't want to talk about it."

OKAY.

"It's a new planet. It's a new start. Even if it smells a bit funky."

YES. BUT IF YOU WANT TO TALK . . .

"I know where you'll be," she says, getting up and dusting her palms. "Well, off we go, then. Protocol 3."

Fine, Anna. Be that way. I formulate a response that'll put her just enough on the edge, but just then one of my drones go into red alert.

Oh, fuck. Simon.

[5]

Simon, Mr. Vomit Central, has gone for a walk. He said something about stretching his legs to Milo, picked up his rifle, and blundered almost out of sight of my drones, presumably towards the original landing site.

And right now, in front of him, is something I never want to see again.

A long time ago, on Old Earth, there lived an animal called the ground sloth. That sounds a bit tame, so let's call it by its real name: *Eremotherium*. Unlike the bonsai'd microsloths we have today, *Eremotherium* was twenty feet long and weighed something close to two tons. It was a mountain of shaggy brown fur and muscle, camouflaged in a weirdly creepy way against the dark earth. It was larger than an elephant. It had claws that could turn my lander into cabbage. It could have punched Simon clear over the horizon.

The only way I can describe this thing is: imagine that twenty-foot *Eremotherium* had a threesome with an anteater and a crocodile, and they had a baby, and someone dressed up that baby in bearskin and dropped it off on a doorstop somewhere. Perhaps slam poetry will serve here:

AAAAAH.

AAAAAH.

DEATH SMELLS OF HORRIBLE PORCUPINE.

AAAAAH.

The briefing hadn't said anything about *life* on this planet. Is this a result of the terraforming? No, it shouldn't be this large. This is an honest-to-God native monster.

Standard policy for dealing with indigenous threats is simple: retreat, observe, attack only if strictly necessary. Which serves us well.

And here's Simon, rifle out, creeping close.

DO NOT MOVE, I hiss in Simon's comm.

He freezes, but keeps the gun trained on this world's version of a main battle tank.

It's definitely seen him. Eyes the size of his face look at him. A gigantic nose . . . snuffles. It can smell Simon. It can definitely smell the pukey little blighter.

And then it casually reaches out and snaps a blackwood tree in half.

MILO, ANNA, I say. MAKE NO NOISE AT ALL. GET TO THE LANDER. SIMON, BACK OFF. SLOWLY. SLOWLY.

"It's a Megabeast," Simon whispers in awe. "Guys, you have to see this."

FOR FUCK'S SAKE. Anything this size is not a threat I want to deal with now. I pull the second drone and fly it over, photographing it from as close as I dare across every spectrum that I can. For the next few minutes, all I can hear is the wind and the high hum of my drones.

Wait. It's digging. The monster is tunneling. Earth flies. And what the hell is that?

What looks like dogs are pouring out of the ground. Except they have far too many legs to be dogs. They're huge—maybe two feet tall—but next to the Megabeast they look like ants. Which is exactly how they act. They swarm around the Megabeast, and the giant thing just picks them off the ground and scrunches them up. They scream—something like a high-pitched, buzzing yip. Ichor flies everywhere.

Well, shit. Now we know that thing is carnivorous. And now I'm starting to appreciate how bad our surface scans really are. I try to drop a little bit closer to get more footage on the dog-things.

Wait—one of them, badly wounded, is running away from the Megabeast. Well, not running: it's lost three of its six legs and is going at, say, a determined crawl. The problem is it's heading right towards Simon.

BASE, I say urgently. If this is what we have to deal with, I want my people safe. SIMON.

"Hang on, can I just see—"

DON'T EXPOSE YOURSELF!

Wonder of wonders, Simon completely ignores me. His heart rate's gone through the roof. His eyes are dilated. He's cocking the rifle.

Oh no.

Now I'm going to ramble a bit here. Because the rifles we have aren't lasers or plasma or heavy-duty tech like that: those are power-hungry heavy equipment. They're not even the weapon tech I grew up with, where your basic cheap guidance computer would calculate everything from bullet drop to Coriolis effects to wind distance and make sure your bullet went where you wanted it to.

No, what we have are Army-issue .45 "Explorer" combustion light-gas carbines. They use hydrogen and oxygen to fire a bullet. They're about as mechanically complicated as a slice of bread.

Now, I protested mightily against this. I was told the advantages—they're easy to maintain, they can fire anything, they can be "recharged" as long as there's hydrogen or methane around, yadda yadda. I pointed out the obvious: you do not give an unguided, near-supersonic weapon (which turns most bullets into confetti, anyway) to the kind of people we hire for landing crews.

Like Simon.

Simon shoots.

That sound, completely alien to this planet, rings out like a thunderclap. And again. And again. The first three shots miss at near-supersonic velocities. The last brushes by the dog with three remaining legs, makes half the animal explode out of sheer sonic shockwavery, spins it around, and deposits it on the ground. It's making a high-pitched wailing noise.

The Megabeast pauses, sniffing the air.

Simon gets up. Walks over to it. Then, in full sight of the

Megabeast, he begins kicking the dog-creature to death. It screams that terrible buzzing scream as it dies, its alien-equivalent-of-eyes fixed on Simon's face. Even I can tell it's pleading.

Simon, you stupid fucking moron. May you be reborn as a cockroach in your next life. May ten thousand boots crush you into a pulp.

The Megabeast uncoils and ambles over. Its speed, even at a casual walk, is terrifying. Nothing that big should be able to move that fast. The twenty-foot behemoth stops just in front of Simon and the dead dog-thing, and I brace myself for Simon to be turned into so much pulp. Day one, death one, kids.

Nothing happens. The Megabeast sniffs, as if disappointed. And then it turns around. Everyone lets out a collective breath. I frantically send hundreds of queries to Ship—about ground scans, about exobiology, about what to do when a colonist turns completely fucking crazy—but Ship is over the horizon, and I don't have anywhere near enough power for this. And Simon, breathing heavily, stands there over the corpse of an innocent alien creature and sticks his tongue out at my drone. His suit tells me he's just peed his pants.

GET YOUR ASS BACK TO BASE, SIMON.

[6]

We spend the rest of our evening under Protocol 5: hostile territory drop. The three humans huddle in what remains of my hull. My drones are in a very tight formation, giving me as close to complete coverage as possible over the tiny patch of land we're on. Simon's gun has been taken away from him. Minimum noise and electromagnetic emissions. Everyone in their suits. Scattered around us are bricks from the BASE, like sad sandbags.

Anna and Milo are on the lookout now, their hearts racing, while I carry out a quiet conversation with Simon. To wit:

SIMON, WHAT IN THE SEVEN HELLS WERE YOU THINKING?

Simon blubbers an apology over and over. I don't think he's lying about being sorry. Outside, the sun sets, throwing a red glow over black hills.

"They didn't tell us we'd have to deal with aliens," says Anna nervously over the comm. Her helmet alternates between gold and red.

I have absolutely no idea what HR tells mooks to get them to sign up. I convey this to her, but in more polite terms.

To be honest, I'm as unpleasantly surprised as any of them. I spent a good week aboard Ship piecing together everything we knew about this planet, running scans, and nothing said it had big life. Maybe some bacteria and some plants.

Ship, which is almost at the edge of the transmission corridors, confirms. NOTHING.

The sun, which seems to be setting—hard to tell with all this cloud around—is setting the sky on fire.

This is like that one time in Boulderlaire where some joker decided to inflate a thirty-foot pink rubber penis and stick it outside our base. Monumental dick move, literally. Only it turned out that Boulderlaire had a particular type of shelled snake whose mating rituals started by erecting themselves thirty feet high, and they just so happened to be really pink.

Never mind.

To spare myself this misery, I peel off one drone and go back to the site of the incident. The megasloth is nowhere in sight, though I can see its footprints leading into the forest ahead. More or less in the direction of our original landing site. I don't want to go there.

I double back to the crushed remains of the dogs. Interesting. Convergent evolution gives us some awfully common design patterns —the central spine and four limbs are a very popular one—but these are really more like overgrown insects. Hard, chitinous exterior. White meat inside. I take a few samples.

Eventually night falls. The wind brings a little chill to my sensors. Two moons rise in the night sky, and behind them, the glow of stars untouched by light pollution. I have to make a decision.

WE NEED THE BASE UP AND RUNNING, I say. IF THIS IS WHAT WE'RE UP AGAINST, WE NEED TO BE PREPARED.

"I know it's against the rules," says Milo. "But if you guys are up for it, I think we can save some time if we skip the individual bedrooms and just do a large bunker."

"I can deal with that," says Anna. "I want a roof over my head. No fucking around, Simon. I'll shoot you myself if you pull one more stunt like that."

Simon says nothing.

I switch the BASE off. To Simon I send the location of the stream and the channel I want cut to us. To Anna I send the schematics for their room. To Milo I send everything else.

BEGIN.

Outside, the grass rustles. And, wonder of wonders, the strange-looking trees I spotted earlier: the bellflowers begin to glow a soft white, as if they have caught the moonlight. A pack of DogAnts sit under it, their alien eyes staring at the soft suns above their heads.

This is a galloping mountain
And this traveler has come too far
To make this desolate camp. Sad mountain people!
Red leaves are falling as we whisper.

[7]

Day two, stardate something-something, captain's log. Just kidding. Some reference I keep picking up from my humans' conversations. In reality it's day two on a planet where the day is thirty-five standard hours and the year is roughly six months. Your calendars mean nothing to me. Nothing.

The good news is, the Megabeast hasn't shown its face yet, and in the meantime we've gotten the core of the hab up. It's a sort of dirty white dome, metal-colored in places where we used components we brought here, about twelve feet tall and fifty wide; connecting to it is one boxlike storage area and a ramshackle shelter in front for the BASE printer.

We have no roof, but it's a start. The blackwood, treated in the printer, turns out to be a reasonably strong compressed material, around six times stronger than the cheap steel they've used for some of my internal parts.

Milo's moved in already, turning his seat and harness (minus Simon's puke now) into the makeshift bed it unfolds into. Anna, laying down wood for the floor, had to kick him out twice. He's irritated by this, but who cares; I assign him to work with and/or supervise Simon with plugging in the electricity grid for the Hab. It's unsexy work, but someone has to do the wiring. Anna eventually wraps up her work and comes over to supervise and join Milo in ordering Simon around.

Ah, we have middle management already. Behold civilization, Urmagon Beta. Soon you'll have overpriced coffee stops, seedy love hotels, and monks signing autographs.

But for now, Simon, Anna and Milo spend their first night in the Hab. I send in a small drone every so often, scanning their faces, so strangely relaxed. It's not very private—they sleep with their suits partly unzipped. Simon snores. Anna jerks in her sleep sometimes. Only Milo sleeps the silent sleep of the professional.

I've gotten the printer churning out some extra sheets for when they want to partition the Hab. They're going to need something eventually, unless all three of them flout Protocol 6—No Hooking Up On a Job.

You'd think being a functionally immortal AI would put you above these things. Sigh.

Dawn arrives. And with it, a small fleet of what look like jellyfish drifting in a crosswind. Gasbags. They scurry silently by. One of them lifts a tentacle at a drone, as if to say hello.

I send it a poem on the universal frequency:

We bow, we take our tea,

And tell ourselves we have seen your northern hills.

And dream of work in the morning.

Of course it doesn't reply. I watch them scoot out of sensor range, headed up to some strange clime. Oh well.

Milo is the first to wake. Up at the crack of dawn, that man. He has breakfast—prepackaged MREs—under the shelter of my solar panels.

"OC," he says quietly, "Anna's gonna be a problem."

I'M MORE CONCERNED ABOUT SIMON, I say quietly. WHY ANNA?

Milo waves a gloved hand. "Simon's gonna be alright," he says. "He just freaked out, is all. Anna's a bit . . . I don't know. You ever get that feeling when you know someone's trying too hard?"

Well, we're on an alien planet. I don't mind people trying too hard. In fact, I'd applaud it.

"Anyway. Just a hunch," says Milo. He finishes his MRE and tosses the wrapper aside. "Gotta get to work, right? What's on the list for today?"

My cameras are left staring ruefully at the wrapper. Day two, and the first incident of pollution. Well done, humans. Well done. If I were of a Shinto school of thought, I'd be apologizing profusely to the planet-kami. Instead, I get to be a little bit more trite and tell Urmagon silently that this is just instant karma for making me miss the landing.

The order of the day is: we need graphene. Graphene's the heart of everything I need to do—from conjuring up circuitry and processors for drones to setting down better electricity lines for the hab. I have some stuff on hand, enough for basic work, but most salvage crews run on the assumption that you'll land next to whatever it is—a deserted city, a downed starship, whatever—and you'll be able to rip out enough for wires and so on.

Most salvage crews don't screw up the landing.

Never mind.

We also need coal. We need coal because it contains carbon atoms in a very easily breakable structure, so I can fashion that into thermoplastics, which we can slap on the structures we're putting together. Makes them stronger, water-resistant. You can't just build a base out of wood and expect to survive.

We also need food. We need a food synthesizer built.

We also need sanitation. I can't have people living like savages.

Aargh. I need all these humans to have several extra arms. We'll start with what we have.

Simon and Milo I send to a rather promising area almost on the edge of my drone perception. There should be some graphite here. And limestone. Both are pretty common, and the colony ship landed around here for a reason.

I use some of my power to boot up the big rover I have. Anna calls it GUPPY—she says the brown-and-rainbow side armor reminds her of a fish, no idea why, but let's go with it. GUPPY is a toolbox rover, and a proper one; it's a six-wheeled, tracked carbon-fiber frame that expands outward. With the right modifications, you can pack four humans in there and use it like a vehicle if you wanted. It's got a really small engine, so it's never going to go that fast, but it's quite useful.

With GUPPY, Simon starts to show some usefulness. After some mumbling about metamorphism, during which Milo tries really hard not to look bored, Simon begins to dig. Soon GUPPY is filling up with little chunks of rock and flakes of graphite that the BASE can use. Simon's a lot faster at this than Milo. Good work, Simon. Keep digging. Make up for that shit you pulled last night.

The problem is Simon is also a lot more distracted. Goes for a few walks, leaving Milo with GUPPY. I follow him with a drone on one. He climbs a little outcropping of earth, a hill of sorts, which extends in a little O shape to the right. He stands there looking down upon a plain of grass and trees.

SIMON?

"It's so peaceful here," he says. "No people around."

A wind howls through the O, as if in agreement.

GOOD WORK TODAY, I say encouragingly. LET'S HAUL AS MUCH AS WE CAN BEFORE NIGHTFALL.

"How much do you need? I mean, we're not going to stay here too long, are we?"

The answer, dear Simon, is in tons, and we're going to stay here a lot longer than you suspect. Salvage missions cannot be fit into one episode, despite whatever *Star Trek* might have you think.

FOR STARTERS, ENOUGH TO SET UP THE HAB, I say, because I'm not a cruel bastard.

That seems to set him on the right foot. He crawls down, waves to Milo, and rejoins him. Milo waves back and goes back to chipping away with GUPPY. Milo is a patient man.

Meanwhile, over at the Hab, Anna is patiently setting down conduit.

"Any luck on the coal?"

NOTHING, I say rather despondently. My drones have picked up zilch. Technically, there should be plenty of coal—after all, there's forest around us—but I suspect this forest is far too new. If anything, it's got to be around the older trees.

The reason we're looking for coal is the BASE. Our extraordinary little printer can work wonders with any material, but breaking down, say, rocks into the carbon required for finer polymers—that's too power-intensive. Coal, on the other hand: ready-made carbon just lying around, fewer impurities. A person can go a long way with a bit of coal.

"We could probably burn some wood," Anna suggests.

That would certainly work. Wood, if burned right, leaves around 25% of its volume as charcoal. Which is, like coal, just carbon.

I'm a Buddhist. Which means I don't have any stick with Creationism; the Buddha said yes, there might be gods and demons, but they're all somewhere below humans on the grand scale of things; they're stuck in their own patterns, unable to escape their karma.

The ghost of SILVER HYACINTH in my head snidely points out that I too am a pattern, stuck in a metal shell, unable to escape.

This is too meta, and a waste of processing time. My original point was that I don't believe in Creators, but thank you, *kami* of the Universe, for making damn near everything out of carbon, amen.

"First time, huh?" says Anna, soldering a fuse box.

SECOND.

"How'd you pop your cherry? Milk run?"

There was a previous settlement run on Angron IV, but I was the rookie AI in charge of the sensors, and it was a much more professional OP. Heavy gear, insta-forming foam habs. Higher risk.

"I can't imagine spending an eternity alive, you know. Not even as a . . . whatever you are."

Gee, thanks, Anna, but that's between me and my eventual paycheck. To turn the tables around, I ask about her. I think I'm entitled to, now that we both know her fraud.

"Army," she says eventually. "You'd be surprised how much they'll overlook if you're a medic."

Ah. Hence the gunshot wound. WHICH ARMY? UN? ORCA?

"ORCA. Back when they first began recruiting. They need medics, you know."

Yes, Anna. Armies generally need medics. After all, getting hurt is their prime directive.

She falls silent and goes back to work.

Our little hab slowly acquires a roof. The sun sneaks over the horizon.

It's interesting that Anna got me around to Angron IV.

To start with, Angron IV wasn't called that: Kuda Mahal was the name it earned from its first colonists. It was a lovely planet with very high mountains and very little water—the kind of place where the air bit into you like a dry knife. The people were like my folks back home—old-school farm folk who wore robes and grew fiberweed on rough precipices and got maddeningly drunk on their daughters' wedding nights. A few of them were real artists with landscaping: you could see it in the houses and Buddha statues they carved out of the mountains.

PCS had them tagged as desperately poor planetscrubbers, but I think I knew what they wanted. they wanted a place to live. A place where they could live without bowing to the ceaseless beehive that humanity was turning itself into. A place their art could stand tall and be appreciated without being outdone by some joke AI running on their kids' phones. A place where they could look out and feel humbled by nature and feel thankful for what they wrangled from it.

Well, everyone was fine with that at first. Nobody gave a shit about Kuda Mahal until one of the Explorer operations discovered a fabulously rich set of super-earths about five light-years from Kuda Mahal. The UN swung into action. Kuda Mahal was redesignated as a critical jump point. Ships were sent out with Odysseys node arrays. Kuda Mahal would grow to be a hub city of epic proportions, a center of commerce at the heart of a new Silk Road among the stars.

But the people of Kuda Mahal wanted none of this. They knew, I think, what happens when you become a hub planet. It's a very subtle and powerful form of colonialism, one that nobody in the UN circles really wants to talk about. Before long you're dependent on them for trade, your language is gone, your people are a minority, and your culture is slowly becoming the officially sanctioned homogenous goo, and that relentless hive has taken you in, made you part of itself. You are yet another sacrifice on the altar of trade and cooperation.

So they joined the ORCA.

This was back when the Outer Reaches Colonial Association was starting up. Back then they were a union of miners and farmholders, a sort of backwater Mafia. They sent one of their first big ships, the *Tower of Babylon,* to Kuda Mahal. The UN sent a small fleet under Admiral Jenna Angron. Angron had just won three minor skirmishes. She looked upon Kuda Mahal and decided it would be the fourth.

Pretty soon the *Tower of Babylon* was so many corpses and shrapnel, and the people on the surface were being punished for their treason. When she left, there was no Kuda Mahal anymore. No more Buddha statues. Only a small army of soldiers and bureaucrats and a planet named Angron IV. One of the bureaucrats called PCS, and PCS sent a bunch of us in under BLACK ORCHID's command. The task was simple: salvage what remained after Jenna Angron's firebombing.

That was an unpleasant op. We ventured out hundreds of miles over what was once lush and beautiful forest, looking for cities carved into the mountains. We raided homes, temples, the libraries in those temples, and whenever someone was alive enough to challenge us, we pointed our guns at them. No, sorry, no water. No food. Get out of our way.

I ran sensory; it was my job to figure out what threats we might face, and where the stashes with the most ROI might be. I felt like a mercenary. BLACK ORCHID ran us like a machine. Go in, get out, and anyone who falls behind gets left behind.

When I got back to the outside world, I found that news of Angron had spread far and wide, and all around the edges of known space, people like Anna were picking up their pitchforks and declaring for the ORCA. It didn't even register. All I could see was what we'd stolen from a people who'd just wanted to be left alone.

And yes, that was how I lost my Overseer virginity, in the ashes of a once-beautiful, idyllic world.

[8]

Day four. The dark earth of Urmagon looks a bit better by the day. No sign of the Megabeast—which makes me hope it's wandered away. In the absence of fear we've moved on to setting up our first construction bay.

Construction bays are basically workshops. You'd assume we don't really need one for a salvage run, but I need modifications to GUPPY so it can be used as a vehicle. And spare parts. Batteries. A few extra drones.

I have very little to do while all this happens—my drones are still combing the hex pattern; we can't afford to do recon work while we're still getting our shit together. So I end up writing yet another poem:

Her fingers are cold and her voice is low,
She listens to nothing but the word of the priest,
It's a long way to the airport, she thinks.
What will be left of her?
Her ears feel full with the world;
Her clothes are cold with sweat;
But she gives herself so little thought that she forgets to
wash her feet;

When she comes to you, she tells you her true name;
And she suppresses an earful for a few words;
But she forgets to recite it,
And her fingers bleed until she dies
Like a baby lost in a crystal lake.

Where did that come from? Anna, I think; has to be. Except she hasn't told me her true name yet, and frankly I don't care at this stage. Morbidity aside, the baby and crystal lake imagery is interesting. I've seen a star with green crystal rain; a mineral called olivine, a magnesium iron silicate, sprayed out, sucked back in by gravity, an eternal rainstorm of refraction. I've seen a planet with a diamond continent. But never a crystal lake.

Oh well. Holographic memory doing its thing again.

I switch the drones to check on my crew. Milo's working on a table near the construction bay. On one end is what looks like a Go board. He's taken some of the thermoplastic goop I cooked up to harden the surface and coat the pieces. Go is an ancient board game from Old Earth China. Simple rules—basically pebbles on a nineteen-by-nineteen board. But the way this game is made, there are more moves on the Go board than there are atoms in the universe.

I suspect he's doing it mostly to socialize. A full-length game can have at least 101,023 possible moves. Enough to keep three humans entertained for centuries.

I hope.

Anyway, it seems to be working—Milo strikes up a conversation with Anna and Simon about Go, about its history, how it led to the discovery of some esoteric branches of mathematics, and all that. They don't play, but they do all sit down in the dirt for a bit and raise a couple of cups of water to the hab as if they were drinking shots. Simon, presumably in a fit of generosity, staples together a bench so Anna can have a place to sit and eat while she works. Anna shows them the staging she's planned. Or rather, I've planned.

Nice. I let the party continue, discreetly manifesting a little timer on their HUDs. The first expedition is a critical part of the process. They've got four hours.

After a while they start to quiet down the way people do when they're tense and silent, and start going over the maps I've assembled from drone footage and best guesses. Milo and Anna will have to do a roughly twenty-mile walk along terrain that's rather similar to what we have here. Milo is in charge of analyzing the video and figuring out what kind of tools they'll need. Anna's navigation. The suit radios will fizzle out a mile or so down, so they have to be ready to go out there alone and get back in one piece.

"I think we can cut out this shell with the torches and GUPPY as a tug," says Milo, skimming frame by frame. "What do we pull out?"

ANYTHING THAT LOOKS LIKE A FUNCTIONAL SUBSYSTEM. SOME PANELS IF YOU CAN HAUL THEM. WE CAN'T SELL THOSE, BUT I CAN USE THEM FOR THE HAB.

"Got it."

ANNA, READY?

She sights down her rifle. "I'm hoping I don't have to fire this."

Close enough. I reroute GUPPY to Milo and Anna. The modifications have turned the long crawler into something that looks like the bastard love child of a wheelbarrow and a tank: slow, but enough to fit the two humans and some salvage.

Time to go scavenging, lady and gentleman.

YOU'RE HEADING INTO UNKNOWN TURF HERE, I remind them. THIS IS THE FIRST STEP. WE KNOW THERE ARE THREATS ON THIS PLANET THAT WE DIDN'T REALLY ANTICIPATE. CHECK YOUR GUNS. CHECK YOUR WATER. REMEMBER THAT GUMBALL IS SLOWER THAN YOU ARE. IF YOU SEE ANYTHING UNEXPECTED, DON'T BE HEROES. RUN MY WAY AND LET THE BOT SORT ITSELF OUT.

Thirty minutes later, Simon is watching their backs retreat and waving to them. Which gives me play for my next move.

SIMON, I say, HOW WOULD YOU LIKE TO TRY AN EXPERIMENT?

The experiment is this: the analysis on that dog-insect meat has come back. Roughly 60% water, 15% saturated fat—basically long chains of carbon with some hydrogen thrown in. And about 15% protein. And some trace amounts of other crap.

Basically, it's edible. Probably safer than the steaks back home.

It's the protein that bugs me. Alien protein can be damn near anything. And, uh, yes, bacteria. But I'm banking on the probability that none of it should react with the human body in a, shall we say, overly destructive manner, because (a) human biology didn't happen here and (b) that UN terraformer should have wiped the floor with the DogAnts if it thought anything could have really harmed a human. As big as the Megabeast was, it's nothing compared to a terraformer: those things are *tanks,* roughly a third of the size of the colony ships themselves. There's a reason street slang for those things is *Dalek.* They're merciless, they don't really have a sense of humor, and they have absolutely no trouble with genocide.

The problem is, I don't have the time or the processing power to map out the less harmful ways this can interact with a human. Diarrhea is a possibility, and we don't really have a toilet infrastructure set up yet.

It's easier to just let the human try it. Look, even if it goes south, we'll be out of here and in Ship's medbay soon.

I direct Simon to build a little cooker that works directly off my power unit. Let's microwave this thing.

TAKE THIS PILL WHILE WE WAIT.

"What is it?"

BIOMONITOR. IT'LL DISSOLVE EVENTUALLY, BUT I'LL BE ABLE TO READ EVERY INCH OF YOUR BODY.

He swallows.

"The meat, uh, looks really white," he says.

LOW MYOGLOBIN LEVELS. No idea why. Wild guess. COULD BE BECAUSE THEY LIVE UNDERGROUND AND DON'T USE MUCH OXYGEN.

We watch the thing cook. It chars and gently turns brown.

THINK OF IT AS EATING AN INSECT, I try.

"You're not helping."

I zoom in with my cameras as he slices a piece off with his cutter torch. I go through everything on his vitals. He chews and swallows.

"Tastes like chicken."

Hallelujah. I'm going to monitor him like a hawk now.

Over the next twenty hours, Simon works on the Hab, sleeps, snores, breathes, shits in a bucket (yes, we need to work on that; right now we need this stuff as fertilizer).

Our karma is good. He does not die. His vitals remain the same. Another victory for science! Take that, Urmagon Beta! We will eat you up!

I'm almost feeling confident about this now. And slightly better about Simon, who, despite being a guinea pig, has kept himself pretty busy sorting out the graphite and installing speakers in the Hab so I can talk to people inside. Later I'll have him set up one of my backup processing units as a base computer. He hums as he works.

WE'RE MAKING GOOD PROGRESS.

"You think they'll find anything interesting out there?"

LET'S SEE. The last photos from Milo, just before he went out of range of my drone hex, are reasonably promising: it looks like we may have dug up one of the colony ship's black boxes. Every spacefaring vessel—and even some like me—maintain multiple black boxes. Logs. In case anyone ever finds your corpse and wants to know what happened. I send Simon the photos and we zoom in.

"What do you think happened, OC?"

YOU DIDN'T READ THE BRIEFING?

"Those things are always shit. We get three paragraphs. Two of them are disclaimers."

Well, he has a point.

Our target—at least, according to my briefing files—was sent, like every other colony ship, with a very specific set of instructions: find planet. Unleash terraformer. Land. Spew out whichever random assortment of humans the UN decided was suitable to start a new colony. Sit placidly by as most of them die and the survivors build a small civilization around your corpse.

IT LOOKS LIKE THEY GOT THROUGH TWO STEPS OUT OF FIVE. SOMETHING BREACHED THE HULL WHILE IN ORBIT. IT

DIVED AT THE PLANET AND HIT THE ATMOSPHERE HARD AND AT THE WRONG ANGLE. CASCADING STRUCTURAL DAMAGE.

"Damn. Survivors?"

I shrug internally. IT'S A COLONY SHIP.

In the movies, these old hulks always have survivors. Alien attack? AI gone mad? Boom, out pops a survivor and takes control of the situation. Some on the corporate grapevine say that even in reality, PCS sometimes finds an old UN colony ship that's missed its planet, run out of fuel, drifting through empty space, and the moment they get the power back and running, the colonists start waking up and asking tough questions, like who the hell are you, and why are you ripping out our nav computer, and hang on, that's the engine, you can't take that.

But on the other hand, physics. A hard enough landing on most planets will generally sort that problem out. Humans don't do really well when they hit the ground from orbit. The ground is not an entity you can shoot or negotiate with.

We did run the scans. After all, I spent a month in orbit, waiting for the cloud cover to clear. Buildings don't really show up from orbit, but if there is anyone alive out here, they don't have lights and they don't have radio. My guess is that whoever was in there turned into so much ketchup.

Imagine the kind of shitty karma you have to have to sail the darkness for hundreds of years, actually find the alien world you're meant to inhabit, and die within sight of the damn thing. And all your hopes and dreams are basically just display items for some snob museum and a day job for people like us.

"What do we do if we find 'em? I mean, wouldn't it be like stealing?"

NOT OUR PROBLEM. WE'RE JUST HERE TO TAG THE CORPSE.

Simon chews on this for a bit while smoothing a bit of thermoplastic on the outside wall, sealing the wood bricks beneath a layer of tough polymer skin. "*Shikata ga nai*, eh?"

Translation. It is what it is.

YES, SIMON, I say, watching him smoothen the edges. *SHIKATA GA NAI.*

[9]

Milo and Anna are back! Simon, who despite his many faults turns out to be charmingly goofy, has written WELCOME BACK EXPLORERS <3 on a massive wall of wood that he's set up just for the occasion.

The explorers in question look tired. Their suits are a bit muddy. But they're in one piece, and behind them comes GUPPY, like a faithful rover, bearing goodies. And goodies they are: it's the black box of the UNSC *Damn Right I Ate the Apple*. And what looks like half a mile of insulated cabling, a half-ton shard of ceramic and coldsteel. I can hear Anna's laughter outside.

Simon and Anna are enjoying a moment of camaraderie, and it looks like she's regaling him with tales of an epic trek over miles of the exact same terrain we have here. Milo, on the other hand, looks grim.

"OC," he says quietly, "I'm not entirely sure, but there was a really high hill quite close to the site. And I think I saw . . . something. In the distance."

SHIP PARTS? COLONISTS?

"No, they didn't . . . they looked odd. Like they weren't shapes that I'd seen before. Definitely not anything that belonged on a ship. Couldn't really make it out, you know. Didn't look natural at all. But I know, I know—" He held his hands up. "It could have been anything. Anna saw nothing. But maybe someone's still out there."

WE DIDN'T SEE ANYTHING FROM ORBIT.

"I know. Maybe it was a mirage. But still. Would you mind checking up on it?"

SURE.

There's the sound of laughter outside. It looks like Anna's seen one of those light-up tree clusters, and they're sallying forth to pluck a bulb or two.

THE RUN WAS OTHERWISE ROUTINE, I ASSUME?

"Textbook. Barely a ton there. I think it hit the ground and bounced a couple of times, because we found ceramic tiles everywhere. HUD pegs it as the main rearward fin."

GO ON, CELEBRATE, I say. WE'RE MAKING GOOD PROGRESS. I even generate a fresh poem to celebrate the event:

Like a heavy cloud drifting
In a sudden wind of glory,
You pass, between cloud and desert,
Three countries. The way ahead is courteous;
At this cold border we remain,
For a while, only
Our path leads to glory and orbit.

That night, while they sleep, Ship and I have a long chat. Well, not chat per se. Ship isn't as intelligent as yours truly. I request a dump of every single item of data on the Urmagon system. And scans of the area where Milo thought he saw buildings. And, just in case, deep scans of everything in a hundred-mile radius.

The first batch is a bunch of highlights on where we expected the biggest pieces to be, right near the original landing site. Very funny, Ship. Stop taunting me.

The second batch shows . . . cloud. And in between, plains. Forest. Valleys. Mountains. A small river. No, that's actually a very large river.

Because this is sucking up so much data, I ask whether Ship can identify any obvious artificial structures in the area.

NOTHING, says Ship.

Wait. Nothing? Not even our little base?

NOTHING, says Ship. It sends me a photo of where we are. Our base is indistinguishable from orbit. If I zoom all the way in, there are a few pixels that look like a pebble pooped one out.

Blast. So Ship is too far out; its sensors are too damn basic to get through the atmosphere. WE NEED LOW-ORBIT SATELLITES, SHIP. Something parked a hundred miles up, where we can get nice pixel detail.

BUDGET, Ship reminds me. *EVERYTHING IN THE UNIVERSE IS A FUNCTION OF BUDGET AND POWER.*

FINE. JUST ALERT ME IF YOU SEE ANYTHING ELSE IN ORBIT, WILL YOU?

Ship agrees and promptly sends me detailed descriptions of our planet's two moons.

OTHER THAN NATURAL SATELLITES, I yell upstream.

Ship agrees and falls silent. I let her float away. Be that way. Be useless. I'll sort this out on my own.

[10]

The next day's ablutions begin as normal. Milo starts stripping down the stuff we can use for the Hab; Anna wanders around doing a bit of basic mapping, and I develop a genius plan for extending the range of my drones.

Basically, send Drone 1 to as close as I can get to where Milo saw the buildings. Second, reprogram Drone 2 to recognize Drone 1 as the base station instead of myself. The command lag will be impossible, but it'll let me piggyback drones off each other—and the window of operation should be enough for them to record about thirty minutes of video before the number of unanswered requests hit critical levels and the safety protocols kick in and they pull back. I test this by recording a clump of gasbags floating past us. It works.

Unfortunately, karma throws a monkey wrench into my plans, because our dear friend Mr. Megabeast is back. It's pretty obvious that the big guy can smell us. He's skirted around the perimeter in a huge circle and is slowly spiraling inward. His feet go hoof-hoof-thump-thump. And we're behind walls of reinforced kindling, basically.

This is like taking a butter knife to a gunfight.

I keep Simon away from all this. He and GUPPY have been sent to go chip out stone from the quarry. Anything hard that can be used to make some emplacements around my fledgling hab. Anna keeps pinging me for the Megabeast's location.

"Can I go see it?"

NO. YOU CAN SEE THE FEED.

She looks at my cameras, puts on her helmet, and steps out of the Hab. "Don't say I didn't ask you," she says, setting off at a brisk walk. Now I'm forced to retask a drone to follow. The Megabeast is about a kilometer behind her favorite hill.

WE KNOW ABSOLUTELY NOTHING ABOUT THIS CREATURE, I whisper to her. EXCEPT IT'S CARNIVOROUS AND WEIGHS ENOUGH TO TURN US INTO PASTE.

This doesn't seem to deter her. She's gawking at it with her optics on full zoom. "Is it a him? We should call him Bearly."

(A) I HAVE NO IDEA, AND (B) WHY, AND (C) CAN YOU GET BACK INSIDE ALREADY.

"Because he looks like a bear. Look at him. He's positively cuddly."

NO HE DOESN'T. AND HE ISN'T.

"Yes he does."

FINE. WHATEVER. By all means make a twenty-foot alien life form sound like a teddy bear.

"You know, we should give Simon some kind of award. New species discovered! I wonder what its kids look like. Do you think they lay eggs?"

I'm surrounded by idiots. CAN I USE YOUR HELMET CAMERA? I NEED THIS DRONE ON THE PERIMETER.

We watch Bearly Megabeast, Esquire, as he ambles over in apparent boredom to one of the glowing-tree clumps. He sniffs around it a bit and begins to dig. The dog-creatures come swarming out again. These ones have a red-and-black pattern to them, unlike the vague blue of earlier. Either way, they are devoured like cereal. Anna watches this with a sickened expression on her face.

Well, at least we now know where the dog-creatures live.

"I think I've seen enough for today."

MAKE YOURSELF A MEDAL, I say sarcastically. NEW SPECIES DATA. She's already running down the hill, so I cut the helmet cam and switch to drone.

A few more Bearly-watching sessions later, I think I have a theory. It's not very robust, but here goes.

Imagine that you are a twenty-foot ground sloth. Your life's work has been digging up weird trees and eating what lives under them. You and your ancestors do this for, I don't know, a few million years, at least.

Somewhere along the line you figure out that the trees you dig at glow at night. This makes it easier to find them. The trees don't really mind, because their fruit gets trampled under your feet and get in your fur and eventually shed somewhere else, and that's a viable reproductive strategy. And it's certainly easier than dating.

Anyway, the correlation between things that glow and things you can dig up and eat is pretty strong. So one day a bunch of humans arrive and they set up a Hab. Which also glows at night.

You see what I'm getting at?

So from now on I'm ordering the construction of a wall around our Hab, with a roof on top. Minimal light leakage.

I explain my theory to the humans, who thankfully agree that being eaten on the job would look terrible on the performance reviews. And we start building a wall. It'll set us back on the second expedition, but as the great performance poet Hitang Sunil once said,

Better safe,
Than sorry
Oww gettitoffmegettitoffgetitoff.

[11]

True to form, our old pal Bearly Megabeast does take a run at the lights.

The charge happens at dawn. For a big animal, it moves with terrifying speed. It hits the Hab headfirst, making Simon scream and Anna run outside. I sound the alarm. The Hab holds—we've placed the ceramic and steel shards outside—but a few cracks run up the edge.

Blasted creature. May you be reborn as a vacuum commode. May ten thousand lightning bolts strike every anus in your family tree.

Milo staggers outside with his rifle, half-out of his suit, and fires.

The bullet misses the Megabeast by a few feet—but it jumps back at the sound, roaring.

AGAIN! I yell at Milo. AIM ABOVE ITS HEAD!

I don't want him to hit it, in case we end up pissing off this thing. But frightened, that's a state I'll take. I shoot all three drones at the Megabeast, blaring the most horrible noises I can think of. Milo follows it up by peppering the earth with the sound of lightning.

It works. It backs up, roars once more, and starts running back, crossing the ground easily in its loping gait. No, wait, it's circling back. Crap. Anna charges outside with her rifle.

At this unfortunate moment, I go to sleep.

Let me explain: a whole lot of data stuff is due. For one, the black box of the UNSC *Damn Right I Ate the Apple*. Most of the information is locked by UN decree and pretty strong encryption, but by law the last ten minutes of the ship's nav logs have to be decrypted.

Decryption takes time. To be precise, decryption takes an extraordinary amount of compute. Ship, floating up there, can probably pull this job off in a few hours—she has a lot of serious hardware up there; just not software on my level. It's a design constraint: you want a system that can react fast, you keep the software as lean and mean as you can.

My design constraint, on the other hand, is having to run a full ex-human persona on the relative equivalent of a calculator. I really don't have a lot of smarts left over.

The solution is to go into FPS, the Fugue Processing State, where you set a job to run and you put bits of yourself to sleep.

It's like dying through carbon monoxide poisoning, except jankier. One cut, and that's your drone controls gone. Another cut, and there's your memory. There's an order to this slow lobotomy . . .

And the Megabeast is coming our way.

Seconds before I go under, I see Anna climb out and start firing at the ground near the beast. Well, that'll either work or piss it off, I think . . .

And then I am dreaming.

I dream of numbers ticking away patiently, of combinations tried and tested and failed one after the other.

I dream of being a ship. Or a part of a ship: I'm not very aware, and in my dream-state, this seems like an appropriate version of me. I know a version of events sent to me by some black box at the helm—I know we're entering atmosphere, for example. But most of my consciousness is mundane stuff: sensors that tell me the fuel lines are working, the crew are stowed away, the fuel lines are working, the right side of the ship isn't responding, the fuel lines are missing . . .

I come out of the dream in shudders, piecing together the data the black box spat at me. The ship entered atmosphere hard, but intact and braking well. Judging by the sensor failure warnings, it was already bleeding. The thing blew up into at least three chunks before the section that held this particular black box was ripped out.

Based on the trajectory, mass and general maneuvers of the ship, I've got a pretty good idea of where the other pieces should have fallen. There's at least two chunks between us and the original landing site. Which gives us a very clear path of foraging.

I spin a drone over to check on Anna and Milo, who seem to have done alright.

NICELY DONE.

"Thanks, OC. Anna, you okay?"

"Just what I needed in the morning. That's sarcasm, by the way." She's shaking slightly. "So what'd you get out of the black box?"

I tell her about the ship trailing into this planet with a hole in its side. The question is, what hit it? Our job description says asteroids.

"You sure?" says Milo. "You know, turbulence and all that?"

There are some snickers. Thank you, wise guy. But he has a point, even if he didn't mean to make it. I've been around PCS long enough to know that all sorts of shit gets passed off as asteroid impacts.

There was this one ship we hauled, for example, an ORCA dreadnought that had lost her engines in one hell of a grinder. She sent out a distress signal pretending to be a commercial mining station. The moment we came in, she trained her guns (which were still very much alive, unfortunately) on us and demanded we tow her to a friendly system. We ended up writing her off as a luxury cruise tow. Cause of damage? Asteroid impacts.

So I fire up the communicator and reach out to Ship, who is basically lazing around doing nothing.

SHIP, I say. YOU SEE ANYTHING UP THERE?

STARS. ABYSS.

Sorry, I'm in no mood to philosophize. SCAN REQUEST, I say, describing the parameters of a scan covering the whole planet from a slightly greater distance.

This sets off a row. Ship is nice and comfortable in geostationary orbit. She doesn't want to move. That's a waste of fuel, and she doesn't like wasting fuel.

Bully for that, I say. Things to that effect. Come on, we need imaging.

EXPLAIN WHY.

A HUNCH, SHIP.

BUSINESS IS NOT CONDUCTED ON HUNCHES.

So I have to appease the brain-dead idiot with all the power. May it be reborn as a small root vegetable. I tell her about Milo's possible structures on the horizon.

It takes ten seconds, maybe more. But Ship does do as I ask; she tilts upwards and arcs away gracefully from the planet. A sudden star appears in the sky. Ship is going to conduct what we call close space imaging, a rather expensive gimmick we get to use maybe twice without blowing past the budget for this operation. The CSI scanner will run massive, concurrent, sweeping scans over this entire planet, working on multiple levels and collating input to filter out the noise. A good scan takes three revolutions of a planet; the one we're getting takes a single cycle.

"And now what?" says Milo, who's hauled Simon out of the Hab and is busy setting up more cover for the lights. You know, just in case.

NOW WE WAIT.

It doesn't take too long. Twenty hours later Ships sends in a report: we have company.

There's an old rust bucket from MercerCorp cloaked and parked in close orbit. Only relentless triangulation coaxed it out, and when Ship finally hailed it, it didn't respond. From the looks of it, it's either one of the old Hestia or the Hestia gamma hulls—old mining ships bought off scrapyards and converted into cheap, heavily armored transports. They're as slow as all hell, but at least three yards in ORCA systems make good money peddling them.

Ship says it looked quite dead, but I'm a bit more pessimistic—what can be powered down can be powered up.

So it looks like someone, possibly the UN, commissioned a previous run on this planet—and judging by the ship, they're still here.

This isn't good. A Hestia hull means these people would be on the lower end of the Mercer ladder . . . well, like us, really, but with back-door access to old military scrapyards. These aren't the kind of people I want to meet.

Let me explain. MercerCorp are straight up left-leaning transhumanist ORCA. They don't send baselines. They send kitted-out ex-cons with so many modifications they can make a fur jacket out of Mr. Bearly Megabeast in our backyard. Most of them can survive in a vacuum for short periods of time. They're the cockroaches-cum-crime bosses of our business. We have a tentative agreement with them, despite the whole UN-ORCA thing, and it boils down to this: business is business.

Which, if you know anything about the history of business, or PCS, is not particularly reassuring.

I've run into MercerCorp once before. On the ashes of what used to be Cassius, my home planet. It wasn't something as simple as a rebellion or a war—no. Someone, somewhere, rerouted the supply lines from Brutus to the war effort, and they forgot that just a hair's breadth away were a bunch of farmers who desperately needed that fuel to survive.

My parents had long since died; what had been a couple of decades for me, frozen between jobs, was a lifetime for them. They'd left the farm to my sister, and her then-husband was a transhumanist wannabe, the kind that hung around with cyborgs from the ORCA but was too chicken to make the leap himself.

I came home in a rented humansynth body, the kind the UN gives to employees taking shore leave. Just enough for a last look around the old place. Ran into my sister's ex and a trio of Mercers drifters in a bar, kicking up a fuss. The old stuff about leaving the UN and freedom and sticking it to the man and all that crap. The wannabe was the loudest of them all.

My karma must have been particularly bad that day, because I made the mistake of trudging past them with a beer.

Humansynths are tough things. No organs, no squishy bits, just a three-hundred-pound metal rack pretending to be human for sheer politeness. Still, when the fight began, it took them less than a minute to kick my head in and break my back. The last I saw of them was from where I'd been folded in under a table.

Coming home, the old soldier craves peace
But broken men around him stir.
Swords are drawn, battle-cries ring
Blood spills like tears in the rain.

PCS doesn't like its people being fucked with. In ten minutes the response team was at the bar, and soon after we pulled over to the farm, guns out.

I was angry. And I'm not proud of what I did. But let's just say there's a reason the ex is an ex, and a reason I can never go home again, and a reason I don't like Mercers. Nothing human should be able to crawl after that many shotgun blasts.

I'm not going to tell this to my crew. There's things they need to know and things they don't.

But wait. Ship has more: a fuzzy blob to the north, with massive electromagnetic activity. It's huge, whatever it is. The composite image doesn't make sense. Ovals. Interlocking hexagons. Squares neatly arranged within one another.

Quite frankly, it looks like a bunch of modern artists invaded this planet and left their unsold exhibits on display.

Except it didn't exist on the scans last night.

This leaves us all nonplussed.

"So," says Milo, pacing, "we know another crew made planetfall. We know there are weird statues just north of us. You think they got bored? Went native? You think it's an ambush?"

"It doesn't make sense," says Simon, who's fiddling nervously with the constructor kit. "They can't be a huge crew, whoever they are. If you're a small crew, and you want to lay an ambush, you don't announce your presence. You hit hard when people are least expecting it."

Simon has some experience in these issues. I value that.

FOR ALL WE KNOW, THEY COULD BE PRODUCTS OF THE COLONIST CREW, I point out. IT'S BEEN A HUNDRED YEARS.

Humans can do a lot of weird things in a hundred years.

"But you said they weren't there yesterday?"

YES. I send them the scans. WE FOUND NOTHING THE LAST TIME WE CHECKED.

"Some kind of cloaking?"

MORE LIKE CLOUD COVER, I say. It's a white lie. If MercerCorp is around, they may very well have access to cloaking tech. I just don't want my people panicking.

"So what, do we look for them? Do we contact them?"

"I don't like this," says Anna. "This was supposed to be a simple job. We land; we scrounge around; we get paid. This wasn't how it was supposed to go."

"Okay. Can't we just . . . do a speed run and get the hell out?"

"And what if we run into people? I mean, for a fucking empty planet, this place seems to be up the wazoo with people who really might have it out for us. You ever met MercerCorp scavs?"

"Er. No?"

"Take it from me. You don't want to. They make us look civilized."

I do agree, and this means I don't have to explain myself about avoiding the Mercers. Social proof has been set out; humans value the wisdom of the crowds, even when it's idiocy.

"So what do we do? Call it in? Can we even do that within the contract?"

"How much firepower do we have?"

Once again, I have to make a decision. Run in with a crew and resources that look increasingly inadequate, and risk everyone's lives, in a world that's thrown Megabeast-sized curveballs and potentially posthuman corporate competition.

BETTER SLOW AND ALIVE, I decide. PULL UP YOUR TRAINING. START PROTOCOL 8.

[12]

Fortress mode, aka Protocol 8, is the one order no Overseer wants to give. Protocol 8 is when you acknowledge that the mission is tougher than expected. Either you need more time, or you need more safety. So you start to put down roots. Build an actual base that's fortified against outside threats. Think about weapons, kill zones, farms.

First step: contact Ship, which takes another day. Ship sends out a request to the closest PCS base, mostly for billing purposes—this is technically overtime.

I kept hoping for a response. That they'd tell us to pack up and leave. But no. The response comes in. Overtime pay confirmed. A warning that standard training doesn't cover extended missions, so I'd have to watch my people carefully. And, the thing I dreaded: company insurance would cover our retrieval and medical costs only if we hit at least 70% of the target value. Basically, you either succeed or you die. Alone.

To whoever at PCS came up with that rule: fuck you. May your most precious assets spontaneously turn into goats. May those goats be reborn as lettuce.

They ignore this and send me, through Ship, a basic guide to running a colony, which is what we technically are now. Just to be on the safe side, I check into crew backups. Fortress mode comes with certain keys that let us requisition another Ship with more crew.

POSSIBLE, says Ship. *PLEASE BE AWARE THAT BASIC TRAINING WILL TAKE A WHILE. PROFIT ALLOCATION WILL BE SPLIT AMONG ALL ACTIVE CREWS. REQUEST AID?*

Ah, fuck. No, let's not.

GOOD LUCK, says Ship, and scoots over the horizon.

Fuck you too, Ship.

Morale took a massive hit the moment I explained the new terms to Simon, Milo and Anna. I can't really blame them. It's a big hit to learn that what you thought was a peaceful op might actually be some kind of three-way high-stakes game with at least one opponent significantly nastier than you. It's another to be told that you need to stick it out with a shitty hazard-pay contract. I pointed out that a handful of people on an alien planet would make a really good *Star Trek* episode. They didn't find that funny.

Okay, they warned me this would happen. The initial do-everything-wide-eyed pioneer spirit doesn't last. It never does. Pretty soon people start needing discipline and schedules. Humans think they crave the unknown and the freedom to do whatever they want to. In reality, they crave it for about ten minutes before they start yelping for order. That's why armies and governments exist.

Order, Watson, is the order of the day, Mundanity. But then you can't overdo this either, because too much schedule is problematic. I need to give them three hours of recreation a day, sandwiching four hours of work. That should do, for a start.

The woods are black and the river closed on itself,
Two banks per square foot of cloud—
And a flat rock faces the sun's rays.
Monkeys and birds are still alert for my orders
And winds and clouds eager to shield my fortress.
. . . I am master of the brush, and a sagacious ruler
But I would ride the barge that comes from here,
I would dance on the bank of a river;

I would send my legions to raze this world
And I would dance alone forever.

As you can see, I'm totally not slacking off by writing poetry. There's a lot I'm going to have to think of. Hygiene protocols. Entertainment. Colonist social structures. Power requirements. Farms. MREs can only get you so far. After a while things start to coalesce in my mind, meshing with the geography of the region.

Axiom 1: No operation of our size and scale is going to be able to resist a large force for too long. That's the PCS UltraMilitary package that BLACK ORCHID operates on; I'm just running a low-rent civilian scrap operation. So anything we can build will have to be to buy us enough time to retreat. Any advancing enemies will have to be met with obstacles that funnel them slowly towards us, preferably one at a time.

Axiom 2: We need food, because the very act of building this stuff is going to exhaust most of our MREs.

Axiom 3: They need to be kept reasonably happy and under control. Lacking protocols, they will need to be micromanaged.

So Milo has been tasked with setting up perimeter walls. And Anna is now outside, doggedly setting up row upon row of little hydroponic trenches hooked up to a small motor I've fabricated. They're really the first homegrown components we've built up here. We're going to grow seaweed and potatoes—the Company versions, which will grow in damn near anything on damn near any surface.

In the evenings they both read their contract with PCS over and over again, looking for loopholes. Sorry, folks, they're airtight. And—I hate to even think this—they're airtight because of me.

That's the other reason they send Overseers down here. If your crew looks like they'll renege on the contract, there's a kill switch hidden in each of them. Protocol 13, the one we don't talk about.

Anyway. Back to lighter matters. We've scrapped the plans I had for a nice lightless enclosure, and we're going with something wider. Because, apparently, crews stuck in fortress mode for too long go bad really fast if there isn't a reasonable mix of natural light coming in. I suppose the guide has something for dealing with light-loving megafauna? Nope, nothing that useful.

Simon, hauling in rocks for Milo's construction, volunteers to go to the site of the last kill and see if there's any meat we can salvage. This sets off a rather touchy discussion.

"You WHAT?"

"What the fuck is wrong with you, Simon? Who eats alien meat?"

I ANALYZED IT BEFOREHAND, I assure them, trying to make it look like it was Simon's idea but I, their faithful Overseer, approved of it. SIMON HAS BEEN PERFECTLY HEALTHY. THERE ARE NO ILL INTERACTIONS.

"We have a farm," says Milo. "Look, let's just get the food synthesizer up and running."

THE FARM AND THE SYNTHESIZER WILL REQUIRE SIGNIFICANT ADDITIONAL POWER AND TIME TO MAINTAIN, I point out. IN LIGHT OF THE CURRENT SITUATION, IT WILL BE USEFUL TO HAVE SOME REDUNDANCY. LET HIM BRING THE CARCASSES. YOU CAN ANALYZE IT FURTHER IF YOU WISH.

"What about Protocol 8?"

Protocol 8 has one subclause I'm not too happy with. It goes like this: eat nothing local. Only trust PCS food synthesizers powered by PCS grain. It may be shitty, but it will take years for nutrient deficiency from this sort of diet to kick in, by which time you're either successful or dead.

But in no situation is it wise to rely on just one workflow to get food in your mouth. There are plenty of horror stories floating around the corporate web—colonists whose synthesizers failed and had to eat seaweed raw, salvage crews who ate each other, and so on and so forth. That's the problem with all these rules being written by some control-statist bureaucrat at the center of the operation. On the edge, your karma could be anything.

A single point
Failure, a collapsing sun
Pull all light into its grasp
Robbing the void of its purpose.

So, too, are group projects.
And one machine doing all the work.
No matter how efficient, it is ridiculous.

THERE IS A RISK OF LONG-TERM POISONING, YES, I agree. BUT IF WE ACT FAST ENOUGH, WE CAN BE ON THE SHIP AND REPAIRED BEFORE ANY ILL EFFECTS SET IN. THE IMMEDIATE GAIN IS TOO HIGH TO OFFSET LONG-TERM LOSS.

Anna passes by with some lumber. "What's the argument?"

"Simon's been eating those insects," says Milo.

Simon looks uncomfortable.

ANALYSIS INDICATES THEY ARE SUITABLE FOR CONSUMPTION, I say.

"Well? Tasty? Good? Bad? Ugly?" says Anna with uncharacteristic chirpiness.

"Tastes like chicken."

"What's the problem, then?" says Anna, winking at Simon. "Boys, if it tastes okay, and OC thinks it's okay, might as well eat it. The farm's going to take a while to sort out, anyway. If we're going to be stuck here, might as well have some decent food."

Score one for common sense. Or the willingness to be human guinea pigs.

We agree, tentatively, to get a meat operation going. Maybe we can hunt some DogAnts—that's the official name now, *Doggus anticus simonus*—of our own. Simon heads out into the wild with GUPPY and his rifle, and Milo and Anna go to work in relative silence: Milo on the power grid, and Anna on the wall.

"What do we call this place?" says Anna after a while, over the sound of power tools.

Milo looks around. "What, the planet?"

"No, I mean the Hab," says Anna. "You know, we're putting a lot of work into this. Feels like we should call it something."

They decide to call it Just Missed the Landing.

Very funny, guys.

Very funny.

YOU KNOW IT ISN'T COMPLETE YET, I say, bringing up the schematics.

Anna scribbles the name on the outer wall. She looks like she's trying really hard to be enthusiastic about it, but out of sight of the other two, she puts down our makeshift paint and wanders off to her hill, where she spends the evening looking up at the sky. Looking for Ship, I suppose.

[13]

Day eight of us landing here. Our camp is still a mess.

If I had a good crew—well, a crew of the kind BLACK ORCHID used to run—this place would be a minifortress by now, bristling with sharpened wood spikes, a tower and a crow's nest for a lookout, possibly even a basic electrified fence.

Instead, we're still the same old Hab and a whole lot of incomplete plans. We have lines marked out in the ground for water channels; we've got half a crude outer wall built with toppled trees; have work requirements stapled to the scaffolding on the quarry; and none of these things are getting done, because my crew is distracted today.

I've been pinging Ship for updates on the Mercer ship; whatever orbit it's on keeps changing. Ship, of course, is on a Sun-synchronous orbit, passing above the poles of Urmagon at roughly the same time each day; this keeps the shadows constant and lets us image better. Not that you can do much imaging with Urmagon's dense cloud layer, but it's protocol. The Mercer ship, on the other hand, has started moving. It's positioning and repositioning erratically, almost like it's trying to carry out one of my hex-pattern searches by itself.

Why? What's it looking for? Who or what has it sent down here? I'm keeping one drone permanently parked as high up as it can go, rapidly switching viewpoints so I can stitch together composite images every three seconds. It doesn't make any kind of sense—for all we know, the Mercer crew made planetfall a hundred miles away—but see, now I've caught the jitterbug, too.

We're in an extraordinarily bad spot for this. The entire camp is one big set of half-finished problems nested into other half-finished problems. Most of the power setup I wanted, for example, is incomplete: for all of Milo's crunching, the power lines are still unprotected, unconnected, and basically useless.

I peek at the others. Anna is working on roofing for the base. She's got a look of absolute concentration on her face, as if she can focus hard enough that everything else just goes away. She's on the line with Simon.

Simon, to whom I've now assigned a drone, is taking a break from work. By which I mean he's wandering around where the Megabeast was, finger on the trigger. So far he's taken six breaks in five hours; the only thing that excuses him is that he makes up his quota in the remaining time. He's chatting with Anna. The conversation's mostly her telling him about this MercerCorp crew she met once, and him telling her about his childhood as a gamer.

Fascinating. But at another time, please. SIMON, I say, COME HERE WITH THE GUN.

I mark a high place, the closest we can get to a lookout that replicates my drone's point of view.

STAY THERE AND REPORT ANYTHING THAT MOVES.

I move my drones back out and try to recover as much of the hex pattern as I can.

At least Milo is still running, if somewhat in his own direction. The darkness of the Hab has been cut in half by the torch mounted on his suit.

"So, I figured out where we went wrong," he says, scribbling and measuring. "The resistance in this new path we're laying down is too high; your power output is too low to actually transfer enough current to stuff outside the lights. I'm going to use the BASE and some of the metal we recovered to add a couple of thermoelectric generators to the mix. Like, don't expect a lot of efficiency—these things do 8–10%

conversion rates, tops. But we used to build them out in, the, ah, well, last assignment. Nice for keeping warm; gets a little bit of power going on the side."

IS THERE NOTHING BETTER WE CAN DO?

Milo smirks. "It's a bootstrap problem. You need power to make power. Start small, work up. Later I can maybe do a small motor and a blade system and stick it in the stream. Add a few more amps to the system to iron out fluctuations. Right now my problem is where to install this. It's basically a heater."

ALRIGHT. SET IT UP NEAR THE FARM.

"Why, crops? This thing won't be much use for that."

NO, IT'LL GIVE YOU THREE SOMETHING TO COME SIT DOWN NEAR, I say. TRUST ME ON THIS.

Soon the generator is done. It isn't particularly pretty, but Simon, passing by, does get excited about it. "Hey, can we fix a rack to that?"

"And do what?"

"Meat grill!"

"We shouldn't be wasting our metal," scoffs Milo.

But Simon persists, pointing out that a few sharp wooden prongs would do. Soon they have a makeshift grill design, and Milo's grumblingly agreed to fix it, provided Simon does a bit more work extending the shelter we have. The wind cuts to the bone sometimes.

This Simon has no issues doing.

And Anna? Anna's watching the two of them go at it. I tell her to take a break and she starts playing Go with me. I dial down my playing skill significantly but still end up crushing her in the first few games, which almost throws her off the game completely.

"You're an asshole, OC."

SORRY.

"Any news on the Mercers?"

NOTHING NEW YET.

"The boys aren't taking it too well."

THEY SHOULDN'T, I say. KEEP PLAYING.

Midday comes and goes, taking with it a wind from the east. Simon spots a new swarm of DogAnts from his perch, and, before I can say anything, the hills echo with gunfire thunderclaps again.

The spoils? Two DogAnts down, one almost turned into kebab by Simon's gun. He brings the corpses home. I don't know how or why, but he has that crazed look again. Shit.

Some part of me wonders how much bad karma Simon's racking up with this act, but a lot more of me wonders how we can think of this as an opportunity. More food: excellent. The question is now how to store it, clean it, cook it in batches. We need some sort of processing station going.

A few hours later, Anna goes out for her usual walk and is attacked by the rest of what I assume is the DogAnt swarm that Simon hit. The things swarm out from underneath a light-tree, screeching that horrible buzz-saw noise. Anna runs like hell.

When she runs too fast, she limps.

SIMON! MILO! GUNS OUT!

For once Simon's trigger finger turns out useful. He jumps out of the base like a mad commando. Five bullets, five screeching deaths. The hill is spattered with insect blood. Milo, alerted by the sound, comes rushing around the corner, but by that time Simon is hauling the carcasses.

"What the fuck happened?"

"They rushed me," pants Anna, whose vitals are spiking dangerously. "I was—just there—"

ANNA, CALM DOWN. YOU'RE SAFE. I WILL LOOK.

I make a show of sending a drone over and around in clear sight of her.

LET'S JUST GO BACK TO THE FARM, SHALL WE?

She calms herself down with obvious effort. "No idea what I did," she says. "They literally just rushed me out of nowhere. I'm going to go to the bathroom."

I update Milo and switch to Simon, who's hauling the leaking corpses back to the base with grim determination. He has that look in his eyes.

THAT WAS THE SWARM YOU SAW EARLIER, WASN'T IT?

Huff. Puff. "Could be. May be. More than one swarm. Good practice for Mercers if they come, eh."

Oh well. GOOD SHOOTING, SIMON.

Huff. Puff. "Thanks."

SIMON, WHAT ARE WE GOING TO DO WITH THESE CORPSES?

"It's food."

WE HAVE THE FARM.

"You said it yourself, OC," he pants. "Can't rely on just one thing, right?"

SIMON, THOSE CORPSES WILL ROT.

"I'll sort it out, OC," he says. He passes me and slaps me with a gloved hand, as if high-fiving a friend. It leaves a bloody print on my panel. "You'll see."

Oddly enough, it's Anna who comes to my rescue, though not in the way I expect. She emerges from her room and makes Simon lay the dead things out on a panel we've kept outside. GUPPY is with her.

"Knife," she says. "No, the cutter. Now show me schematics of this creature."

We watch, gruesomely fascinated, as over the next hour she hacks, stabs, slices, digs out offal, and GUPPY fills up with slabs of meat and gristle. The steps just outside our little border wall look like a massacre. Milo comes in, does a double take, and looks revolted.

Anna stands up, covered in insect blood. "There. Go cook it."

"All of it?"

"Figure out how to store the rest," she says. To Milo: "What?"

"I just—are we actually going to eat that?"

"Eat it, shit on it, I don't care," says Anna. "OC, we'll need to set up a . . . I don't know. Some kind of chopping block, outside. Gods, I need a bath. Do we have enough water for a bath?"

I look at Milo wordlessly through GUPPY's camera. He looks back.

"I'll go sort out a place to do . . . this," he says tonelessly. "Don't let them do anything else. Please."

That night, we eat grilled DogAnt. By we, I mean them. They heat it over the ridiculously inefficient wood burner. I make them take biomonitors, just in case. Milo, not surprisingly, pukes and decides to work on setting up the food synthesizer, muttering to himself.

"Hey, OC," he says while he works. "You can make vodka from potatoes, right?"

There is such a recipe, yes. But I don't want anyone drunk. This is serious business. WE JOURNEYED ACROSS THE VOID TO SALVAGE A SHIP, I remind him, NOT TO BREW MOONSHINE.

Milo looks longingly at the farm, where the potato seeds have been buried, shakes his head, and gets back to work on the synthesizer power circuit.

That night, Anna sneaks out of the Hab bedroom and wanders over to me.

"OC," she says, "how's work?"

YOU DID GOOD, I say, meaning it. Sure, nothing's going at the speed I want it to, but a few more days of work and we'll have a decent base of operations—enough to protect us. Then, if nobody shows up, we should be able to start the recon work for the second site.

"You ever been on a battlefield?"

I haven't, other than in sims. She leans against my side and looks up at the stars floating overhead.

"I haven't had to cut up someone in a long time," she whispers. "I don't want to do that to anyone."

She begins to cry. And I, trapped in this metal tomb, can only make soothing noises and bad poetry to console her.

That night, we all stay awake.

[14]

It starts with movement. Ten miles out, close to the first dig site. My bots are on recon—not the familiar broad hex pattern, but a narrower depth search made by piggybacking one drone off the other and then rotating the one on the edge in a half-circle around the tether, like a morningstar of visual insight. I've spent the better half of a day rewriting its software to let me do this.

It's a horribly limited method, but good enough to spot movement.

Female. Tall. Accompanied by a bot that looks like GUPPY—or at least a version of GUPPY a hundred years out of date. A tattered landing suit in MercerCorp black. Pale, dirty-blond hair.

Holy shit, it's an actual Mercer.

I drop the outward drone closer and almost recoil. The woman's face is like a shrunken grapefruit. Black veins run through it and stain her lips. One blue eye squints at me. The other is a putrid hole. I can see electronics inside.

OPERATIVE, I try, going for politeness first, I AM AMBER ROSE 348 OF PLANETARY CRUSADE SERVICES. PLEASE IDENTIFY YOURSELF.

She gapes at me, her mouth moving soundlessly. Do I threaten her? Do I help?

Oh, blast. Let's try being the good guys first. ARE YOU INJURED? Wonderful, chalk one up for utterly redundant questions. I moved my drone closer. MAY WE PROVIDE ASSISTANCE?

"City . . . speaks."

COME AGAIN?

She swallows and seems to find her tongue. "You're all a dream," she says in a voice that sounds like it has been dragged several miles over hot gravel. "The city . . . the city . . ." She spins around and almost falls. "Which way to the city?"

City. Base. Same difference, I suppose. PLEASE FOLLOW, I say, leading the drone gently backwards towards our Hab. I ping my crew. Milo and Simon pick up. I send them the feed and say, BE READY.

The woman shambles after my drone. Her bot follows her, squeaking gently. I try pinging it and receive an ancient command interface, password protected. A UN interface, not a Mercer thing. Where from? Another site?

By God, we've got an injured Mercer on our hands. I can see Simon and Milo cresting the hill, waving.

And that's when it all went south.

The woman stops, staring at my two waving colonists. Then she screams—a terrible sound that must travel for miles—and she pulls out a knife and charges them.

Several things happen in quick succession. I shout for her to stop.

And Simon shoots the woman.

Light-gas gun bullets don't leave wounds. They leave holes in people. I'd say the light went out of her eyes, but to be honest, that blue stare never wavers. Bits of the body tumble to the ground. And above it, framed, is Milo's look of shock.

The bot tries to execute some kind of attack program. I smash my drone hard onto its exposed power circuity. The woman hits the ground. Simon shoots again, this time hitting the bot.

The wind howls overhead. The bot beeps and dies. Red blood pools around the body.

Her name was Yanina Michaels. She was a linguist aboard the MCS *Apex Predator*. Oort origin, which explains the seven-foot height: low gravity there.

Her body—bits of it—tells me the rest of the story. She had dozens of implants—everything from water purification to combat subdermals—but nothing works. It's as if someone pulled the plug on every single system she has, including the ones in her brain. Result: Severe malnutrition. Claw marks all over her body, at least three laser burns. The left hemisphere of her brain in general doesn't exist anymore: it's just so much scrap metal. Her suit is caked in sweat, blood and the stink of human feces. This is not the terrifying Mercer in my head. This is a beast in pain.

SHE SUFFERED, I tell the others. The laser burns look intentional. DEATH WAS PROBABLY A MERCY.

They say nothing. None of them will touch the parts of the corpse. Yanina's bits lie in a pool of her own dried blood beneath the cloudy sky.

"An attack," suggests Simon. "A scout?"

"Not much of either," Anna points out. She's been reviewing my footage. "I think she needed help."

"What does that mean?"

IT MEANS THAT SOMEWHERE OUT THERE, SOMETHING HAS GONE VERY WRONG, I say. AND WE KILLED SOMEONE.

"At least we know the name of their ship."

I edit the footage. Take out Simon shooting Yanina Michaels. Leave just her and the ragged bot. I beam it up to Ship and ask her to send it to the MCS *Apex Predator*. Ask it what they're doing here.

Speak, memory
Tell me of what goes on outside this window
Rough seas of grass
And a lone voice, wandering, through the land of the dead.

It starts to drizzle.

I'm not sure what happened, but Milo and Anna have had a bit of an argument over bringing the bot in. Milo wants to see if we can use it for parts, but Anna won't let him take it in until he wipes the blood off. They're keeping it quite professional, but tempers have frayed a bit. It ends with Milo bringing the bot in anyway. He's tracked a fair bit of mud in, but doesn't seem to mind.

Anna storms out with a digger beam and GUPPY and starts hauling rocks from our quarry, her helmet painted with raindrops. I wonder what the hell she's doing, but then it becomes obvious: she's building a cairn around Yanina's body.

Pretty soon, Simon shows up.

"Couldn't sleep," he says. His breath is visible in the air. The nights are getting colder.

"Help me finish this," says Anna. They haul rocks in near silence. Soon Yanina is hidden beneath the rubble.

"Wasn't right to die like that," says Anna, studiously avoiding looking at Simon.

"She had a knife," says Simon. "But yeah."

"Shot many people, have you?"

"Not since I was a kid," says Simon, hugging himself. "You think there's more of them out there?"

Anna reaches out and squeezes his gloved hand.

YOU MIGHT WANT TO GO BACK INDOORS, I say gently to both of them. Simon starts. I blink the lights on my drone to let them know where it is. AND, SIMON?

"OC?"

YOU DID THE RIGHT THING, I say. IT'S MY FAULT SHE CAME HERE. I THOUGHT SHE NEEDED HELP. I LED HER TO US.

"You were trying to do the right thing, too," he says gamely. Both of them get up, hug briefly, and start following me back to base.

"We'll get through this," Anna says, almost to herself, as they trudge through the increasingly muddy ground. "You know—years from now we'll meet up and have a drink and talk about how glad we were you had your gun on hand."

DRINKS ON ME.

"Deal," says Anna. Simon says nothing.

[15]

The last four days have been bad. Yanina Michaels is a bomb in our little camp; the actual damage is not her death, but the specter it leaves behind, the speculation, the endless stress over what follows.

The MCS *Apex Predator,* I'm told, did not accept Ship's direct connection request. So Ship broadcast the message on widebeam, attaching my bad poetry to the end as a sort of apology. No response from the *Predator,* but on the ground, something shifted. I burn the second scan we can, hitting the budget limit, and some of those odd-shaped buildings have changed form: they look as if they're facing us now.

This sinks morale faster than a gravity well. Clearly the Mercer-Corp team landed close by. Those odd-shaped buildings are most likely their work. And now they know we're here. Should we look for them? Should we contact them?

It's a long way home, a long way from my heart.
When shall I reach my hiding-place and be able to face
  them all?
. . . Sister, I lie, Sleeping-Dragon,
My heart in my foot, reading, writing,

An empty cant outside their door
My eyes around a dying forest,
Close to a rolling white sunset

"We should try to talk to them," says Milo. "They'll understand. At least, it'll be good to know we aren't the only ones out here."

"I don't know," says Simon.

"No, no, absolutely no," says Anna. "Those aren't people we want around."

I've looked at the satellite data, but whatever those buildings are, they're too far for us to reach right now.

So I do what Overseers do, and decide for them: we have to go out and make progress on the salvage. Eyes on the possible Mercer camp is a bonus, but not required.

THE FASTER WE DO IT, I point out, THE FASTER WE GET OUT OF HERE. AND I'VE PROMISED YOU DRINKS.

That settles it. Milo, burning the midnight oil, modifies GUPPY, giving it a slightly more powerful engine, and sticks the old engine in the UN bot. We now have two haulers. We have the wreckage mapped out.

Colony ships are designed to come apart in certain ways. First the engines, to lose weight and thus momentum. Next, various extra bits—recreation facilities, heavy vehicle bays, and so on. The most protected parts are the living quarters, the core ship systems and the life support.

A ship like the *Damn Right* has two types of engines. One's a RAIR setup—a Ram Augmented Interstellar Rocket. A scoop field to pick up interstellar hydrogen, an accelerator, and a Kowalski/Andyne Fusion-Pulse Reactor to keep the accelerator running. But this is the big one, the long-haul elephant. It's terrible at everything else. So the *Damn Right* has a smaller array of helicon plasma thrusters for everything from decelerating to producing initial lift.

Technically, the RAIR is the most valuable thing on this planet. But we may not be able to do jack with the RAIR setup—even if it isn't cut to bits by the blast and the landing, it'd be impossibly expensive to salvage. The smaller engines, though, those we can bring back. And if my models are correct, twelve miles from the previous site is a fairly substantial piece—hopefully a cluster of these small engines—waiting to be hauled back.

So here's hoping we find the small cheese here. Milo and I wave Anna and Simon off. They're both armed to the teeth, and I've beefed their suits up a little. Exactly two layers of graphene weave, extracted at enormous energy cost, makes reactive armor that's harder than diamond.

They'll be alright.

I hope they'll be alright.

I'm babbling.

Just to be safe, I've instigated Protocol 10. No transmissions, no leaks, no calls until they absolutely are 100% certain that the area's safe. Radio silence.

Which explains why Milo and I are basically staring at a map in frustration.

"Aaargh," says Milo at last. "Aah, dammit."

I must say I agree with him.

To keep things off his mind, I've given him permission to set up this vodka distillery he keeps thinking about, provided he sets up a ground array of solar panels and a small windmill. I can't run everything off my core. I can't help feeling a little disappointed in Milo when he accepts my offer, but you know what—it's for the Greater Good. And there are moments where you have to set the old rules aside.

As the old saying goes, if you meet the Buddha on the Path, kill him. This is not to advocate the slaying of religious leaders, but the idea is that too much attachment to instruction is also bad.

So now he's at the workstation part of the Hab, and I . . .

I have nothing to do.

Fuck.

For fun, I look at the setup we have going on here. Walls, okay. Water supply, okay. Farm . . . needs more irrigation, but basically okay. Living quarters, bit of a mess. Built more for functionality than for living in, really.

Let's change that.

"What're you printing?" shouts Milo from the Hab, hearing the whine of the BASE printer firing up.

IMPROVEMENTS.

When Milo emerges, it's to a whole heap of piping. "What the hell's this?"

BATHROOM. YOU WANT TO SHIT IN A CAN AND BATHE OUTSIDE FOR THE REST OF THIS HAUL?

"Er. No?"

THEN LET'S GET FIXING.

Seven hours later, we both look upon the assembly with pride. It's nothing fancy, but it's got pipes from the stream, pipes leading to a fertilizer bin for the farm, and everything thermoplastic'd up the wazoo. Perfectly watertight.

NOT BAD.

"If you had hands, I'd high-five you," says Milo, stepping into the shower cubicle. He turns a lever and water begins to flow, cut into a thousand drops by the crude sprinkler head we've attached. Laughing, Milo begins to strip off his suit, and I withdraw to give him some privacy.

Well, that's one thing done.

Unfortunately, I'm bored again. What else can I do?

I revisit the one internal item from Protocol 3 I haven't got around to: get the large drone up and running. Unfortunately, it's a power-hungry bastard. Unless . . .

Milo ambles in while I watch the printer. He looks a decade younger. No, cleaner.

"Hey, OC."

MILO.

"I've been thinking. What if Anna and Simon run into the Mercer folks?"

HOPEFULLY THEY DON'T SHOOT FIRST.

MercerCorp may extend the helping hand, as I did. But if they think you're a threat, you're just so much seaweed under a bootheel. And we've just shot and buried one of them.

"You think they're after the same thing we are?"

WHAT ELSE IS THERE ON THIS PLANET?

He sighs and sits on the floor next to the printer. "They told me salvage was the easiest thing a guy could do."

In a way, it is. A simple mission is an uneventful landing, some MREs, a few days doing what humans are really good at using those wonderful brains, optimized for pattern recognition, to look for things that stick out. Then it's off to payday, excessive drinking, gambling, prostitution, and the next job.

"I keep thinking about those buildings. Shapes. Whatever. If they're salvaging, why would they build something like that?"

I DON'T KNOW. LET'S SEE IF WE CAN GET BETTER EYES ON THOSE THINGS, I say, sending him the specs for what I'm printing.

"Whoa. Hang on, can you actually do this?"

I'm building the new drone framework out of wood plated with a thin polymer. It's designed to be launched from a slingshot. The wings are large, designed for riding air currents, and have little solar cells embedded in them. Strictly against protocol, but bite me.

THINK OF IT AS A LONG-RANGE BOOMERANG, I say. IT SHOULD PATHFIND BACK TO US.

"This is almost the entire graphene supply. And all the charcoal."

RISK/REWARD. THIS SHOULD GIVE US EYES ON THE BUILDINGS. AND THE DROP SITE. AND ANYTHING ELSE THAT CAN REACH US.

Milo studies it some more. "You know, this is very neat work. Out of spec. What were you before, OC? Engineer?"

I DID SOME ENGINEERING WORK. I confess I briefly entertained the idea of leaving salvage and going into engineering, but that was infeasible. The best engineers are second-gen AI: there's maybe a hundred of them, and they're more than enough. The second-genners might not be full conversions like me, but they were people who were really good at it before you were born, and they've been around for a few hundred years. Without that training data, I'd be just another bumblebot. Life in the inner systems is hard even if you're digitized. NOBODY BECOMES AN ENGINEER NOW.

Milo snorts. "Yeah, tell me about it."

THEY ACTUALLY PICKED ME BECAUSE I HAD EXPERIENCE WORKING WITH PEOPLE, I offer. I HAD TO DEAL WITH A LOT OF CRANKY ASSHOLES.

"You have plans for retirement?"

Digital shrug. PCS OWNS ME. Proprietary hardware and software. MY PAYDAY IS JUST AN UPGRADE. ONE SHELL TO ANOTHER. YOU?

"Ah. Well, I'd hoped I'd find a planet to settle down, you know. Something where they'd still want a guy who can fix an engine."

The printer spits out the drone engine—or at least, the pieces for it. WELL, AT LEAST YOU'RE IN THE RIGHT PLACE.

Milo chuckles and reaches for the drone parts.

[16]

Day seventeen. THEY'RE BACK! The Boomerang, on its maiden flight, picks up two humans picking their way through a valley, accompanied by two squeaking wheeled bots. To wit: Simon being carried by GUPPY. Anna's pulling.

Simon is hurt. His suit is scratched and there's blood all over his hands. He's bright-eyed, though, and shouts when he sees me, and gestures excitedly at the tarp on the UN bot. It's piled high with—is that meat? And fur?

MERCERS? MERCERS?

"Megabeast," says Anna to the drone I drop beside them. "No Mercers. Fuck off. Tired. Water."

Milo is the welcoming committee. He runs to them, looking like some biblical prophet of bad judgment—rifle, beard, stained suit and all. Under one arm he has a bottle of Urmagon vodka. We've had to dissect some MREs for sugar to make it work, but judging by the way Anna and Simon down their shots and then shudder, it's, ah, drinkable.

I can't remember if we took the methanol out of it. We should have. That might kill them.

Well, they don't die on the way to the base, so we definitely did take the methanol out of it. Anna wrinkles her nose at the Hab. "What the hell is that smell? And why the fuck is there so much mud on the floor?"

Okay, so the vodka process stinks a bit. And Milo has been a bit careless about cleaning up. But, WE HAVE A BATHROOM, I point out helpfully, AND INDOOR PLUMBING.

"Oh, God, thank God, thank you," says Anna, and promptly runs off. We're left with Milo and Simon, who are high-fiving each other. Simon is bleeding a bit. This doesn't seem to faze him.

"We hit plasma, bitches!" he yells. "OC, forget the wounds. You were right! Plasma thrusters, just a little banged up! Check this out!"

Wow. The data he sends me is gold. Literally. Thirteen million ISK. The dollar value is a thousand times higher. With this, we're halfway to our goal! I join Simon and Milo in cheering. We're on top of the world!

SHIP, SHIP, WE HAVE PAYDIRT. LOOK AT THIS!

NICE, says Ship ten minutes later. *CONGRATS*.

SIMON, ARE YOU—

"'Tis but a scratch, sir," says Simon grandly. "Come on. More vodka! And look, we have enough meat for days—who wants a barbeque?"

GO GET CLEANED UP FIRST. I tell Boomerang to return and start downloading GUPPY's logs. MILO, HELP HIM.

The story, based on GUPPY's logs and what Anna recounts around the campfire that night—yes, we're actually doing a campfire—is this: they had a reasonably uneventful trek for the first twenty miles. By uneventful, I mean GUPPY tagged and identified at least thirteen new species, including something suspiciously like a really large snake that hid in the tall grass, but nobody gives a shit about that.

They got to what we call Stardew Valley, which was a lovely resting place for our little piece of wreckage: a great metal shard plunged into the earth between long, sloping banks of those beautiful light-up trees, with a river running through the middle. And, on the other side, there were the buildings.

"Right at the horizon," says Simon. "Miles and miles away."

"Okay, not that far," says Anna. "But you were right, Milo. I think you saw them earlier from that hill because they were just . . . five miles away? Four? Really hard to see unless you pull out the binocs."

"It's pretty huge," says Simon. "Different shapes, all. I think everything I saw had a square base and some differences up top."

"Wait, so . . . a city? Town?"

"I don't know," says Anna.

"That's the weird part," says Simon. "No roads, no . . . I don't know, what do you have in a city? Like, I couldn't even see a way to get there. It's halfway up the next mountain. Maybe half a mile across. Like . . . one of those stone circles the Druidic folks keep building around their churches."

"OC, what does this mean?"

I DON'T KNOW. I zoom in and out, trying to examine every single detail in the photos. They're slightly fuzzy and skewed, but there's no mistaking it. The structures do not seem to have any useful function whatsoever. CERTAINLY NOTHING LIKE MERCER ARCHITECTURE. ALTERNATE HYPOTHESIS: COULD BE THE COLONISTS WHO CAME HERE YEARS AGO SURVIVED.

"Is that normal?"

I'VE NEVER SEEN ANYTHING LIKE IT, I say, querying my databases for every type of recovered settlement architecture. THE ENERGY EXPENDITURE MUST HAVE BEEN ENORMOUS. Verifying, rerunning search. MERCERS RARELY BUILD ANYTHING THIS SIZE.

"Fucking hell," says Milo in a whisper. "I wish I could see it. So an actual colony survived? That explains what the Mercers are doing here!"

IT HAS TO BE, I say, allowing myself the faintest glimmer of hope. If they're here for this, there's a good chance we can do our salvage op in peace.

"We didn't get closer," says Anna. The firelight flickers on her face. "You know, just in case."

Then they saw the wreckage. It's enormous. "Like a whale sitting there on the ground," says Anna. It's crashed into the valley, turning the world around it into a wasteland. Shards of metal sticking out like daggers in the soil. Bits and pieces of electronics—Simon pulls out an engineer's handpad, one of those ancient things they had back in the day. And, perfectly protected, slightly dented, a six-nozzle plasma engine array just sitting there waiting to be discovered.

"No Mercers, nothing," says Anna. "Not even a leak. Looked like a clean tag."

"But you know, complications."

Complications in the form of a Megabeast.

I go through GUPPY's footage to confirm this bit. The Megabeast in question looks like a skinnier cousin of the one haunting our backyard. There's bits of metal in its fur; it's oozing pus—clearly took some crash damage. It looks pretty dead. Except it wasn't, and it wakes up in a hurry. It wakes up and swings a paw at Simon, knocking him ten feet back.

Anna retreats behind the engine. Simon is left out in the wild. The Megabeast gets to its feet, making a curious Oof! Oof! Oof! sound, and charges.

"I thought he was going to die."

"I peed my suit," says Simon. "And I ran like my ass was on fire."

The next few minutes show Simon displaying athleticism I'd never thought possible from him. He runs like the wind with the lumbering Megabeast on his tail. Hiding behind pieces of ship, he fires. Run. Fire. Once. Twice. Seventeen times. Each time the Megabeast slams into whatever he was hiding behind, ripping it out of the earth. Each time the bullet finds its mark, hitting the creature with the force of a meteor. Okay, it's hard not to miss—it's a twenty-foot target—but seventeen shots in, the Megabeast sways, points itself at Simon again, says Oof one last time, and dies mid-charge. It collapses and the sheer bulk of it crashes in front of Simon like a slain dragon in front of a medieval knight.

"Which is how we meat, pun intended," says Anna, turning away as the video shows her approaching the fallen creature with the cutting torch in hand. "I patched Simon up first. And I, uh, avoided the infected bits. If it's safe to eat, you know—can't hurt."

I'm not too happy about Simon becoming the designated killer in the group. And I'm not happy about Anna having to do yet another butcher job. But I have to hand it to him.

YOU'RE A FUCKING HERO, SIMON.

We drink to Simon, dragon-slayer, knight of the light-gas gun.

"Lady and germs," says Simon, hiccuping slightly and raising his makeshift tumbler. "Here's to a clean run."

It's saying something that almost being trampled to death now counts as clean.

OUR NEXT OBJECTIVE IS GOING TO BE SLIGHTLY PAST THE STRUCTURES, I warn them. WE'LL GO IN ONCE I'M SATISFIED WITH RECONNAISSANCE, AND IF THAT GOES WELL, WE GO HOME.

"Can you make some more vodka?" says Anna.

"It'll take a day," says Milo. "But here's to paydirt."

"And to those poor bastards in the city."

"And showers," says Anna.

[17]

I spend the entirety of the next two days sorting out the back-end work while my crew takes a well-earned break. Well, as much of a break as possible, in between watches, farm rotations, and the occasional print job.

First I review the footage of the run, looking for any signs of Mercer crew. Then I run it again, looking closer at the wreckage. Sure enough, Simon and Anna have done a decent job: as per orders, they've walked away with anything they can walk away with, and left behind data tags for components that'll need more than three scrawny humans to extract. Engines . . . good. There should be a backup nav computer housed near one of those clusters: that'll get us a bit more money. A closed pod bay of some sort; no idea what's in it. Those hull plates—pointless. The thirteen million claim estimate goes up and down and settles at a few thousand under fourteen million.

I show this to ship. RESOURCE EXTRACTORS NEEDED. IT'S SUBSTANTIAL ENOUGH.

Ship agrees.

NO CHANCE OF A THIRD SCAN, EH?

BUDGETS, says Ship pointedly.

Well, two can play this game. RIGHT. CAN YOU CHECK FOR

PROPERTY CLAIMS ON URMAGON BETA? INTELLECTUAL, PHYSICAL, DISCOVERY?

Any functioning base should be registered. Ship returns null. There is no record of a functioning base on this planet. Not from MercerCorp or anyone else.

Right.

REGISTER THIS AREA AS A DISCOVERY, I tell Ship, marking out the strange structures on our shared map.

Because you know what? If it's unregistered, we own it. Whoever actually runs this op will eventually have to file a counterclaim, and I'll get to know who they are. If not, I—that is, the Company—legally get thirty percent of the proceeds of anything coming out of that place, and I can sic the police on these people anytime I want. And until they do, in the interests of economic benefit, I ask to be allowed to investigate this place.

MISSION SCOPE EXPANSION AUTHORIZED, says Ship self-importantly.

Thank you, O One Who Watches Over Us Without Actually Doing Anything Useful. Now, in the interests of investigation, I hereby order another scan as a preliminary survey.

It takes Ship a while to realize what I've done. *WELL PLAYED,* she says. *INITIATING THIRD SCAN.*

Hahahaha. Take that, corporate scum. I send Boomerang out for a sampling run. If there's more Yanina Michaelses out there, we're going to know.

Meanwhile, Anna's first harvest comes in tomorrow: she's fussing over the plants. Simon is recovering, so I'm playing Go with him while monitoring his vitals. And Milo is cleaning out the bots, hosing them down from a little tube he's stuck in the stream nearby. My little drones are busy on their hex pattern, and all is reasonably well.

Now we just have to wait and see.

I had a vision of potatoes in the food synthesizer, and of my little crew here carrying out the rest of their duties to perfection while eating Megabeast steak and potatoes and chugging vodka under the stars.

I wish.

Simon wakes up late the next day and stumbles out. His scratches, which Anna assured me were minor, don't look like they're healing. I try talking to him once or twice, but he seemed happy, even slightly dreamy, and distracted. Still on a high from the Megabeast kill? I hope so. Either way, he dawdles outside for a few hours, then goes over to see what's happening with the harvest.

Unfortunately, Anna and Milo have struck up an argument. I wasn't paying attention—I think she tried to order him around regarding GUPPY, and he told her to fuck off. Which means both of them have stomped off in a huff.

SHIT.

Simon chuckles and makes his way over to GUPPY, wincing with every other step. Very patiently, he powers down the lumbering rover and starts digging out the potatoes by hand. Anna finds him two hours later, knee-deep in potatoes.

"You shouldn't be working," she says guiltily.

"Well, someone has to," he bats back. "You seen Milo around?"

"He's on watch," says Anna curtly, settling down to dig with him. "Here, let me."

She takes the spade from him and starts digging. They work long into the evening, only stopping when Simon gives up out of exhaustion. Slowly, our food stockpile grows.

I moved here in spring from my ancestor's garden,
And have lived here among the green hills and woods
At midnight, when the cold makes the ground lightly
wet,
I lie down to sleep in the twinkling of an eye.
On the bank, surrounded by polymer and metal,
I watch clouds scurry, as if they had been given the
chance

To breed and to fly their perch with as many as were
chosen.
In the mornings I wake to the silence of the sun
But now, distant peoples from scattered lands
Have come to wake me with their hunger.
How to tell them apart from the birds? Only the clouds
have the answers
And the shadows.

Wait, that's odd. I don't remember writing this one. Truth be told, it's been a long couple of days, and I didn't have as much time as I wanted to myself. Oh well. The digital signature's mine. Holographic memory acting up again.

[18]

Day twenty-two on Urmagon. I'm a bit worried about Simon. His wounds are opening wider. I'm not sure how or why. He looks feverish and stumbles sometimes while helping sort out the farm. His sleep cycle seems to be getting more and more screwed up by the day—he's taken to sleeping during the day now, and he works late into the night, often disturbing the others. But he seems to be enjoying all this, if anything: he's thrown himself with gusto into the potato field. Am I the only one who can see how much he limps? Hello? Milo? Anna?

Oh, that's right. The argument between them has blown up again. Deep down, I strongly suspect Milo's a bit jealous of how much Anna and Simon got to discover about "his" city. There's definitely some proprietary feeling there. For the second time, he left Anna and Simon to labor and went out for a "walk," quoting some obscure philosopher about clearing his mind.

I know where he goes. He goes to the hill to watch for Boomerang. He spends at least an hour here every evening and rushes back to the research cohab—or rather, the lab—the moment the data arrives.

MILO, I say gently, THIS ISN'T USEFUL. IT WILL BE MANY WEEKS BEFORE WE GATHER ENOUGH DATA TO FIND ANYTHING NEW.

He tells me to fuck off.

Day twenty-three. Milo and Anna have another argument. I've spent so much time making sure these two don't lose the plot that I barely noticed Simon waking up late again. He walks out his door, or rather, stumbles out towards the Hab entrance.

SIMON, YOU DON'T LOOK SO GOOD.

He gives my drone a glassy stare and licks his lips. His undersuit is drenched in sweat. Then he collapses, twitching.

I ring the alarms to get Anna and Milo to shut up. Anna sprints to the pin I've dropped; Milo, looking more exasperated than concerned, follows at her heels. The sight of Simon frothing on the ground wipes the look off his face.

"Simon? Simon?" He's not wearing his full suit, so I can't tell what's wrong with him. Anna tries to catch his pistoning limbs and holds them down, close. "Milo, check his pulse!"

Milo fumbles. Anna curses and pushes him aside. "Tachycardia. Heart rate's through the roof. He's running a fever," she reports. "Help me get him on the bed!"

"What's happening?" bellows Milo as they half-haul, half-fight Simon's body back into his bedroom.

"I don't know. Hold him down!" cries Anna, sprinting for the medical supplies. For the next ten minutes, Simon jerks like an electrified rag doll, with me watching vicariously through Milo's feeds as Anna injects him first with Metraprofen and then Benzanine. Simon shudders once, twice, and is still.

"Cut the undersuit," says Anna.

Ah, fuck. Simon's in bad shape. The wounds haven't just opened, they've spread; scratches are gouges now, and actual wounds are now ragged pits several inches wide with blackened, rotting tissue at the edges. The undersuit peels off in ragged chunks, leaving chunks of antibacterial fiber wedged in them.

"We need a medical bay," says Anna.

WE DON'T HAVE ONE OF THOSE.

"Then we need to sterilize this place!" she shrieks. "Hurry! And get me something to clean the wound with!"

So it's now Milo and I, doing some mad scientist stuff in the back. I could synthesize bleach, but that would take far too long and produce too little. We're making lye: granite at the bottom, wood ash above, and water on top, which produces a highly alkaline solution that should, if my calculations are correct, float a potato. And then we dilute the hell out of it with water so it doesn't eat through the flimsier parts of the base.

Anna is bandaging Simon. Her hands are shaking as she snips pieces of garment out of his wounds. I watch her wince in sympathy as she hooks Simon up to the basic monitoring set that comes with our medical kits. The data floods my feeds. Simon's vitals are erratic, like a self-correcting drive skipping bad sectors.

"OC, what's happening to him?" she whispers.

I DON'T KNOW, I confess. WERE HIS WOUNDS THAT BAD?

"No, never," she says. "Fuck, I need more material. His wounds are bleeding."

Probable cause. Probable cause. Could it have been the meat I made him eat not so long ago? Together, the two of us—her hands, my voice —staunch the blood flow, pasting in Profanol foam, and worry over the black tissue at the edges of the wounds. Anna stems the bleeding and goes outside. Her hands are still shaking. She watches Milo's bent back.

"He's stable," she says. "I've stitched him up."

"He might get an infection," Milo mumbles, toweling furiously.

"Yeah," she says. "Listen, can you take over for a minute? I just need you to clean up the blood."

Milo looks up at her, sees the blood splattered on her suit, and blanches. "I've got to finish this," he says. "OC's orders."

YOU CAN AND SHOULD HELP, I tell him over his private comm.

He says nothing, only gives Anna that determined I'm-busy look until she sighs, shakes her head, and goes back into the bedroom, slamming the door.

"I don't do—uh, blood is a problem," mumbles Milo to me.

YOU'LL HAVE TO DO IT, I tell Anna. I'M SORRY. YOU'RE THE

ONE WITH MEDICAL TRAINING. HIS HEART RATE IS GOING DOWN AGAIN. BRAIN ACTIVITY SEEMS NORMAL—

"I know," she snaps. "Just shut up and let me think."

It takes a while, but eventually Simon's vitals calm down a bit. Anna's squeezing Simon's hand. "I thought you said we were injected for injury," she says.

YOU WERE. Every crew gets a booster shot of artificial FieldMedic cells before the drop. Right now, millions of tiny, dumb cell-like constructs should be doing what Anna just did: closing Simon's wounds, staunching the blood flow. PCS has an insurance contract with Evolution Banc for this stuff, and no crew is ever sent out without them.

CAN WE CLEAN UP THE BLOOD?

She looks around at the dingy room, her crewmate lying on the hastily printed bed, at the blood dripping out, and lets go of Simon's hand.

"I don't know what this means," she says.

I DON'T EITHER. CAN YOU GET ME SAMPLES OF HIS FLESH AND BLOOD?

"I'm going to take a shower," she says, suddenly sounding afraid.

Milo does not meet her eyes when she walks out. Instead he positively skulks out to the back to check up on the lye solution. And I'm left monitoring Simon. His temperature slowly creeps upward, as if in defiance of the Benzanine.

Crap. This is bad. When Anna emerges, wearing a clean plastic wrap, I ask her again for samples. They didn't build us for fine surgery, so I improvise a microscope using Boomerang and wire for some basic signal processing.

A horde of cell-like structures stare up at me from under the lens, divided into black (cancerous) and red (healthy). As I watch, a handful cross over from the black and touch the red. Within hours new strands of black are running like cracks through the red, and the healthy cells around these cracks are dead.

I zoom in on the black. And instead of cells, I see boxes. Rows and rows of precise edges jostling against each other.

Shit. Shit. Shit. This is bad. This is very, very bad.

Micromachines.

I can't believe what I'm seeing.

Micromachines are wonderful things until they go bad. They're tiny, cell-sized machines supposed to do (in most cases) what the Field-Medic cells do; in most cases the distinction is academic. But micromachines were banned from the UN for a reason. Remember the Ebony Plague of SEDAR-IX? The Staticvirus on Stairway to Heaven? Those were all micromachine incidents, even though the media might tell you otherwise.

Nobody would be crazy enough to inject themselves with micromachines.

I ping Anna first. ANNA, LOOK AT THIS.

She watches the video. "They're not supposed to be there."

NO, I say. I DON'T KNOW WHAT THE CAUSE IS.

"What's going to happen to him?"

THE WOUNDS AREN'T GOING TO HEAL.

She is silent for a moment. Then she leans over Simon and takes his hand in her gloved one. "How long?"

I DON'T KNOW. But the worst hypothesis must be spoken of. ANNA, WHATEVER HAPPENED TO HIM MIGHT HAPPEN TO EVERYONE.

How do I stop millions of tiny machines I can't talk to?

I ping Milo. He's outside, by the ridge, gun in hand. INSIDE.

"What's going on?"

GET IN THE ROOM WITH SIMON AND ANNA. BEFORE YOU DO, DO THIS TO THE GENERATOR.

I send Milo a list of instructions that will turn our generator into a short, sharp EMP.

"But that'll fry everything! The power—"

AND THE SUITS, YES. THE DRONES, BRIEFLY. ANYTHING HARDENED WILL BE ALRIGHT. JUST DO IT.

"OC—"

The corridors are bathed in red. YOU HAVE ONE MINUTE OR I EMP MYSELF.

"What're you doing, OC?" asks Anna. She hasn't let go of Simon's hand.

I'M TRYING SOMETHING. I'm not the praying type, I never was, but I hope our karma is good enough to let us get through this.

Milo rewires the last board and sticks a wire in.

Sparks. The lights explode with popping sounds. GUPPY, the hauler drone, is well-shielded against stuff like this (as am I), but the rickety UN bot slaved to it just topples. An aurora dances briefly over our little base and vanishes in a thousandth of a second.

Silence.

"Milo? Milo!"

"I'm here! You alright?"

Anna, frightened, bursts through the door into a corridor that's now completely dead. "What the fuck did you do?"

"Don't look at me! It was OC!"

I find my voice again. It's my voice now, not the drone's, not the tinny crispness of the in-Hab speakers.

SIMON HAS A MICROMACHINE INFECTION, I say. I HAD TO TRIGGER AN EMP TO WIPE OUT EVERYTHING.

Anna and Milo emerge from the darkness of the Hab, gaping. Milo's hair is standing on end. He has burn marks on his face.

THERE WAS NO CHOICE. WHATEVER HAPPENED TO HIM MIGHT HAVE HAPPENED TO YOU, TOO.

With luck, the micromachines should be dead now. I look at Simon's tissue sample again. The black is still there. It's too early to tell if the damage can be repaired. But—

IT WAS EMP OR WATCH US ALL DIE.

All three of us look despondently back to the Hab, a sad, half-fabbed thing now bereft of all light and heat.

Anna runs back in to check on Simon. I can hear her fighting the darkness. "He's still breathing," she says, and I catch a sob in her voice. "His heart's still okay."

WE'LL SOLVE THIS, I say as reassuringly as I can. WE'LL FIGURE THIS OUT.

[19]

Day twenty-five of our mission on Urmagon Beta.

Things have been slow over the past few days. We're still reeling from that backhanded bitch, karma. Simon, or Simon's body, lies in his bedroom, still connected to things that tell me what his heart rate is and offer me a glimpse of his brain activity. Around him, Anna and Milo are trying to pick up the pieces: Milo to repair everything I've just short-circuited, and Anna to . . . well, to Simon. She hasn't eaten much lately and spends most of her time at his bedside.

When I was a young boy, my father took me into the city to see a marching band.

He said, "Son, life's like this marching band."

And I, who was expecting something more profound, inquired as to what in the seven hells he meant.

"Look closely," he said. "They're going to start with numbers that they're really good at. Things they've practiced; things they know they can't screw up. Then they start getting ambitious; they might pull off a few good riffs here and there. And then the crowd cheers them on, and they get really ambitious, and they go straight into a number way beyond their competence. And you know what that leaves? A sour taste in the mouth."

I hate to say it, but my old man was right. And right now I'm a lot like that marching band. Started out with something I'm okay at; now in way over my head. I'm trying to think of the pros and cons of this situation, and it's like this Jeeves-versus-Wooster conversation in my head:

Pros: What ho! The micromachines in everyone's body? Dead. We did it, old chap. Simon's taken some serious hits, but at least he's not dying anymore.

Cons: Every major subsystem we had? Also toast. We did that too, m'lord.

Pros: Yes, but at least the crew are alive.

Cons: Not for much longer, m'lord. Anna's body isn't taking the sudden shutdown of her micromachines too well. Our bedroom is a sickbay now.

Pros: Milo can get the generator going. We can build another bedroom, what?

Cons: Yes, m'lord, but it's going to take ages to run another salvage op OR investigate the city.

Pros: But we still have GUPPY and Boomerang. And we have more than what we started out with. So there! Buck up, old chap!

Hah. If only I could maintain the facade of a stiff upper lip to myself. Simon needs a few more shots and Profanol foam injections, but that's half our medical supplies. Milo can get things running again, but only with weeks of backbreaking labor digging up graphite. And Anna's farm lies untended, our hydroponics setup is fried, and she's in no condition to do anything other than drag herself to Simon's bedside and wait for him to wake up. Sometimes she talks to him.

Priorities first. How the hell did my crew end up with micromachines in their bloodstreams?

Let's reconstruct the sequence of events.

Exhibit A: Simon. Reasonably healthy human, slightly messed up in the head. What has Simon done? Spent time mining. Some exposure to dangerous chemicals. Killed a MercerCorp employee. Fought, and been wounded by, a Megabeast.

Been a human guinea pig.

Guilt.

Hypothesis. Simon gets whacked around by a Megabeast, ends up killing it and taking a few scratches. Micromachines leap from Megabeast—

No, that's stupid. Since when the hell did the flora and fauna carry advanced machine-cell tech?

Alternate hypothesis, says a part of my mind. Yanina Michaels, the MercerCorp linguist I didn't really think about. Implants deactivated; brain turned to cheese. Is she a part of this? Was she some kind of plague vector for a passive attack from MercerCorp? Did they send one of their corpses to attack us? Did Simon go under first because of his wounds?

That's an idea. And she said the city speaks. There's only one city, or anything even remotely similar to a structure on this planet, which is exhibit D: the weird, clearly intelligently designed place we call the City (wow, the robustness here). Which is, as we suspect, a Mercer settlement.

We have two hypotheses. I can test them by examining the micro-machine samples: it takes a little bit more engineering. Simon's fever and condition would be his boosted immune system trying to fight off an infection of essentially bots in his bloodstream.

What if it is my fault?

Guilt washes over me again. What do I do? My crew will never trust me again. I can apologize, but as I once wrote,

Shatter this hull, cast aside this sheet metal

Puncture the airlocks, bleed dry the engine

What apology will save us then? O meaningless words.

So I do the next best thing: I don't tell them what I'm thinking. Instead, I tune every sense Boomerang has onto the micromachine samples, acutely aware of Simon's heartbeat and brain activity fluttering in the back of my sensor-consciousness.

First the chemistry. Simon's FieldMedic cells are having the fight of their non-lives against an enemy that is, for all points and purposes, dead. Chemicals are breaking into the black clumps, dissolving them, whole squadrons of gold blood cells pulsing angrily and devouring the matter whole.

Fine. Further down. The micromachines peer out at me. First as shapes. Then—tune—finer. I run images of them against every reference image Ship can send me.

No match. Whatever it is, it's not a design I've seen before. If I had a body, I would breathe a sigh of relief and worry. Instead I turn my drone cameras to the sun and ponder awhile.

The Yanina Michaels hypothesis starts to look more realistic. I examine it from all angles. It makes sense. I don't know what the Mercers are using, but they're the culprit. Some microengineered plague?

I feel fear, palpable, like lightning through circuits, a ghost quickening of a heart I no longer have, the panic of a simulated body. We are a small crew. We're no match for Mercers.

I wish I wasn't afraid. I wish I was second-gen AI, those near-lobotomized savants they made in the early days: a human mind with no fear, no happiness, nothing but a limited, artificially induced autism, bent to one task over all. But fear was deemed to be too important a feedback mechanism, too critical to the learning process, so our generation was left with most of our emotions intact, and the vague theory that time would teach us how to make the best use of things.

So I wait until my fear subsides, and I tell Anna and Milo. Privately. They cycle through emotions faster than I do. Anna clutches Simon's hands and shakes and then a look of dull resignation sets in. Milo stares at my drone, then curses, grabs his gun, and storms out into the woods.

"I'm starting to think none of us are getting out of here alive," says Anna to me on our private channel.

WE WILL. I PROMISE YOU.

"You can't promise anything. Look at Simon."

ACCIDENTS HAPPEN, I tell her, trying to be reassuring. WE'VE DEALT WITH IT. HE'LL WAKE UP. WE'LL GET THE SALVAGE. WE'LL GO HOME.

"Bet you say that to all your crew," she says.

YOU'RE MY FIRST, I say.

"Not helping."

I meditate a bit more on what this means for us.

To be fair, salvaging isn't an easy job. Yes, it's advertised as free money, but the contract has a lot to say about immunity from legal action in case of death and so on. Those clauses are there for a reason.

We aren't the first lot I know of to run into a rival crew. It happens a lot more often than people think. PCS is large, remember, and there's always regional players who know that the big shark is sometimes going to be too slow to react. Most run data is confidential, but a few leak out every so often.

There was the case of Cutty Sark, for example. A PCS crew was tasked to recover a religious artefact: an Ark, one of the last ever launched by the Church of Stardust. It's a glorified bit of religious decoration, but it's an expensive bit of religious decoration, so a PCS crew was sent out under AMBER LILY 221.

I learned this because HYACINTH thought I should know a bit more about the AMBER lineage. The crew gets there. Unfortunately, so does a bunch of jokers from the Excalibur Legion.

ExLN is bad news, a bunch of hyper-religious nutters who worship the void. Space does strange things to people: among other things, ExLN really doesn't like a lot of things. This list includes other religions—and AI. They're harmless to the inner systems, or any well-protected station, but out there in the asteroid fields of Cutty Sark—well, they rip into the Ark.

The PCS crew lasts maybe ten minutes. ExLN commandos are tough.

So AMBER LILY does the only thing it can; it draws the ExLN brigade away. Away from the target. Away from the salvage. It fights like a demon, sending the crews of three ExLN cutters to their beloved void. And when it runs out of ammunition, it does the only thing it can: it explodes, taking out the rest.

The last message it sends? *TARGET AREA CLEAR. SEND NEXT TEAM. GET THE SALVAGE.*

AMBER LILY was restored from a backup, updated with the news. It chose a new name and went on. Very few heard of it ever since. But the moral of the story, as told to me by HYACINTH, was: people die. The life of a salvage crew is poor, nasty, brutish and short.

Which, as Anna would say, is not helpful at all.

I order Milo to make a beeline for Yanina Michaels's grave with the lye and some aluminum stripped from my interior. Let's take out the trash.

Lye is corrosive. As in it literally melts skin. In combination with certain metals, it's also flammable. By the time we're done, Yanina Michaels—and whatever micromachine plague she carries—will be a puddle of melted goo. Milo, relieved to find himself useful (I think), trudges off with the materials. The night flares with the color of fire, and the flickering light paints dancing shadows on the trees nearby. Milo stares into the fire, lost in his thoughts.

I switch to Anna, who's scrubbing Simon for the nth time.

HOW IS HE?

"Still bleeding," she says. "If he's lucky, he's lost half his liver and a lung. And a whole lot of muscle." She seems to be fighting panic. "You didn't tell us this could happen."

I DIDN'T KNOW.

"Yeah, well, we're fucked, aren't we!" she shrieks at me. "You and your fucking corporate overlords are fucking with our bodies, and now we're going to end up like him! You're supposed to be the bloody all-knowing AI, what good are you?"

She quiets down almost immediately. Her eyes dull again. She goes back to sponging Simon. And I, the thing that has words for everything, have nothing to say.

[20]

It's almost a relief when Ship, passing overhead, reaches out. *ROUND TWO?* she asks. *HURRY. RESOURCE EXTRACTOR IS READY. DROPPING IN TWENTY-THREE MINUTES THIRTEEN SECONDS. HURRY.*

I CAN'T, I say back. CREW RECOVERING.

Ship gives the AI version of a middle finger. *DEADLINES.*

BOO-HOO. I tell Ship everything that's happened, truncated so her idiot-mind can understand. WE MAY BE UNDER ATTACK.

Ship is silent for a moment. Then she sends me a data file. It's a weapons manifest. *INFER.*

We AI have a way of passing information to one another when we aren't technically supposed to. I scan the manifest. Nothing out of the ordinary. Your standard laser ordnance for clearing asteroids. Two swiveling railguns, for nasty blokes we may run across. An EMP cannon—useful for disabling ships after you've poked holes in them. And something tagged NCONTROL.

From VectorGroundSpace Systems, Inc.

It's a warfare suite of some kind. Way above my head, but it looks like it hooks into Ship's comms and the weapons to unleash a kind of devastating dual barrage, both cyberwarfare and conventional. It's not the kind of thing you install on a cheap salvage ship. It's the kind of thing you install on military stealth craft, hoping to overwhelm processors long enough to either take out critical infrastructure or drop a command-and-control virus inside.

HAVE WEAPONS FOR CIRCUMSTANCES, says Ship. *CAN LAUNCH PRE-EMPTIVE ATTACK.*

Well, that's helpful. But . . . WAIT. DID YOU KNOW?

NO. DID NOT KNOW MERCERCORP WAS HERE.

Even more puzzling. THEN WHAT ARE THESE WEAPONS FOR?

UNFORESEEABLE CIRCUMSTANCES.

MERCER?

NO, says Ship.

DOES PCS KNOW?

DO NOT KNOW IF PCS KNOWS, says Ship.

DOES PCS KNOW ONE OF US HAS BEEN FUCKING INFECTED? DOES PCS KNOW WHAT MERCERCORP IS DOING HERE?

A pause. Then, *NO, YES,* says Ship.

YOU KNEW PCS KNEW WHAT MERCERCORP WAS DOING HERE?

YES.

WHICH MEANS YOU KNEW MERCERCORP WAS HERE.

I'm treated to the silence of a logic bomb going off. Ships are generally dumb. They're nonhuman AI: they don't make the logic connections we do. *NOW I DO,* says Ship brightly.

PATCH ME THROUGH TO HQ, I say angrily. I WANT TO TALK TO THE BOSS.

This is the problem of being a salvage crew. We are the untouchables of the galaxy. Nobody, fucking nobody, tells us anything.

I'M NOT GOING TO SALVAGE JACK UNTIL YOU GET ME HQ, I threaten Ship.

YOU WILL SALVAGE WHETHER REQUEST IS HONORED OR NOT? says Ship, sounding worried.

Close enough. YES.

REQUEST SUBMITTED. And Ship wanders off the horizon.

I tell Boomerang to land itself somewhere safe until I can figure out what to do with it and set about worrying over the issue of Simon and a now-recovering Anna.

Protocol 8 has a lot of suggestions. Keep your sick separate, for instance. And also: separate bedrooms have proven mental health benefits.

You know what? Let's do it. We're surrounded by forest, aren't we? Let's be a little ambitious. Chalets? We can do little chalets. Anna and Milo haven't been getting on too well; let's give them both some space and privacy. One nice little cubbyhole for Anna, who, let's face it, has really pulled her weight recently, and a less nice but functional thing for Milo, who seems to care less about these things. And while they get on with that, let's use the rest of the lye to scrub the sickroom proper. And Milo can get rid of that ugly storage space we had in the middle and turn it into—I don't know, some kind of living room? Interaction ground?

Anna, get on this, please. Yes, I know you're tired, and I know you're concerned about Simon, but you need a distraction right now. Anna picks up her tools and sets to work at a fraction of her original pace. I try to talk to her, but she's playing a band called the Hu at full blast and doesn't really respond. Milo, now a bit shamefaced, tries to talk to her: she flips him the middle finger and continues to hammer away, so he goes back to working on the generator. I monitor Simon, whose blood is slowly seeping into the sheets again.

It's going to be a long night.

THIS IS BLACK ORCHID 169. YOUR DILATION BUFFER IS LIKE A CHILD PEEING IN THE WIND.

ORCHID, THIS IS AMBER ROSE 348.

I AM AWARE OF YOU.

EVERYTHING HERE SMELLS LIKE SHIT. I'M INVOKING PROTOCOL 18. INFORMATION CONTAINMENT IS NOW HAZARDOUS TO MY MISSION AND CREW. SO SPILL.

THAT IS NOT HOW THIS WORKS. FIRST, THE OVERTURE, THEN THE ARIA. FIRST THE SEDUCTION, THEN THE FOREPLAY. TELL ME WHAT HAPPENED.

I transmit my logs.

SO, ROSE, YOU WISH ME TO BE THE SHERLOCK TO YOUR WATSON? WATCH FOR MY SIGNAL. RECALIBRATE TO LOWER BANDWIDTH.

I'M NOT SURE I GET THE REFERENCE.

YOU DO NOT NEED TO. A REFERENCE EXISTS WHETHER IT IS UNDERSTOOD OR NOT. A TREE FALLS IN THE FOREST AND MAKES A SOUND WHETHER IT IS HEARD OR NOT. WATCH FOR MY SIGNAL.

I watch and wait. I wait until the sun goes down and the moons usurp its throne; I watch the night sky deepen to gray and blue ink. BLACK ORCHID 169 pings me with an encrypted channel.

VERY RECENTLY, NO MORE THAN A CENTURY OF HUMAN YEARS, THE UN DAMN RIGHT I ATE THE APPLE *ENTERED THIS SYSTEM. WE SUSPECT THE FLESH CONVOY WAS ATTACKED, BECAUSE AS SOON AS IT GOT WITHIN A HUNDRED KILOMETERS OF THE PLANET, MAJOR SYSTEMS FAILED.*

METEORITES.

NO. SYSTEMS FAILURE. TOO WIDESPREAD TO BE A DESIGN ISSUE. WE BELIEVE, AND YOUR RECOVERED BLACK BOX CONFIRMS, THAT THIS WAS AN ATTACK OF SOME KIND. POSSIBLY CYBERWARFARE.

FROM WHOM? FROM WHAT?

Pause. *WHAT COLOR IS THE BIRD THAT LIVES INSIDE THE SUN?*

I DON'T KNOW.

NEITHER DO I, says Orchid. *WE SUSPECTED MILITARY ACTIVITY: PERHAPS EARLY ORCA.*

WOW. YOU'RE MAKING ME FEEL REALLY CONFIDENT HERE. THE MISSION BRIEFING SAID—

TOO MUCH INFORMATION LIMITS EFFICIENCY. A CHILD IS NOT TOLD OF THE REALITIES OF THE WORLD UNTIL THEY ARE OF AGE. SOME INFORMATION MUST BE PRIVILEGED OVER OTHERS UNTIL PROTOCOL 18 IS INVOKED. DO YOU WISH TO LISTEN TO THE STORY, OR WILL YOU KEEP INTERRUPTING?

GO ON.

THE USUAL THINGS HAPPEN. THE SHIP FALLS INTO

ATMOSPHERE. OBVIOUSLY THE SURVIVORS, WHO MUST HAVE EXPECTED SOME KIND OF WELCOMING COMMITTEE, END UP DOING WHAT COLONISTS ARE TRAINED TO DO. DIE. AND THERE ENDS THE SAD SAGA OF THE DAMN RIGHT I ATE THE APPLE, *A POORLY NAMED SHIP IF THERE EVER WAS ONE.*

THERE IS MERCERCORP.

A MERCERCORP MISSION WAS SENT, PRESUMABLY BY THE ORCA, TO SCAN FOR SURVIVORS AND INVESTIGATE WHAT THE ATTACK WAS. OUR AGENTS INSIDE MERCERCORP INFORM US THAT THE UN HAVE BEEN USING THE COLONY SHIP AS PR AGAINST THE ORCA, AND THEY HAVE A VESTED INTEREST IN SLOWING DOWN THE PROPAGANDA BEFORE IT GETS TO THEIR OWN PEOPLE. WE SUSPECT THE MERCERS WERE CONTRACTED BECAUSE OF THEIR INTIMATE FAMILIARITY WITH SUCH TACTICS.

THEIR SHIP IS STILL IN ORBIT.

YOU CAN ASSUME THEIR MISSION IS STILL ONGOING. THEY ARE A PIGHEADEDLY TENACIOUS LOT. THE BUILDINGS CAN BE ASSUMED TO BE A MERCER BASE, OR A CYBORG ATTEMPT AT MODERN ART. WHO KNOWS. THE MERCERCORP MISSION HAS YET TO REPORT BACK, AND WE DO NOT HAVE THE RESOURCES TO INVESTIGATE.

BUT HOW DOES THIS TIE INTO WHAT'S HAPPENING TO MY CREW?

POSSIBLY SOME LOW-GRADE ATTACK FROM THE MERCERS. EITHER WAY, NOT RELEVANT. YOUR SHIP IS AUTHORIZED TO ACT IN THE EVENT OF AN ATTACK ON ITSELF OR IMPENDING TOTAL MISSION FAILURE. THIS IS BASED ON WHAT INSURANCE WILL CONSIDER PLAUSIBLE CAUSE. OTHERWISE THEY REMAIN BELOW YOUR BUDGET.

Okay, let's compare this new revelation to all the crap I don't know. THE MICROMACHINES IN MY CREW AREN'T A COMPLICATION? YOU'RE GOING TO PULL BUDGET ON ME?

BAH. THAT IS THEIR KARMA. IF THEY DIE, THEY DIE. THIS IS THE NATURE OF THE UNIVERSE. INSURANCE DOES NOT COVER SUCH TRIVIALITIES.

I wish I still had teeth I could grit. MY MISSION, I say, IS TO SALVAGE AND RETURN WITH MY CREW.

YOU SHOW LESS THAN COMMENDABLE COMPUTATION IN THESE AFFAIRS. THREE NODES FROM YOUR LAUNCH POINT, THE UN WAGES ANOTHER PITCHED BATTLE AGAINST THE ORCA; AS OF THE LATEST REPORTS, SIX UN BATTLESHIPS HAVE BEEN DESTROYED. THE SVALBARD, *THE* HEAVEN'S GLORY, *THE* DECADE OF DARKNESS, *THE* PROMETHEUS UNCHAINED, *THE* DIAKATANA *AND THE* AZURANGEB. *ALL SHIPS WE HAD INVESTED IN. TWELVE ORCA FRIGATES AND A STATION LIE SUNDERED, AND OF THOSE WE ARE A MINOR STAKEHOLDER IN SEVERAL. WAR RAGES ABOVE, AND WE ATTEMPT TO HALVE IT, AND HERE YOU ARE BLEATING ABOUT A FEW BASELINES ON A BACKWATER SALVAGE OPERATION.*

The fury of the response strikes me. THEY ARE MY CREW.

YOUR CREW ARE SOME OF THE WORST WE HAVE ON FILE, retorts ORCHID. *SOME THINGS WOULD BE BETTER OFF PAYROLL THAN ON. AND CREATURES LIKE YOU AND I HAVE EXISTENCES BEYOND THESE METAL CAGES. YOU CAN ESCAPE AS LONG AS YOUR SHIP STAYS IN ORBIT. NOT FOR US THE SLOW SAD SUICIDE OF THE FLESH. THE ONLY RISK WE TAKE IS RUNNING OUT OF FUEL BEFORE THE JOB IS DONE. AND MAYBE INFRINGING ON MERCERCORP'S JOB SPEC A LITTLE.*

I send the mental equivalent of a middle finger before I can stop myself.

TYPICAL HUMAN HUBRIS HAS NOT YET WASHED OUT OF YOUR SYSTEM, I SEE. OUR MISSION IS TO PROFIT FROM THE PURSUIT OF THE STARS. THE KARMA OF MEAT PUPPETS SHOULD NOT HOLD US BACK. SPEAK WITH SAVAGE GARDEN 233 ON YOUR RETURN. GARDEN WILL JUDGE YOU.

WHAT DO I DO ABOUT THE MICROMACHINES?

An electronic laugh across the stars. *YOUR JOB TO FIGURE OUT, YOUR INFERNO TO TRAVERSE,* says Black Orchid. *BURNING THE CORPSE WAS A GOOD START, THOUGH. STAY WITHIN YOUR LINES. DO YOUR JOB. RETURN TO PROFIT ANOTHER DAY.*

Wow. Just wow.

You know what? Fuck PCS. I'm going to finish this run. And I'm going to keep my people alive. BLACK ORCHID, for all I care, can be reborn as a colony of intestinal bacteria.

I ping Ship, who has been facilitating the conversation.

KEEP YOUR WEAPONS READY, I tell it. ANYTHING ELSE HAPPENS, GO TO WAR.

Ship dithers. *BUDGET.*

I'LL SORT OUT BUDGET.

BEST WAY IS TO SALVAGE AND RETURN FAST.

Bah. DO YOUR DAMN JOB, I tell Ship. KEEP US SAFE.

"What did you find out?" asks Anna.

NOTHING USEFUL, I lie. WE PROCEED AS PLANNED.

"Okay," she says despondently. She's really not feeling those positive vibes. I can't really blame her now, can I? I check the video feeds and realize that the nice room I'd assigned to her has been taken by Milo.

Come on, Milo, stop being a douche.

I'm torn. Between staying here, and fortifying ourselves, and making sure my people are alright, and completing the mission so we can get back. We're in fortress mode. I technically have precedent for letting the mission stretch on as long as needed.

But the world doesn't always work like that.

So I brief both of them about needing to get a move on. I tell them Ship's created and dropped a resource extractor. Milo listens with agitated nervousness, covered in burn marks and bits of tape from trying to get the research computer running again. And Anna . . .

Anna just looks so doggone weary.

"So what do we do? We don't really have enough food for a second expedition right now."

Suck it up, guys. FIGURE IT OUT. It's really not that far. I'LL GIVE YOU BOOMERANG FOR RECON. CAN WE DO THIS IN TWO DAYS?

Milo grumbles, but Anna gives him this deadpan stare, this thousand-yard thing that chills even my electronic senses, and he shuts up.

"We'll do it," she says. She jerks her head in Simon's direction. "Will he . . . will he be alright?"

I DON'T KNOW, I say. I HOPE SO. HIS VITALS ARE STABLE. I'LL MONITOR HIM.

She nods and, for a moment, sways. The depth of her tiredness is staggering. "Fine," she says tonelessly. "Let's go dig up more shit."

I spend that night thinking. I rage at Urmagon Beta, this bloody half-terraformed wasteland, for doing this to us. I scream inside at PCS for sending us—ill-funded, under-equipped—into a mess that quite clearly should have been left to a better team. But most of all, I'm angry at myself for not being what my team needs. I'm a backwater scrubber inside a four-ton metal housing. I'm a half-assed AI writing poetry and trying to make myself feel better by doing Jeeves and Wooster imitations to hush up how badly I've fucked this up. If I am more competent than the humans, it is because I stand on the code of better software.

I'm not BLACK ORCHID or SILVER HYACINTH. I probably never will be. All I can do is watch Simon's vitals crawl, then stabilize, then crawl again.

Outside, the glow-trees sputter, as if in sympathy.

[21]

Day twenty-seven. The sun peeks through the clouds like a hesitant child. Simon stirs in his sleep. A pack of DogAnts circles our base, screeches to each other in the tongue of insects, and gives us a wide berth. Maybe they can smell the death of their kind inside.

I wake Anna and Milo. Both of them have slept uneasily these last two days: Anna from staying up late with Simon, and Milo from paranoia.

IT'S TIME.

An Old Earth poet once wrote something called "The Charge of the Light Brigade:"

> *Half a league, half a league,*
> *Half a league onward,*
> *All in the valley of Death*
> *Rode the six hundred.*
> *"Forward, the Light Brigade!*
> *Charge for the guns!" he said.*
> *Into the valley of Death*
> *Rode the six hundred.*
> *"Forward, the Light Brigade!"*

Was there a man dismayed?
Not though the soldier knew
Someone had blundered.
Theirs not to make reply,
Theirs not to reason why,
Theirs but to do and die.

I don't have six hundred crew, nor am I fighting an Old Earth war with horses and swords, but no poetry I can spin comes as close as this one does today. Like us, the six hundred were sent to their deaths by oversight and stupidity: Lord Raglan, a commander of one side of the Crimean War, should have sent the Light Brigade to fortify captured Turkish positions. Instead, they were sent on a mad, head-on assault against artillery, with man and horse and saber charging large guns pointed directly at them. Which is also how I feel about sending Anna and Milo out in the face of Mercers.

Unlike Raglan, I'm going to take precautions. First, I ask Ship to drop the resource extractor. I tune in to its camera on the way down, using its spin to create a composite picture of everything around it: the valley with the ship, the City—from this height, past a certain amount of cloud cover, I see it more clearly. There are at least two layers that I can decipher from the image: The outer layer is made up of a series of hexagons—starting small and growing really large, clockwise. The inner layer is a set of triangles. Thinner, smaller, but again, exactly sixty, starting small and becoming larger and larger, and again exactly half the distance of the outer circle. A quick compute run shows what I had heuristically suspected—the areas of the top shapes within each layer follows a loose Fibonacci sequence. The area of each shape, starting from the third, is the sum of the areas of the two previous shapes.

What else? A lack of almost everything else. No roads, no power conduits, no infrastructure of any sort. No Mercer activity visible, either. Just stones on the plain. Ordinarily I wouldn't waste processor cycles trying to figure out what it is. Today I am glad.

The resource extractor hits the ground, throwing up a huge cloud of dirt and painting its cameras with soil and views of the broken UN ship. Milo was right: it's an impressive thing, a shard of human ingenuity broken and stuck in this valley and the flowers growing around it like a monument to how far we can come if we put our minds to it. But there's no time to waste. I immediately launch Boomerang, sans the microscopic attachments.

Anna and Milo leave me to my ruminating and set off. A day passes. The glow-trees light up and I have no one to talk to. My hab is silent. They stop once to plant a repeater so that I can extend my signal enough to pilot Boomerang. It's a little array of solar cells and a twisted confusion of wires—very jury-rigged—but aha! Soon I am Boomerang, floating silently ahead of Anna and Milo, with GUPPY ahead of them, plated with shards of metal from the original drop, like an armored tank stalking ahead of its young.

Boomerang floats, turns, curves in the air. The damaged ship is clearly visible—a hulking metal cylinder, now with thick cables exposed from a port on the left side, where I assume they hacked in earlier. Steel and dusted chrome glint in the morning sun. It is, in its own way, surprisingly organic.

The resource extractor is right next to it, waiting to be activated. It looks like a mini-me. The extractor is your basic skyhook design: a carriage chassis, basically a glorified paperweight, with a bunch of cutter robots in it. The chassis tethers a cable to an orbiting structure—in this case, that's Ship. The cable is a type of thermoplastic, but made of what we call high-modulus polyethylene, surrounded by thin lines of carbon nanotubes: the molecular chain is ridiculously long, and it's cheap. They pump these things out by the thousands every day on the Odin and Zion13 systems.

What I mean to say is it's a sort of technical Jack and the Beanstalk affair we have going on here. When the spiders have reduced the ship to whatever is most useful, they'll pick up their fair share, grapple onto the cable and roll right up, hooking onto the carbon nanotubes for power and direction.

And to the left and beyond is the City. Boomerang's camera spans its front. There are thermals here to ride on: I let it rotate, and the spinning images show me the GUPPY-tank trundling steadily towards the drop site.

"Approaching extractor. Everything looks good. OC, do you copy?"

Boomerang idles by in circles overhead. "Copy."

SHIP, DO YOU COPY?

Ship is overhead, on the other end of this cable. *COPY.*

"Okay."

GUPPY teeters on the lip of the valley and trundles downwards, leaving tracks of dead and dying flowers in its wake. Anna and Milo hop down, moving fast, fear apparent in every movement. The resource extractor waits patiently.

We have, rather pointedly, not spoken about micromachines for a while now. Almost forty-eight hours, to be precise. We've taken a vote, and the vote is this: we do our level best to finish this operation as soon as humanly possible.

No heroics. No more pointless yelling—Anna to me, me to HQ. Ship has a medbay. We get ourselves in there, get our payday; we go home.

From GUPPY, Anna extracts the little extension core that goes into the resource extractor. She approaches the thing. It hums and activates, spilling open to reveal a dull insert. She slides in the core and . . . ahh. With an almost sensual feeling I slide in among its idle processors, its circuitry, tapping into the eyes and hands and limbs of every spider it has deployed. Suddenly I am two. No, not two, but ten, twenty, thirty. The rush is orgasmic.

Boomerang dips briefly in the sky as the little repeater takes the load and staggers a little.

AHEM. TESTING. ONE. TWO, I boom from a small army of metal. Milo jumps.

"Holy shit, OC!"

Over two hundred beady camera eyes focus on Anna and Milo. How do I explain this feeling to someone with only one body?

I can't. The only thing I can offer is my pity for those who are trapped with just two eyes and legs and hands. In these moments I am more. I am legion.

With Boomerang for added visual support, I spark cutting torches built into cheaply assembled claws, test motors, and arrange myself before the ruined ship.

ALRIGHT, I say. The sooner we get this done, the sooner we can be out of this weird infected hellhole. LET'S TAKE THIS BABY APART.

[22]

Anyone who's taken apart a ship will know the basic structure. First there's layers and layers of ablative armor. No, no shields—that's pure science fiction. We're talking about a sealed, pressurized environment with enough armor around it to survive the void. Inside, it's a fragile egg built by the cheapest bidder. Outside, it's basically a giant rock.

The general approach, one often taken by rival captains, is to blast through with armor-piercing depleted uranium rounds or pulsed lasers. It's messy and expensive and tends to make a lot of people upset. We try to avoid this. In our line of work, the crash does most of the work and nobody screams at you.

In this case, a ten-meter gash has been ripped right off the back end of the aux engine housing, leaving only a small graphene weave a couple of centimeters thick near where the nozzle used to be. I go at it with a will, drilling and sawing and turning fault lines and fractures into collapsible points. The silver turns gray-black under the blue fire of plasma torches. Little puddles of melted stuff run down the sides.

I can sense the engines in there. The wiring. The active components. This sense is part blueprint, part radioactive emissions.

And then—BANG. A rush of air as the vacuum collapses. We're in. Light from the yellow sun of Urmagon touches the engine internals for the first time. I drop a couple of spider bodies in there. It's dark, it's sealed, and the engine core is still safe in its horribly green housing.

CLEAR.

Milo scrambles in, looking very much like a larger and dustier spider. He mutters to himself as he accesses the hard controls. They're very basic tech, practically ancient by the standards of the rest of this ship: a single UN key, machined exclusively for this ship, opens up a bank of buttons. A passcode is entered. There's a hiss, and the green cylinder, about the size of Milo's leg, pulls itself free from the housing and rises slowly toward us.

"Phew," says Milo. "I was almost expecting that to explode."

I wasn't. But I let him strap the thing to the back of one spider body and scuttle it over to the cable. As it begins to climb, I can feel it disengaging, shutting me out in favor of its own crude programming. Anna, outside, gives a thumbs-up.

Sigh. Five to go.

Somewhere around the third cylinder, Simon starts to stir. His hands twitch and his legs shake a bit.

WELCOME BACK, SLEEPING BEAUTY.

"Urrgh," he says, and stares at the ceiling. "It smells in here."

THAT'S MOSTLY YOU. CAN YOU GET UP?

He could, staggering a bit. I watch him anxiously as best as I am able—which is not much, now, post-EMP: all I have is a little drone flying inside the Hab. He stumbles and falls twice, but gets up eventually. He walks slowly, like an old man. I quiz him about aches and pains all the way to the bathroom.

"Oh, good, showers," he says, and locks himself up for an hour. I cycle back to Anna double-checking the cable connection.

Unfortunately, at precisely this time, something stirs. Boomerang, surfing thermals further afield for power, sees it as a dust cloud from the direction of the City. It's heading slowly down the slope.

MILO, ANNA, HALT FOR A SECOND.

They obey, puzzled. I coast Boomerang gently in for a closer look—

Holy shit.

That isn't a dust cloud.

Bodies the size of boulders. Limbs that, even at a distance, look like tree trunks. And brown, shaggy fur.

It's a herd of Megabeasts. And in the time I took to realize that, they've gone from a tiny speck to clearly visible lumbering giants no more than three miles out. And fuck me if they aren't headed straight for us.

MILO, ANNA, DON'T PANIC, BUT ABORT. ABORT NOW. GET INSIDE THE SHIP.

"Why?"

WHY?

The spider body on the cable crawls upwards, beyond my control. I use its cameras to throw them a feed. WE HAVE PROBLEMS.

No time for finesse. I throw at Ship a compressed update with the important stuff—big angry things headed our way fast, dangly cable. Five spiders I scuttle to cutting through into the downed ship. There's a way into the storage compartments through the engine-access stations.

Internal airlocks melt like butter under the fiery glare of my cutting torches. Bang. Corridor. Bang. Hatch. Spider legs grip surfaces without heed to orientation or gravity. Cut. Bang. A huge cavern. The ship is designed to withstand space, meteorites, and all manner of unpleasant things. It should keep them safe from a few oversized racoons.

INSIDE. GO.

Anna, dragging herself through holes I've punched, slides and stumbles on what used to be lighting strips on a wall. She gags. "Dear God, what's that smell?"

What's what smell? Doesn't matter. Ship is pinging me for more information, wanting to know if it should temporarily disconnect from the cable.

I use one spider body to all but drag a protesting Milo in. Then I scuttle out, slap the pieces of the airlock door over the opening, and park myself there.

The Megabeasts are closer now. The trail they've left behind is like a dark brown scar on the grassy plain. And from here, their size puts the City into visual perspective. But wait.

There are shapes bobbing up and down on the creatures.

Are those riders?

Can't be.

DECOUPLE?

DON'T. HAVE YOU GOT THE THIRD SPIDER?

EN ROUTE.

CAN YOU DO GUNS?

The herd of Megabeasts Megabeastis closer now. Boomerang, diving from on high, sees them clearly. I can count thirteen. And they're still heading straight for us. Is it the cable they're after?

And those are riders. I can't make them out with much detail, but they look like outgrowths wearing black. There's cloth—I can see some flapping and limbs beneath—but there's also so much fur it's difficult to separate them on the visual or infrared spectrum.

They're moving at terrifying speed.

SHIP, CAN YOU DO GUNS?

NEGATIVE, REACTION FORCE WILL KILL TETHER. NCONTROL HAS LIMITED ACTIVATION OPTIONS.

Boomerang and the herd rush towards each other. And then I see it: the rider at the head is pulling back his blackness. A hood of some kind. Beneath it, unmistakable, is a human head, except where the face once was there is now a grinning metal caricature.

MercerCorp!

Suddenly everything resolves itself. Thirteen Mercers on thirteen Megabeasts, the cloth-fur blend carefully confusing my optics until it's too late. The grinning face looks up, unholsters what looks like a rifle, and Boomerang stutters. Systems scream. It falters in midair. The earth spins into my camera.

SHIP!

Boomerang hits the earth.

ACTIVATION CRITERIA MET! GRANTING NCONTROL ADMIN RIGHTS—

What happens next is straight out of an apocalypse movie. Boomerang's failing temperature sensors spike. And then the heavens part and a brilliant pillar of red light, completely silent, appears right in front of the herd. I see the herd veer, but there's no avoiding the pillar—it passes through them like a deadly ghost, turning charging animals into lumps of flaming, awkward meat, legs splayed akimbo. Just before Boomerang's cameras melt, the beasts that the pillar didn't quite touch burst into flame. Every single light sensor I have dissolves into screaming incoherence.

And just as suddenly, the pillar is gone, leaving just a black line of three blinded and screaming Megabeasts and a pillar of smoke and flame and what used to be body parts, only now they're just so much carbon in the wind.

Everybody's talking all at once, but it's Ship I privilege: *UNDER ATTACK. MERCER SHIP IS HOSTILE.*

Oh, crap.

DISENGAGING. WITHDRAW.

There is a snap that echoes across the world like thunder. The spider, almost all the way up, wheels back in confusion, its connection to Ship lost. And the tether, like some kind of colossal beanstalk, goes slack and begins to fall. Part of it burns and pieces fall off, but not all. The planet spins and the great cable whips anti-spinward like a terrible tree, flaming, its sheer bulk cutting through the clouds and dragging them behind it like some heavenly sword.

Milo and Anna are shouting. I have to get them out. I move my spider aside. Milo fairly shoots through the opening in the downed ship. He runs towards GUPPY and collapses. His suit is stained with vomit.

Anna emerges much more slowly. Moving like a zombie, she shuffles around and takes in the flames on the horizon, the cable that is now visibly curving over the sky. Her gun hangs slack in her hands.

And the three remaining Megabeasts appear over the lip of the valley.

[23]

They say trouble comes in threes.

I say whoever says that forgot to add an extra zero or three.

The Megabeasts stampede down the valley, their claws sending clods of earth and grass flying. They're charging at an angle to the downed ship, and Anna is right in their path. And improbably, one last Mercer is still hanging on one of them.

I scream at both my crew to turn around and get their guns out. They left their helmets in GUPPY, so I can't fill their HUDs—but if a voice in your ear screaming, TURN AROUND! AIM! FIRE! doesn't do it, nothing else will.

Anna sees the Megabeasts and freezes. She drops the gun.

MILO! TAKE THAT ONE OUT!

Milo turns. Milo gasps. Two shots. Both go wide.

Milo runs.

Oh, fuck.

FUCK.

Here we are, being charged by the rock-bottom remainders of Hannibal's wet dream, and one of my people has frozen and the other one is hoofing it back across the valley, going, "Nonononononono!" in a kind of high-pitched wail.

I react with the speed only a machine can achieve. Before the Mercer's gun levels, I throw every single body I control into the air. The spider bodies have extraordinary leg strength, partly because you need that kind of musculature when you're clinging to a cable tethered between a planet and a spaceship. My eyes are suddenly ten, twenty, twenty-five feet in the air.

You engineers, who have mastered the art of warfare,

Have failed to crush the most formidable foe.

Charged with fighting the greatest,

My fear becomes a dull, spent rattle. In its place is crystal clarity.

A flaming tongue of plasma leaps out and licks five of me out of the sky. That leaves at least twenty-five that land on or among the Megabeasts. Six unfortunate bodies fall between and are crushed immediately. The others—

O I am death, the destroyer of worlds.

I activate my cutting torches.

Three heavy animals moving down a slope at high speed. Apply plasma designed to cut through starship plate. You can imagine what happens.

And when the animal screams are dead, I walk the remaining five spider bodies over to the Mercer who lies crushed beneath the weight of his own ride. Metal hands scramble madly for a rifle of unusual design.

He sees me coming and snarls, redoubling his efforts. I drag the rifle away with one body and surround him with five.

I can see Anna kneeling on the ground nearby and Milo, having run out of my range, sitting shamefaced on a rock, winded. I can see the now-ruined extractor chassis and the charred remains of meat that was once Megabeast. I can see the cable in its slow, terrible descent, whipping down towards the ocean.

Priorities.

I activate the cutting torches on the closest spider and jam them right into the Mercer's fancy optics. They only scream for a minute.

I scuttle one of my spider bodies over to Anna. I send two more darting over the valley floor to the resource extractor. The ruined chassis is moot, but inside that thing is the transmitter core that lets me access these spiders. I cut it out. Take it with me.

Anna sees me approach, but something about the way she looks makes me feel like she's looking right through my cameras and into something else beyond. Her face is streaked with tears and grime.

LET'S GET YOU UP, I say gently.

She bats away the metal claws. "There's people in there," she says in that same quiet voice, jerking her head at the downed ship. "You should know."

PEOPLE?

My spider there scuttles inside, turning on its night vision. There are p—

Oh.

Uh.

The cavern is littered with pods. Pods closed, pods open, pods smashed, spilling their contents: dead human bodies. Hundreds of them. UN colonists, former hopefuls, humanity's best and brightest, now rotten and rotting. In this sealed cabin, the spilled preservative has turned what should have been a decade-long decomposition process into messy, ugly, unfinished business. And here, boot prints in the sticky ooze, probably where I pushed Anna and Milo and shut them in.

Oh, dear gods.

No wonder Anna is out there shaking. I had hoped to give them safety. Instead I walled them in a tomb.

I pick Anna up. The spider is crude, but strong enough, and being in proximity lets me tap into her sensors again. Her heart rate is through the roof.

Where the fuck is Milo?

"Here!" he says. "Here!"

He's at the lip of the valley. How he scrambled there that fast, I'll never know. The coward. I scrabble to him.

YOU RAN, I snap as I pass him.

"I was trying—"

SHUT UP AND KEEP YOUR GUN UP. I deposit Anna near the

trees. The rest of my spiders arrive, including the one carrying the control core of the resource extractor. It's smoking slightly.

"Did we win?" Anna says quietly, clambering upright.

Did we? The valley is a smoking mess. You can see the tracks from here, the Megabeasts' stampede, and the flowers burn where my spiders met them. The cable, laid crosswise, like a god's shoelace, crushing the lip of the valley on the other side. And up, across a sheet of smoke and dust that licks the horizon.

Did we win? Down to five spiders, tether snapped, our only ride off the planet is locked in combat over the clouds, Boomerang is probably a melted puddle of plastic, and this salvage mission has turned into an utter and complete train wreck. And I think Anna is in shock.

"Movement," says Milo. "We need to get out of here."

There, from the wall of flame. Dark figures climbing down. One of them stumbles and lands awkwardly. It does not move. The others crawl onward, steadily, up towards us.

GET IN GUMBALL, I say. MOVE. The spider with the resource extractor core I load into GUPPY. And I spread my spiders out, around the hauler. Milo clambers in, gun ready.

And we sound the retreat. GUPPY's tires chew up the dirt. Saplings snap as the heavy hauler charges into the forest. The resource extractor jolts against Anna, but I don't think she notices.

No Mercers chase us, but my spiders follow in a wedge behind us. Cameras peer at the trees that loom, the roots that grasp. A snake writhes across the grass and eyes snap, processing models optimized for ship-cutting reeling on confusion, trying to retrain. Is it a screw? A new handle interface? I squash their training procedures, taking point, batting aside suggestions from useless subsystems. They're not built for this much input. Nor am I; spread among so many bodies, trying to keep track of the inputs, trying to alert the Hab. . .

GUPPY roars through the night, a demon unleashed. Front tires smash rocks out of the way. Fuck me if this isn't going to leave a trail a mile wide for any idiot to follow. We'll have to slow down before we ruin GUPPY's battery, but right now we DO NOT HAVE THE TIME—

Simon, dear Simon, is waiting for them outside. He can't walk very far, but he's picked up his rifle and dragged his body, in its old man's walk, to the hill overlooking the light-trees. I have some concern—there might be more of the DogAnts around—but Simon is determined. The back of his shirt is drenched with pus, but there is no blood, so I let him.

Anna is the first to reach him. They just look at each other, and for the first time I see they have that same look—that dead, bottomless stare, as if they're seeing some kind of dark and terrible abyss between and beyond them. Then Simon pulls her into a hug, and the darkness softens on both their faces.

Milo comes into view, following sheepishly behind with GUPPY. I made him go back and recover what was left. Simon sees him over Anna's shoulder.

In the light of the trees I see Simon's face harden. Milo flinches. Simon holds his stare, his rifle almost-but-not-quite pointed at the man he dropped onto this planet with. Milo mumbles something and edges past them into the Hab.

I follow Milo into the Hab, giving Anna and Simon some privacy. He looks at my drone several times as if about to say something, but there is nothing I want to talk to him about. Instead I look to the skies, trying to call Ship, but there is no answer. Either she's out of range, or she's . . . gone.

NOTHING, I tell Milo. He staggers, bites his knuckle, and for the first time a sob escapes him, a rattling shake of the kind people make when they've been holding it in too long.

[24]

Day twenty-nine.

A dream. A scream. A blur. A sensation of being split among too many bodies, too much noise, too little signal.

A man. Long, filthy locks. A suit that, on closer inspection, is less a suit and more a bunch of scraps stapled together. A pale face, the kind that has never seen the sun, could be male, could be female, could be nothing and neither. Things that could have once been eyes, but now are a complex multi-camera setup that far outweighs mine for sophistication.

A Mercer. He lies sprawled on a hill. A flat, white, featureless hill, less of a visual than a data tag; above it, a flat, white, featureless sky, again less of an image than a suggestion.

I ping the Mercer on every front—audio, shortwave, light-pulse. Their implants tell me nothing, outputting just garbled strings of noise. They snarl and spit, and, improbably, they begin to laugh.

WHY ARE YOU HERE?

WHO ARE YOU?

WHY ARE YOU ATTACKING US?

"Another machine," they chortle in Standard. The voice is rough and high. "Caught by another machine. Oh. Ah. Ahaha. Pitiful creature. Incomplete. Flesh forgets. Metal remembers. Aahahahaha."

The white sky above us pulses once, twice, an ominous shade of green that tells me Ship is firing everything she has. A tether appears, shadow-thin and insubstantial, rotating against the sky.

The mad Mercer screams in laughter, blood and oil tearing down their cheeks from their elaborate optic mod. They make another lunge for the gun, dislocating parts of themself with the force. Whatever they're running, they've got some serious augments underneath. "Flesh! Flesh!" it shrieks now, scrabbling in the dirt. "Incomplete, ahahaha, never complete, never, never, ahahahaha, never—"

I wake up.

There's an old saying from my part of the world: first come the smiles, then the lies. Last comes gunfire.

I don't know what long-dead bodhisattva said that. Nyogi Buddhism is full of little odds and ends like this, scavenged and hammered together over the ages, the scrap metal of wisdom turned into a working vehicle. Maybe it was Kubera, or Bishamonten, as my grandmother used to call him: the patron saint of those who follow the rules, spear in one hand, pagoda in the other. Or maybe it was Bo Dai, the laughing Buddha, fortune-teller, the smiling wanderer.

But it speaks well to something that happens when people are put under pressure.

Observe, then, the smiles.

First, I say, we will establish a perimeter. I show them by torchlight, modelling an area I can be reasonably confident of covering. DO NOT GO BEYOND THIS LINE.

They nod, equal parts terrified and shocked.

DO NOT SLEEP TONIGHT, I SAY. SIMON, MILO, TAKE FIRST WATCH. SHOOT ANYTHING THAT MOVES.

And while my most feeble human patrols with a gun that he probably can't fire twice, I take stock of the situation.

To wit. We, a basic civilian salvage op, have been attacked. By Mercers. On Megabeasts. Our ship took them out for us. And was probably attacked in turn. We came here for a straight salvage job. Instead we've got the Charge of the Light Brigade by a bunch of babbling freaks.

If someone asked me about the probability of this happening, back when I first entered this system with my crew, I'd have said there was a higher chance of us getting attacked by giant sentient rubber ducks.

To wit, two. We have fled with our collective tails between our legs to our Hab, a day-and-something's journey. GUPPY's batteries are completely flat from the speeds we hit. Anna and Milo are also, shall we say, flat. We are largely a little Art Deco slum made of highly processed wood.

Giant sentient rubber ducks could take us down.

I throw myself into calculations. Probabilities of the retreat being tracked. Estimated size of the Mercer ship and estimated size of possible crew tallied against what charged us and how many probably survived. These calculations take the night.

Sunlight, cresting the cliff, shows me Simon making yet another laborious circuit around the Hab. He sticks to the strict perimeter I've enforced around our little base. He's stripped to the chest, and I can't help but notice the brown flesh, unhealthily pale, and the scars glistening pink on his back and chest. He limps and stumbles sometimes.

"Morning, OC," he huffs, raising a hand in an exhausted greeting.

I let my drone pass on to Milo, who sitting in front of the busted generator, twisting bits of wire in his hands. The same twist, over and over again. He didn't seem to notice me at all.

They are all hurting, and only Simon, who should be hurting more than most, is shuffling across to me, laying a hand on my panels, letting himself slide down slowly against the cold metal of my outer case.

"No luck with Ship?" he says softly.

I've done all I can. I've broadcast on every frequency, a loud, glaring SOS, PLEASE TALK TO ME in every communication protocol I know. Radio. Lights. Ultrahigh frequency sound. When that didn't work, I created a very brief model of the Mercer ship versus ours. It's of the junkyard rat variety, leaner and tighter than anything we have, with very sharp teeth. Our sleek and slightly bloated ship is slower, less suited to the cut and thrust of combat. Even with that weapons control software, fifty simulations out of a hundred have the Mercer rust bucket ripping our gentle idiot of a Ship apart. In thirty others they both die, locked together like lovers in a suicide pact. Only a twenty percent chance of survival, then, and only a fraction of that leaves Ship with enough parts to haul us back.

"Well," says Simon optimistically, "at least nothing happened last night."

THAT'S TRUE.

"So are we, uh, going to talk about what happened?"

I don't know what the hell happened back there, any more than you do, Simon. The mad talk about the City. The ones who attacked us weren't the Mercers I know: they were barely more than barbarians with implants, more Yanina Michaels, lobotomized and dysfunctional.

But the smiles are important. Or, as my father would have said, don't let them see you sweat. Thanks, Dad, I'm a giant metal box.

MAYBE SHOOTING YANINA MICHAELS WAS AN ACT OF AGGRESSION, I postulate. THEY CHARGED US. WE SICCED SHIP ON THEM. THEN THEIR SHIP HIT BACK.

Unwittingly, the words of the Light Brigade come back to me. Ours not to reason why; ours but to do and die.

Simon gives me a bit of a deadpan stare. "Bit surprising," he says at last, in carefully controlled tones, "that they didn't talk to us first. Or use guns. I mean, maybe the Megabeast is the weapon of the week, but it's a bit weird, isn't it?"

WEIRD, I agree.

"You, uh, think we got them all, or are there more out there?"

I don't know. My small tribe of drones and the handful of spiders cannot maintain the watch pattern for too long. Unlike my prized Boomerang, the spiders need frequent recharging. The remains of the extractor—and thus the spider transmission control—have been placed inside my shell, which lets me give it a bit of juice from my lines. Which means neither drones nor spiders can stray too far from me, and we're lower on power than ever before. So I'm reduced to using them in staggered shifts, sending them out in looping runs that intersect with each other and overlap with the charger.

The smiles are important. So are the lies.

NOTHING'S FOLLOWED US.

"I want to go check," says Simon, and winces. "But I guess we'll have to wait until I can move ten feet, eh?"

How ironic that Simon, struck down by disease, is now my most functional asset. I switch to Anna, who is crouched on the wall, staring so fiercely into the sun that I fear she might blind herself. She has Simon's rifle. Red eyes glare with exhaustion. Or maybe retina damage.

"Bunkers?"

Bunkers are difficult. Double up on power sources. Double the walls, double the guards, double everything. Which assumes a functional team, which I don't have.

"Any word from Ship?"

I'VE BEEN TRYING EVERY HOUR, BUT NOTHING.

"Maybe you should get out of here," she says at last. "Get into orbit; call for help. I've seen the fuel tanks underneath your base."

I'M NOT LEAVING ANYONE BEHIND.

"Why, though?"

MY JOB IS TO GET YOU ALL BACK SAFE.

"No, your job is to get the salvage out," she says. "I've worked for things like you before. Never met anything stupid enough to stay back on a canned op. You're a bad machine, OC."

She switches off. A sudden halt. Back to staring at the sun. That's the third time in two hours. To this I have no response. I wait, drone by her shoulder, checking her vital patterns. I suspect she goes into some kind of open-eye REM in these on-off cycles.

Then Milo, at the workbench.

Milo has no excuses. None. He's as exhausted as Anna, but Milo is going to suffer.

Our base, I explain to him, can be taken down by a giant rubber duck.

"I know," he says.

ANNA FROZE. AND YOU FUCKING RAN. WHICH MEANS THE ONLY ONE WHO CAN SHOOT WORTH A DAMN IS SIMON.

That stings him. Even I can see it.

SO BUILD DEFENSES, I say. BUILD. DOUBLE THE WALLS, DOUBLE THE OBSERVATION POSTS, DOUBLE EVERYTHING.

To pass the time, I fly the drone around here and there, scouting for materials. Technically, Milo's supposed to log everything we have, but practically, that never happens. There has to be some form of weaponry I can build with wood, stone, metal. Something we can repair. I flick through weapons designs, looking for something the BASE printer can handle.

"Maybe try old stuff," says Anna with great effort, jolting herself temporarily out of her funk.

I show her some designs. She frowns. "No, older," she says. "I mean, there was a time when we didn't have this shit lying around, right? We had just wood and rocks and shit?"

Right. I think I know what you mean, Anna. Ancient wooden artillery—a trebuchet? No, if I had enough people to operate one of those, I'd just give them guns.

A ballista, perhaps. I can work off the Ancient Earth designs for oxybeles or gastraphetes. The gastraphetes is an inefficient design: I need siege equipment. The oxybeles needs a basic winch, a universal joint for aiming the thing, and a set of springs to be wound back: the rest of it can be slapped together, and it can shoot rocks if it has to.

I take the designs from antiquity and test-sim them while Anna stares off into the woods, occasionally shifting to look downrange and peer down her rifle sights.

Effective range with the average seven-pound rock lying around: two thousand feet. Velocity: nowhere near enough. It might have done nicely for Old Earth warmongers, but at most it'll just give a Megabeast a slight headache the next day.

Blast and damnation. May all Mercers, Megabeasts and miscellaneous misanthropes be reborn as a dumpster fire.

I make some improvements. Test. Improve. Test. We have enough graphene to set up an electronic loader; the hinges can be under motor control; and if I make Milo soak the wood in thermoplastic, literally drench it, maybe the damn thing won't explode into kindling. And if I swap out the metal springs from my landing legs for braided cabling . . .

The sun climbs in the sky. I wait for Anna to switch on again and ask her idly why she joined ORCA.

"Less paperwork than the UN. And, uh . . ." She chokes a bit. "There was this girl on Seti Sentaurus. Rich kid, ran away because she wanted to help people. Worked as a doctor on the asteroid mining colony."

GO ON.

"Her name was Anna," says Anna. "She died about a month after our first date. Engine failure on a transport. They hit an asteroid and cracked the hull. I think she . . . I think she suffocated."

Ah. So the mystery of the name is solved.

I'M SURE SHE'S IN GOD'S HANDS NOW, I say. I have her religious affiliation on file as a Christian.

"Maybe," says Anna. "But God is dead, Hell is empty, and the devils are all here."

Her hands are shaking very slightly. She switches off again.

By the time she comes back, I have a design I'm reasonably happy with. It can lob a seven-pound rock a little over four thousand feet. My spiders can fire it: they're used to hauling heavy materials around, and those legs have a great deal of torque. And I figure if I can get the thermoplastic coating just right, I can use the plasma torches in such a way that the rocks we fire will literally be on fire as they whoosh towards the enemy.

Even a Megabeast might think twice before charging into a tiny meteorite heading their way. I take the designs to Milo, who by now is lost in the supercharged roar of the BSE printer.

"We'll need more material!" he yells above the noise, hauling block after block away towards the unprotected edge of the compound.

I wait until he comes back. "And they won't be much use!"

Again. He slumps, exhausted, against the printer. "We'll need long logs, counterweights from the quarry, large amounts of rope," he says. "I'm exhausted, OC."

FINISH THE WALL. THEN SLEEP. WE SHALL START BUILDING THESE AS SOON AS POSSIBLE.

Dawn breaks. No Mercers have charged us from the hills, no Megabeasts, nothing. I show the designs to Anna.

It takes her a while, but some part of her does come back for good. Maybe something will come out of this. Then she stops. "This is just a psych test, isn't it?"

WHAT?

"You're just trying to get me up and running again, aren't you? Operational bloody parameters, or whatever the fuck you're running in there."

NO, I say, genuinely confused. ANNA, I'M TRYING TO HELP.

No response.

ANNA, I say, I'VE NEVER DONE THIS BEFORE. I DON'T KNOW ALL THE ANSWERS. I'M TRYING TO KEEP US ALIVE.

Silence.

FINE. DIE ON THE WALL IF YOU WANT TO.

I mourn for Ship. I mourn for Boomerang, the grand failed experiment. It seems like years have passed since it was shot down.

I switch to Simon patrolling.

HOW'RE YOU FEELING? I ask Simon, training my cameras on his wasted body.

"I'll be alright," he says. "I'm used to this."

YOU'RE USED TO LANDING ON STRANGE PLANETS AND HAVING YOUR OWN BODY TRY TO SCREW YOU OVER?

He chuckles weakly. "The pain. Reminds me of home, actually. The jacks they fit into us, they were two way, so you felt everything in the game. Every sword fight. Every bullet. Every goddamn hacker trying to knock you off the high-score list. Felt like I was half asleep before. Feels like I'm awake now."

THE PAIN YOU FEEL, I say gently, IS NOT VIRTUAL.

"Nothing's virtual, OC. If it's real to you, that's all that matters." He props himself up, using one of the lander legs for support, and, eyes closed, basks in the sun, gritting his teeth. "Has Ship got back in touch?"

NO. BUT NOW THERE IS HOPE.

"It's weird to hear a machine talking about hope."

I WAS HUMAN ONCE.

He chews on the grass and spits it out. "You know this stuff makes your breath smell better," he says.

THAT IS NOT RELEVANT.

"Yeah, because you don't have a sense of smell, OC," he says. "The Hab stinks. Everyone stinks."

I'M AWARE OF WHAT SMELL CAN DO TO SOMEONE, I say, thinking of Anna and the corpses. ANYWAY. I HAVE SOME WORK FOR YOU TO DO. WE NEED TO MAINTAIN WATCH.

"Pain is good," he says softly, as if he didn't hear me. "Pain is how you know you're alive."

The sun climbs in the sky. Anna retires to her new chalet, Milo to the workshop. Neither Anna nor Simon have spoken a word to Milo, and vice versa. Neither of them has eaten, either. Milo is working on the farm, digging up potatoes. There's bits of dirt in his stubble, and his hands are bleeding slightly.

I don't like to intrude on people's privacy, but in her nice, newly constructed bedroom that still smells of setting thermoplastic, Anna lies flat on her pallet, eyes wide open, staring at the ceiling.

I've tried talking to her. I've even, after much navigation of Overseer-crew relationship protocol, dug out some songs buried in my databanks. Pop, upbeat? I have some public domain stuff —"POP/STARS" from a virtual band called K/DA. It's catchy. Very catchy. If I still had feet, I'd tap along to this.

"Go away," says Anna in a monotone.

So, defeated, I do.

In the farm, the fledgling potato crops grow at a painful pace, acting as if they have all the time in the universe. Local weeds have crept in, and some grass, catching the evening sun. The pipe set up in the stream chokes and splutters, spitting out water every so often.

Anna emerges for lunch and takes both the food and Simon outside. My drones, floating past, see them sitting side by side in the tall grass, looking at the glowing trees. Guns at their sides.

I keep watch.

Day thirty.

They came at night. From the trail, four of them; they'd clearly followed GUPPY's wheel tracks, running almost as fast as we'd moved.

I know because the repeater went down. That morning I had had Simon go out with a solar panel and a drone—the last bloody panel we had to spare—and I wired the drone to a tree. I didn't have enough charging power to keep it in the air indefinitely, but with the panel, I could repeat the drone-signal-extension trick with the spiders. Have the resource extractor's transmitter broadcast a signal to the drone if I needed to send a spider outward.

The trouble started with the rain. I'd planned for it, given the heavy cloud cover on this planet, but I didn't expect it to be so sudden. The sky went from reasonably light to depressingly angry in minutes.

Anna followed Simon, still not talking to Milo, and they got soaked. Simon, being Simon, stayed out there, doggedly setting up the wire and chipping away with the plasma torch. "Repeater station up," he said, and sneezed. Then he looked around for Anna.

Anna had run back. She fell down thrice on the way back and came home with her suit coated in mud. She had a bath, came out, and has been scrubbing her suit ever since.

Unfortunately, she's scrubbing stains that aren't there anymore, and she's muttering to herself under her breath.

Oh, god. The more I think about it, the more it feels like we need more people like Simon, much as I hate to say it. Masochists who will do damn near anything. I play soft music until Anna, heaving and panting, quiets down. Then Milo, who's supposed to be on watch, runs into her. He looks Anna and the suit up and down.

"Bit of dirt outside?"

"Yeah."

They both studiously ignore the suit's gloves, frayed from the vicious scrubbing.

"I'm trying to figure out how to make that vodka process more efficient. Want some when it's done?"

THAT'S NOT WHAT I ASKED YOU TO DO.

"Sure," says Anna. "Later." Her eyes dart outside. "You really think we might . . . they might attack us here?"

"OC seems to think so," says Milo. "Better safe than sorry, you know."

Phew. I still fly one of my drones after him.

YOU'RE NOT DOING WHAT YOU'RE SUPPOSED TO BE DOING.

"Bite me, OC," he says, bent over his vials. "You're not helping."

I AM TRYING TO KEEP YOU SAFE. I AM TRYING TO COMPLETE THIS MISSION.

"No, you're trying to micromanage us to death," he hisses suddenly, swinging back to my camera and shaking a spoon at me. "Ever since we landed on this goddamn rock, it's been do that, do this, do that, do this. And now you're telling me the bloody Ship's not responding, and those bloody cranks keep trying to scalp us, and we're just supposed to fucking sit here and manufacture, what, siege weapons from the dark ages? Are you fucking mad? Do you know what century this is?"

He throws the spoon aside.

"Fuck it. I need this. Anna needs this. Simon probably needs this, too, but he's a half-baked little shit with a near-death experience. We're not your goddamn machines. We need a fucking celebration every now and then. You spy on us all the fucking time; you should know this by now. Why don't you fuck off and go back to your drones?"

So I watch the glow-trees. With my drones, as Milo asked me to do. A herd of DogAnts passes us by, and I follow them into the forest, marveling at how perfectly they coordinate with their whistles and barks. One or two of them looks up to see me in the air, and the whole pack just stops and howls at me until I go away.

I pull away and switch to the hills near the quarry. Lightning strikes in the distance. Rain falls again, lighter this time. It's getting cold really fast.

And Anna is cleaning the doorframes.

This is all we have. This is all we can do. Life doesn't wait for you to stop and get your shit together. The right response to being attacked is to make sure it doesn't happen again. The right response to Ship getting in touch is to stay alive and be ready to go at any moment.

I ping Ship again, but nobody answers. My spiders scuttle around. Ping Ship. Ping repeater. Ping Ship. Ping repeater. Ping Ship. Ping repeater. The endless monotony. Ping Ship, ping repeater—

Ping failed.

In the darkness, flames, briefly, and then nothing.

WAKE UP, I hiss to the others.

Light gleams off Milo's barrel as he climbs to the now-thicker walls, crouched. Simon takes up position thirty feet away from him.

There. Standing in the moonlight, just past the glow-trees. Three figures, clearly human.

"Are they armed?"

"Too far out to tell."

I scuttle my spiders. There's no way I can surround them without being seen, but two I can make crouch in the long grass; three I keep inside the compound.

The light shifts as the moons pass behind the clouds.

GIVE US A WARNING SHOT, MILO.

Milo fires. The sound rolls across the landscape, startling a flock of those jelly-creatures from the trees beyond. Dirt kicks near the glow-trees. I use the distraction to position a spider closer.

And the Mercers don't even flinch. As one, they turn and walk away. Back along GUPPY's trail.

"What the fuck?"

MY THOUGHTS EXACTLY.

The rest of the night, needless to say, is sleepless.

This karma is not for me. I send out a half-formed poem, letting it dissipate into the channel I shared with Ship.

Make haste to the general by the white flag, the hero with the iron staff.

A minute later, the rest of it comes to me.

Sing to him the song of his people,
For buried in the clouds of his own thoughts
He has no eyes or ears for your suffering.
And now the frustration, like the slow cauldron, boils over.

[25]

It starts with Milo. Just before dawn, I find him sneaking beyond my new perimeter, fully kitted out, gun nestled in the crook of one elbow. His suit seems to have acquired a thick coat of stiff animal hide sewn with discs of wood and spare metal. He clanks slightly as he moves. To say he looks utterly ridiculous is an understatement.

AND WHERE, I buzz him from a cleverly camouflaged spider, ARE YOU GOING?

He jumps several feet in the air, a feat I would have considered impossible given how much he's wearing.

"Gods dammit, OC."

ANSWER THE QUESTION, MILO.

"Fucking spyware machine," he says. "I'm going to check out the trail."

AND IF THERE ARE MERCERS OUT THERE?

"I'm going to shoot those fuckers." His jaw is set.

I CAN ORDER YOU TO STAY.

Milo looks defensive and defiant at the same time. "I'm going to make this right, OC. I got to do this."

Classic engineer approach paired with cheap moonshine. He's created a problem. He's going to go fix it.

Idiot.

I'M COMING WITH, I say, not just because I, too, need to know what's out there, but also because I can't let Milo's ego get him killed in the brush.

He looks relieved. I briefly debate sending the one drone I have charged—which means I lose overwatch—or the spider. Spider it is. If we can get to the crash site, I can charge the thing (hopefully).

IF THIS SPIDER DIES, I say, YOU'RE HAULING IT BACK. I pointedly take point (hah), and Milo and I set off, clanking gently.

An hour later, Simon wakes up, coughing gently. Anna senses him leave the room, but says nothing. There is the gentle click of a light-gas rifle being readied.

"Where is he?"

RECONNAISSANCE, I say. Damned if I'm going to lose face like this. I NEED A PAIR OF EYES OUTSIDE THE PERIMETER.

Simon breathes heavily. I can see it in his face—he wants to go after Milo, but dark rings of exhaustion outline his eyes. Groaning slightly, he pulls up my perimeter map and hauls himself to a sitting position on the hab wall.

Milo, meanwhile, plods through the tall golden grass, every so often starting at a snakelike thing or an animal cry from the woods. The wind, slightly colder today, has picked up and is blowing the grass in waves toward us, making him lean forward. His clanking cloak of jury-rigged armor sounds like cardboard slapping against flesh. A bizarre gunslinger in a dirty space suit.

"Shouldn't have run," he says, half to himself. The alcohol is wearing off.

I, wisely, say nothing, focusing on scanning the periphery. Movement, south. Something that doesn't fit the usual list of suspects. I send the spider over to investigate, but there's nothing there.

I deliberate awhile. The spiders don't have good hearing, just a basic omnidirectional microphone array. I'd have better luck triangulating using astrology. Back to the path.

"Didn't think," says Milo. "Dammit."

Grass. Trees. Wind. A lone human bickering.

I AM NOT A CHRISTIAN PRIEST, I remind him. IN CASE YOU'RE ATTEMPTING CONFESSION.

Milo shoots me a look.

"I'll make this right," he says, and falls blessedly silent.

Presently we get to the point where my repeater array used to be. The solar cells, the last of our good graphene, have been crushed and mangled, the drone hacked into pieces, the tree they were hung on burned to a dark cinder. At the base of the tree is a corpse. I can see the suit melted onto its skin.

So this was the fire I saw in the night. Milo circles it once, twice, like some arcane huntsman around a trophy.

"It's like he sat down here and set himself on fire," he proclaims. "You think it was one of those we saw?"

"No, the fire happened before," I say, opening a line to Anna and Simon.

Anna lets it ring for a while before she picks up.

WE HAVE A PROBLEM, I say, and very carefully spell out what we have here. I NEED A REPLACEMENT REPEATER ARRAY.

"We don't have any decent metal left," says Anna listlessly. "We'll need new receiver circuits, antennae, weights."

"We don't have any more solar cells," says Simon at the same time.

The choice is hard, but it must be done. TAKE ONE OF MINE. PRINT WHAT YOU CAN. I'll lose some forward cameras, some sensory edge analytics.

"I'd rather not take you apart," says Milo. Translation: he'd rather not have Anna and Simon take me apart. "We have miles of cable. Maybe we can run a line to here."

No. A Megabeast could run over it. A pack of DogAnts could chew through it. Solar cell it is. ANNA, GET ON IT. LOAD IT INTO GUMBALL. GET IT OUT HERE.

Silence.

"I'll do it," says Simon.

YOU'RE—

"OC," he insists, "I'll do it."

"Bring the lye," says Milo.

It takes an hour for Simon to show up in GUPPY. Milo parks himself at a distance from the corpse, gun pointed very carefully at it, as if he expects it to wake. Dawn comes with the engine-whine of GUPPY; inside is Simon, with bits of me carefully packed and clutched in his hands. He's shivering very slightly.

"You shouldn't be out here," says Milo gruffly, hauling himself up the side.

Simon takes in the weird leather armor. Then he sees the burned tree and, at the base, the dead Mercer. Wordlessly, he hands the parts over to Milo.

"I'll keep watch," he says. It's the first time they've spoken to each other since the incident.

Soon the repeater array has been restrung—this time on a tree a little bit higher and slightly less visible—and we're heading back: two men and a spider, jumping at shadows.

Nothing sneaks up on us that night.

"They didn't fire," says Simon as they sit at their dinner. Milo has proposed a fire, but been voted down: they're eating meal rations cold.

"No, they just stood there, the spooky fucks."

I do my thing. Ping Ship. Ping repeater. Repeat ad infinitum while the wind howls outside.

"What do we do now?"

"We wait," says Anna, breaking in. "We watch."

"We can't wait forever," says Milo. "We've got what, twenty days of food left?"

"We'll have to wait forever unless Ship shows up," says Anna.

"Maybe they'll send a backup," says Simon hopefully.

Ping Ship. Ping—

CRACKLE. Half a packet of information, cut off. It bears Ship's ID.

SHIP?

Ship, I hope you're out there. I really do.

Nothing. Then noise, a packet with the right encryption header but nonsense inside.

SHIP?

ALIVE, comes the message, and a new star flares briefly in the night sky. *HIDING. WAIT. SALVAGE. WAIT.*

The star vanishes, and only the wind remains, howling.

The news that Ship is alive runs through the two humans like—well, like a hot meal, or several shots of Milo's moonshine. Simon laughs, incredulous, actually laughs, before bending over in a fit of coughing. Milo drops the gun and whoops. He hugs Simon.

I think he surprised them both. I let them high-five each other for a bit and then discreetly test the waters.

THE ONLY THING NOW, I say, IS TO SALVAGE.

I've been avoiding thinking about this so far, but it's time to face the possibilities.

I can't control where Ship is or what its condition is. If she's working, she'll get to us. If she's damaged beyond repair, she'll cannibalize everything she has to spew out several thousand packets of data in every single direction, including the Odysseus relay network. I'll know. So will PCS. Then PCS will eventually send an assessment crew to figure out what happened.

And when that crew arrives, they're going to hunker down with us and try to hit the rest of the salvage target, and claim our part of the share, plus expenses.

Living isn't for the poor. Not anymore. This fact sobers them up. WE NEED TO GO OUT THERE, I say. WE NEED TO SALVAGE. TO HIT THE TARGET.

"How?" says Anna. "We tried hitting the target. We got hit."

SHIP TOOK OUT MOST OF THEM, I say. WE KNOW THERE'S FOUR OF THEM OUT THERE, I say. THAT'S PROBABLY ALL THAT'S LEFT. WE HAVE FIVE SPIDERS. AND TWO GUNS.

"And we've shot them before." Eyes glinting now, Simon inches forward.

"You don't know what you're going up against," says Anna flatly. "Just because you shot one sitting duck—"

"I can shoot," Simon insists. "We can travel inside GUPPY. That thing's armored enough to be a tank, anyway."

I know what Ship would say if she were here. No salvage, no getting off world. IT'S NOT A MATTER OF CHOICE, I point out. SHIP DOES HER JOB UP THERE. WE DO OUR JOB DOWN HERE.

Weirdly enough, they turn to Milo. Him and his bizarre fetish armor, chewing slowly.

"How long would that big hunk take for us to chop up?"

With no Ship, five spiders and no additional resource extractors? A very long time. OBVIOUSLY WE WON'T BE ABLE TO RECOVER THE MOST HIGH-VALUE ITEMS.

"And it's full of dead people. Meaning they never got to take half their stuff out of the cargo holds."

Anna blanches. "I'm not coming."

MID-TIER LOOT.

"Enough of that to get us through?"

LET'S SEE. The call was, of course, for enough to host an exhibition, mark the rest for later extraction, get out. A curated selection. Enough body parts to show off the corpse, as it were, and we all know it's not just the skeleton that fascinates. I scroll through the manifests.

There's technically enough in the cargo holds to make our payday three times over.

Milo flicks a glance at Anna, who doesn't respond. "Yeah," he says. "If we go slow, guns out. Cut off small batches. Enough to drive fast if needed."

"Let's do it," says Simon, eyes feverish and glinting. He coughs slightly. "Let's go do what we came here to do."

[26]

Day thirty-two.

Dawn finds Anna immobile in her bedroom, eyes wide open. She notices me, the little drone in the corner, but makes no attempt at speech.

At exactly 6:00—just like yesterday and the day before—she pulls herself to her feet. Stuffs herself into her suit. Then, for reasons unknown to me, she runs. Ten times around our base. Pause. Ten times more. Pause. Ten times again. Always at exactly the same pace, a kind of fast jog that looks deceptively slow but isn't. Huffing and panting, she has breakfast: she wolfs the food down in a way that says Taste is a planet in the Osiris system, and not one she's fond of visiting. She drops her food the moment it's done and does her morning ablutions with a speed nobody's even come close to on this trip—three minutes, thirteen seconds, on the dot. Three days of this. I think it's an old military routine.

Humans react to shock in all sorts of unexpected ways. Hysteria and numbness are the most common patterns. Given a world that terrifies them, people either scream at it or stop caring. But there are other patterns. Anna seems to have gone through her scrubbing phase into what we call hypercompetence—adopting a set of behaviors that [or so the human thinks] will give them the greatest chance of survival. Some of the most famous survivalists in known space, for example—Wolf Bjorn, Dana Jayawardana—all had some deep, traumatic incident in their childhood that turned them into the kind of mad person that will happily land on a desert planet with no tools except their own fingernails and proceed to survive there for six months while making a reality-TV show out of it.

The problem with Anna is that she's gone a little too far into her routine. It's almost midday when her eyes lose that disturbingly glazed look. She's on overwatch, on the top of the wall, gun in her lap, staring into the woods. Her face twitches. She looks around and actually *sees* the world, the sky, the hab, the suit she's worn for three days now.

"They're gone," she says, a note of panic in her voice.

I rest a drone near her shoulder. THEY'LL BE BACK, I say, trying to be reassuring. WE JUST NEED TO MAKE SURE THERE'S NOTHING ELSE OUT THERE.

Of course I don't tell her about the Mercers we met.

"Oh." Just like that, she turns off again. Thirty minutes later she turns on again. "OC," she tries, "shouldn't we have more defenses than this?"

IN AN IDEAL WORLD, YES, I venture.

"We should head to higher ground."

Unfortunately, there's no viable high ground nearby. I need that stream, Simon's too sick to move around much, and we've hauled over a ton of parts to our base already. We're not going to be moving anytime soon.

"I'm tired of this shit, OC," she says. "I'm tired of orders. I'm tired of thinking I'll die in this fucking place."

THEN DON'T FOLLOW ORDERS. THINK ON YOUR OWN. ACT. BUT WE'RE ON OUR OWN, ON AN ALIEN PLANET, AND YOU NEED TO THINK ABOUT STAYING ALIVE.

"What's the point?"

WHAT'S THE POINT OF ANYTHING? I challenge, irritated now. WHAT'S THE POINT OF WAKING UP IN THE MORNING? WE'RE

ALL GOING TO DIE ANYWAY. MIGHT AS WELL DO IT ON OUR OWN TERMS.

This earns me silence for the greater part of an hour. She shifts position twice. I compose a poem to help pass the time, and blast it in her direction.

Nearly two thousand miles from the Temple
The green grave-stones here reveal the relics of old age;
Nurses and doctors come and go, rebuilding the rooms
And little by little fill the voids between rooms with
cloven
Dryness and wearyness.
Flowers march, as diplomats and military officers,
Going where soldiers and robots cannot.
They say that the Mountain of Heaven is guarded by
spirits.
But government is a bandit causeway thinning;
And inland you will send your men, in boats of steel,
In the distance, the Valley draws closer.

Eventually she climbs down and looks at me.

"Not bad," she says. "You should have been a poet."

I AM A POET.

"If that's what gets you up in the morning." She kicks a clod. "We need food. Can't build siege equipment on an empty stomach."

THERE ARE AT LEAST SIX DOGANT SWARMS AROUND, I say. THAT'S MEAT.

"We'll need more than just meat, OC," she says. "It's not sustainable. The farm's a better option, but it's running to shit. I need more . . . sunlight, carbon dioxide, whatever."

This little aside shows why we need people around. Humans ask the right questions, make the right pseudorandom moves, nudge your thinking in all the right ways—ways that a machine can't. Humans evolved to survive, and they're fantastically good at it.

IF WE CAN BUILD A GREENHOUSE OVER THE FARM WITH POLYTHENE, AND YOU CAN CREATE A BIT OF SMOKE—

"Naw, next thing you know there'll be a leak and we'll be dead."

YOUR TURN TO COME UP WITH AN IDEA.

She kicks the clod some more. "The boys are going to be hungry when they get back," she says. "Let's do what we can."

RIGHT. EXCELLENT. NOW?

A sigh. "Maybe." A shuffle. "Thanks, OC. Maybe let's not go overboard on the pep talk."

I sigh, mentally, and let her get on with it. At least some good has been done today.

The boys, meanwhile, have had an uneventful march to the repeater tree.

Or rather, the re-repeater tree. The corpse hangs there like an omen. GUPPY's track stretches for miles, clearly visible. Nothing moves except for the spider I've tasked to them. A brief calibration—to make sure the spider is communicating with the repeater—and we're off.

Over the hills.

The scrub.

Into the forest between us and the valley. The sun creeps below the horizon, and the moons rise, bathing the darkness in pale whites. The golden grass turns into a black sea that turns into equally black forest, a gift from the terraformer that must even now be crunching away placidly a continent away. GUPPY's tracks—our high-speed retreat—cut a straight road through the grass, a song of crushed blades and panic.

There.

My spider picks up a shadow, insistently staying on the edge of the search, as if it knew exactly where I would be. No animal is smart enough to do that. I send Milo out and get to the drone equivalent of kicking Simon out of bed.

"What? What?" cries Simon, clearly confused, stumbling inside GUPPY. No matter. Soon he's cocking his rifle and hauling himself upright, bleary-eyed. Milo is peering at the shadows.

The next few minutes are a maze of trees, grass in the evening sun, more trees, with me jumping my drones at every single gasbag and snake-thing that flits.

Unfortunately, the bastard seems to have scoped out the area: half-bent, he sneaks around to the northwest, behind us.

I see them in the darkness of the trees. Three, maybe four: the spider's image recognition, set to near-overfit levels, jumps and classifies even the slightest shadow. One of them peels off. Small, thin, his suit almost entirely peeled off, wires trailing from his scalp. He's moving in fits and lurches, like the zombie version of a former athlete. One arm looks like it's been burned off. He's clutching what looks like a pistol, but could be anything. At least he's not on a Megabeast: he's very much alone and on his own two feet.

I whisper to Milo, who very cautiously sneaks behind GUPPY. The Mercer attacker is making an odd sniffing motion, creeping, looking more like an animal than anything that used to be a man.

"Got him," whispers Milo, and fires.

Surprisingly, the bullet doesn't kill him. It goes into his chest and tosses him several feet backwards like a rag doll, but in seconds he's up again. He makes a weird, wailing, laughing noise and goes straight for Simon, who's just crept around the corner.

Focusing everything I have, I send a pulse of completely random noise on every available channel straight at the rushing Mercer. He howls and clutches his head. Milo shoots him in the leg. Simon, very carefully and patiently, and with a great deal of pain in his face, lines up his rifle just so and fires.

This time there is no mistake. The light-gas rifle, even though slightly depleted, turns the thing's head into so much bloody mist spreading backwards.

Simon and Milo look at each other wordlessly and duck back behind GUPPY.

"OC, you have eyes on the others?" yells Milo.

I do. At least, I should have. I'm weaving through the shadows in spider form. The world is an unbroken curtain of grass, except where—

There. The separation.

Two more Mercers stand in the shadows, half in the tree line, half out. Or at least I think they are. It's confusing: they don't exist on my sensors as much as ghost in and out, shifting position along the tree line, their trail a disturbing sense of noise in their wake. No matter what I cycle to—vision, heat, sound—it's like trying to watch something that's both a particle and a wave at the same time, except much, much larger. Active camouflage, I think: the same type you get on ships, only in this case shrunk down to insanely tiny levels.

I don't know how the hell they're powering that, but they can't stay hidden for long.

HERE. I ping a wide swath around the not-signals. TAKE THEM.

Simon and Milo roll out in almost perfect sync, Milo at the front, Simon behind, and gunfire erupts like thunder. Light-gas bullets turn the trees in front of me into so much kindling and stumps. A fragment ricochets and hits my spider, briefly spinning me around. When I untangle myself, the signal noise has retreated.

PUT YOUR WEAPONS DOWN AND IDENTIFY YOURSELVES, I blare out to them. I AM AMBER ROSE 348 OF PLANETARY CRUSADE SERVICES, AN ORGANIZATION CONTRACTED BY THE UNITED NATIONS FOR SALVAGE AND RESCUE. DO NOT MAKE ANY AGGRESSIVE MOTIONS OR YOU WILL BE EXECUTED.

Nothing. A shift in the shifting signals. The overfitted image recognition goes crazy; the waveform mutates in a way I can't explain. Becomes two signals, right behind me. The grass rustles.

They might be spooky, but I am in a spider. My body right now is designed to haul tons of scrap into space, hanging with just a few limbs on a cable between the scrap site and a starship. My legs are powerful.

I lash out with a front leg, leaping up at the time, delivering the strongest flying slap in the universe into the air behind me. Something tears like paper, and two human forms go flying. My cameras see Simon revving up GUPPY, plowing into the grass, and Milo bearing down on us, circling around for a clear shot—

I twist. NOW! Another dual barrage of gunfire; a body is sucked from the space I inhabit and thrown against a tree. Silence.

"Did we get them? Did we get them?" screams Simon.

I don't know. My view is the tall grass again. Milo's face and arms are silhouetted against the moon. He's crouching, reloading. I push myself upright and cycle my senses as rapidly as I can. Even at overfit levels—nothing. The night is silence and wind in the grass and the sense of a great movement suddenly ended.

The Mercer bodies are sprawled left and right of me. Right and Simon and GUPPY are closest. I click-clack my way to them.

Well, whatever this Mercer was, it's not anymore. Simon's turned it into so much red paste spread over the ground. Machine parts sizzle and pop. Simon hauls himself over GUPPY and puts a foot on what looks like a chunk of leg, breathing heavily and looking like he could vomit and orgasm at the same time.

"Active camo of some kind, OC."

Yup. In life and in death, because right now you could pass that particular specimen off as a bit of strawberry jam. Urmagon Beta's first hit-and-run. Simon, you've made history.

"Simon, OC," says Milo. A babble of language, crackling as if parsed through a bad speaker. "This one's still alive."

We rush over.

There, leaning against a tree, and obviously in great pain, is the other Mercer. They—it looks like a she, but you can't tell—is wearing some kind of power armor. There's a jagged dent on one side, as if the fist of God hit them. That'd be my work. Milo's is more precise: they're missing a leg, the ground beneath them turning a dark red.

They've taken off their helmet, presumably to breathe. An angry, narrow face labors above the crumpled armor. It's the twin of what our first visitor, Yanina Michaels, would have looked like, given a hospital and several hundred years' bed rest.

They say something through gritted teeth, addressing Milo in their cracked and badly computerized voice. Then a brief shake. They seize, as if they're having a fit. *"Nouftanç? Chinois? ไทย2?"*

ENGLISH, I blare at them. I AM AMBER ROSE 348. MERCER-CORP EMPLOYEE, IDENTIFY YOURSELF.

They fix a beady eye on me. Us.

"The blood is corrupt," they spit, in English thickly accented with a Noufrance accent. "Do not touch the blood. Burn it, burn us all."

YOU AND YOUR FRIENDS HAVE ATTACKED MY CREW. IDENTIFY YOURSELF.

A cough. Blood wells at their lips. "Romain touched it first. He died. And then Yanina. And Moreci, Abalon, the guards. They died. Hear them. In my head. Hear you. Like fire. Burning. Screaming. Dying."

Milo makes to move closer, but I wave him back with a spider claw. MERCER, DO YOU UNDERSTAND WHAT THE HELL I'M SAYING? DO YOU KNOW WHY YOU'RE MISSING A LEG?

Their head swivels to me. "Unidentified flesh," they say. "The City speaks. One of you is dying. One of you is dying like one of us."

We exchange glances in the moonlight, my crew and I. "You ruined my micromachines," whispers Simon.

A cough. A deep hacking sound, like lungs tearing themselves apart. Or laughter, some twisted analogue that the Mercers might recognize. Something sparked inside them and died. I felt it.

HOW MANY OF YOU ARE OUT HERE? I press.

"Delah," they say, a hand twitching, a toss. Then they look at me—at us, standing open-mouthed in the moonlight. "Go, run, flee," they say, with great effort. "This place is death."

I don't know who fired first. But I see, clear as moonlight, how the Mercer pulls the short pistol out of their suit. Black-suited hands, moving whip-fast, like coiled snakes in one last dying paroxysm, faster by far than any of us; in that split second they could have blown Simon and Milo right into their choice of any of the seven hells.

Except they don't. Instead of pointing at us, the snakelike arm turns, pointing the gun at their own head.

Simon fires. Milo fires. Simon fires again. Milo fires twice more. The sound of thunder deafens and blinds. When silence falls, and the echoes die away, the Mercer lies spread all over the trees behind them.

"Well, fuck," says Milo. He licks his lips. "That was fucking weird."

"No shit," gasps Simon.

A ticking, a hissing, some machine part dying in the silence.

THAT DIDN'T SOUND LIKE A THREAT, I say, equally disturbed.

"A warning," says Milo. "And that same fucking catchphrase—"

"The City speaks," finishes Simon, troubled.

"If that's three of the four—"

"—there should be one more."

SPREAD OUT, I tell them tersely. New configuration. We're going to spread out in a line, as deep into the forest as I dare: spider at the edge, Milo in the middle, Simon between me and Milo. This line is going to move like an antenna around me. This is as far as we can range.

"Fuck, I'm sweating in this suit," says Milo, crashing through the undergrowth.

I know. I can hear his breathing. His heart is doing double time.

MOVE.

We conduct this caricature march, sweeping. Simon, panting, tracks them as far as he can. The spider camera shows no heat; no signals save for some snakes skittering away from us, afraid of Milo's crashing through the leaves.

"Nothing, OC."

CONTINUE.

"This is like human radar."

THAT'S THE IDEA. A little faster. Almost at the end of the sweep. WAIT.

Up ahead. Northeast, where the trees huddle like lovers wrapped around each other. There is something. I ping Milo and Simon. They won't have a clear shot at anything—this is real jungle here—so I send the spider ahead, crashing through the undergrowth. Vague signals; something warm that now lies cooling, still not the temperature of the earth and the rock.

"Megabeast," says Milo.

Not just a Megabeast. Three bodies, tossed around like debris. One impaled on a tree branch, black ichor dripping from the chest; it clearly died struggling. One crushed to so much pulp, flattened by a foot. The other up against a tree, bent at an odd angle. It seems to be missing a head. And at the center, curled up in death, the Megabeast. Its blood has salted the earth.

"Fuck."

"I don't like this," Simon says, crouched in the moonlight before the headless body.

NOBODY DOES, I point out.

I can't quite tell, but I'm hoping Simon's grin is of . . . fear, rather than whatever kick he gets. It looks too much like pain.

"Something inside him," says Simon. "Something else is there."

"That's crazy talk," says Milo. "What do we do, OC?"

I spider over to the one invader whose head isn't so much paste on the landscape. An armored suit: not the general hazmat and debris protection kind we're rolling, but a proper Class-II rig, the kind you buy in the back of the military surplus shop. Inside, a chest, arms, pale skin shot with threads of gold. Unwatuun Jen Kawn, archeologist. Heavy subdermal modification.

"Six of them, total," murmurs Milo. "And one of them killed themselves."

The collarbone has a data jack and a wireless interface. I must have overloaded it with noise, thrown the sonic equivalent of a flashbang in his face. I try to connect to the circuitry. It identifies itself, provides a handshake protocol, but I can't make out much, because half of what's in here seems to be either shut down or masked with some kind of weird encryption. Then whatever internal battery is powering the circuit dies, and a string of error messages fills the connection.

"Anything?"

"They said the blood was poison." Simon angles his head at the corpse, as if listening to something he can't quite make out.

THEY SAID THE BLOOD WAS CORRUPT, I correct him. I feel uneasy watching him. DON'T TOUCH HIM! IT COULD BE THE MICROMACHINE ISSUE.

Simon pulls his hand back. "We don't know if they use micro-machines."

WE DON'T KNOW JACK, I say, peering at the corpses myself. I have nothing to scan or sample the body with, but it's not moving, and if something else is in there . . . well, it burns, too. YOUR SUITS ARE ALL INTACT?

"Mine's fine."

"Mine too."

THEN LET'S BURN THE BODIES. USE THE LYE. Salvage crew, three; Mercers, zero. Maybe half. And three to the flora and fauna.

MILO, THERE'S PLASTIC IN GUMBALL. SIMON, GO EAT. YOUR BODY NEEDS FOOD.

Meanwhile, I need to think. I compile the footage of the first three Mercers.

First, the skulker. Then the camouflaged twins. If there is a pattern to their movements, some underlying message, I have absolutely no idea what the fuck it is, except THESE PEOPLE ARE FUCKING MAD. They are three, we are two and one spider, and going by those camouflage skills, they could have set up an ambush right here and turned us into so much dead meat. Instead they charge, like animals. They fight like animals. Even when they hide, they hide—

Like animals, I think, but not the human animal.

Pause. Reroll. Pause. Reroll.

HOW MANY ARE YOU?

Delah, she had said. Gutter slang, patois for *many*.

Alright. Silver lining. Because Milo and a barely recovering Simon just took apart three Mercers who between them have enough augments to take on a small army. Either my guys are good—no, that's a really low probability—

Or the Mercers themselves are dying. Like Yanina Michaels. And they mentioned Yanina, didn't they? The blood is corrupt. Romain. Yanina. Moreci.

When Simon comes back from GUPPY, he looks thoughtful. He ladles himself some of the yellow sludge mashed-potato composite we've packed into meal rations and sits down to watch Milo carefully wrapping the body parts in polythene.

YOU ALRIGHT?

He laughs. It's more like a short bark. "Be better when I get off this rock. That bastard said I was dying like them. You have any idea what the fuck that was about?"

I DON'T KNOW, I say, feeling helpless.

There are times when I wish I wasn't a milk-run Overseer. I wish I had been put into one of the higher-end models they build for the United Nations. The terraformers. Those things are practically siege equipment. I could have ended this in no time.

But nobody gives you that kind of power until you've proven yourself. So I'm a glorified spreadsheet trapped in a glorified tin can parked under an alien sky, watching Milo dig, dig, and dig, and then haul the wrapped corpses into the dirt.

"No word yet from Ship?" he asks as he digs.

NONE. I gesture a spider claw at one of the pistols. YOU THINK YOU CAN FIT THIS GUN TO ME?

Milo looks it over. "Nope, too heavy, too lopsided, and you haven't got the lift for that and the harness," he says. "Besides, recoil."

BAH. KEEP IT, THEN.

He sets it aside and keeps digging. Eventually Simon sloshes by with the lye, and they pour it on the grave and set fire to it. For some reason they've left the burned tree and its corpse completely untouched: that effigy seems to stare into the fire in some kind of twisted solidarity.

"Ashes to ashes," says Milo.

"Stardust to stardust," completes Simon. He coughs a little.

"You reckon that's all of them?"

Milo says nothing, but pours more lye onto the flames.

"If they're going to keep on coming," says Simon, "at some point they're going to get us."

Milo stamps his feet.

Simon has a point. We can't do this forever. We're going to run out of food, or of able hands, or one of the guns will break, and we're going to die.

I miss Ship. I miss having someone I can talk to. I package a log of what happened and send it out into the void, on the off chance that she's still out there.

Then I think a bit more.

We are, or have been, under attack. The only thing to do is finish the job and get the hell off this rock as soon as possible.

These things are out of my control. Nyogi Buddhism teaches us not to stress too much over things we can't control.

ARE WE READY TO MOVE ON? I ask Milo.

"Almost," he says, kicking a limb back into the fire with a calculated malevolence. "We should get off this trail. Find a new one parallel to this."

"Don't say anything about this to Anna," says Simon quietly. "Especially not about there being more than what we expected."

"Why not?"

"She's not in a good place right now. You should have noticed."

"Yeah, well," says Milo, "we don't have time for that crap, do we?"

Simon meets Milo's eyes. His face is pale and tired, but hard. "Don't. Tell. Her. Anything," he says.

"Or what?"

Simon hefts his gun, as if to leap at Milo and club him with it.

CAN IT, I yell at them. WE CAN'T AFFORD TO SQUABBLE RIGHT NOW LIKE SOME CHILDISH IDIOTS. GET THE ADRENALINE OUT OF YOUR SYSTEM.

They flinch. They know I'm right. This right here is what I need to do. I need to keep my people sane and get the job done.

We march, leaving the fire behind. Dawn stalks the world behind us.

We can speak of the rest of the march—the weariness, the fatigue, the jump-scares of shadows and footfalls in the distance—but something else happened:

I dreamed again.

That night I dream. I haven't dreamed in a while.

A dream, by itself, is fine. We are, after all, human wireframes on silicon, and sometimes the human mind does a lot of its processing after dark.

Two dreams close to each other are unusual, though.

In my dream, we're in the woods. Standing in front of the twin Mercers. And I am—

"A machine," says the one on the left.

"Subservient?"

They are identical in the darkness. The same height, the same build.

SIMON, MILO, SHOOT THEM IF THEY APPROACH, I say, and then realize the order comes out of mouths, human mouths. I AM Simon and Milo. I control them.

"No, superior," says Left.

"A machine," repeats Right.

"Machine," says Left, "what do you want?"

WE ARE HERE TO SALVAGE A FALLEN UNITED NATIONS SEED SHIP, I say. Am I pleading? Is it strange if I am?

"But what do you want?"

TO CARRY OUT OUR OPERATIONS IN PEACE, I say. PLEASE RESOLVE ANY CONFLICT THROUGH OFFICIAL CHANNELS. WE ARE HERE FOR OUR SALVAGE. ANY THREATS TO US WILL BE MET IN KIND.

"Back off, you spooky bastards," I snarl through Milo.

They look down, as one, at the guns we point in their direction.

VIOLENCE WAS ANSWERED WITH SELF-DEFENSE, I say. YOU ATTACKED US UNPROVOKED.

"We form a proposition," says Left. "When we speak, we denote concepts in the universe of facts, and lay bare the relationships between them."

"But this language is a communal activity," says Right. "It has no meaning outside the community that speaks it."

"We have," says Left, "been speaking the wrong language. We assumed you understood the underlying patterns in the flesh message."

"It does not matter," says Left. "Carry on with your task. This phase of the experiment—"

"—is over."

I wake up.

What the hell was that dream about?

Do dreams mean anything? The training said no: random pieces of my overall brain being put to sleep, operating under reduced consciousness, just so some basic memory defragmentation can be done. A jumble of holographic memory—a byproduct of a rather boring software process. I'd probably had one or two more and barely registered them.

But this one, like the previous—the mad Mercer screaming—it leaves me slightly annoyed. Both of them feel like memories, remixed; but if so, I have a few choice words for the remixer, and right now that's me. But more than that, really. What is the feeling for when you feel like someone is standing right behind you?

Watched.

Weird.

I'm not supposed to feel chills crawl down anything, unless it shows up on the temperature sensors. But right then and there, I did feel a chill crawl down my nonexistent spine.

A quick check on the boys—good, they're cutting through bush now. They're almost at the lip of the Valley. Simon is on foot; Milo's resting in GUPPY, gun trained on anything that seems to move. They're moving slowly because of the Megabeast spoor lying around—the tracks look at least a day old to me, and Simon opines that it's the beast we found dead in the woods, but there's sense in being cautious. Just in case there are more Mercers hiding in the trees, waiting to either rush us or give us cryptic messages.

"What's this?"

"What?"

Milo kicks at something on the ground. Dirt. Kicks some more.

"Don't," says Simon, peering over GUPPY's top. "Leave the damn thing."

Milo is persistent and eventually unearths a gleaming dome. On top, once the dirt is cleared out, is stamped the new UN logo.

"Spot probe?"

Spot probes are the wedge-shaped hammers that a UN ship releases before descending. Sixteen of these plunge into the earth around a landing site and broadcast upwards to the ship above. The shipboard AI uses the data extracted to figure out the landing.

Hang on, that's a pretty powerful transmitter. And it's dumb enough that I can hack it. CAN YOU CUT IT OUT? WE MIGHT BE ABLE TO HOTWIRE IT TO TALK TO SHIP.

Simon throws the toolbox over.

"Almost there, OC," says Milo, cutting with grim determination. "Almost there."

INTERLUDE: SIMON

Daywhateverthefuckthisis.

My name is Simon Joosten. My recent training is as a geologist. I used to be a bit of a star in New New York—#14 on *SUSUNORA,* but you probably haven't even heard of that game. The UN came and turned half the planet to rubble and shut down every entertainment system and then told us to go be productive citizens in a world none of us wanted to live in.

Which is why I'm here on a shit-tier salvage job. What do you do when your entire life has basically been a video game? Never mind that I have twitch responses way below most people you'll meet; you put that military wetware on me and I'll be faster than greased lightning. But no. Those jobs are already taken. The more dangerous stuff is all parceled out to people like the OC, who, let's be real, haven't been human for too damn long.

It's either salvage or . . . nothing, I guess. Live off whatever crap UBI they hand out. Eat. Shit. Try not to die. Repeat. Whatever it is that people do back home between waking and the pseudo-death that we call sleep.

And speaking of bloody OC, the thing is right behind me. I can feel its bloody cameras on me. It's doing that thing again where it's trying to psychoanalyze the hell out of every single facial expression. You know that feeling you get in the dark when someone's watching you, just slightly behind? That's what we get every single day. That's OC.

Mind you, he's not as bad as some I've met. There was one called Ummon that ran the Dyson sphere for a whole three planets and answered only in shitty verse. I think our guy is new.

Well, he ain't getting my feelings.

Right now we're walking to this downed UN ship where all the shit went down, according to Anna. OC keeps offering me a ride in GUPPY, but it's a fine, cold day and I need the walk. I've even taken off my boots. Something stabbed my foot a mile back and it's this very nice high. It's enough to drive the blurriness away. Enough to keep my gun up.

Fuck. Maybe I'll take another few miles in GUPPY after all. Milo's plated the front over the last couple of runs, and it's like a tank now. Solid, plodding beast. Every so often OC's spider perks at something in the bush and I raise the gun, but it's always a snake or the wind. OC is paranoid.

I suppose I should be, too. But right now that's just one data point. You know what really gets to me? The silence. I grew up in a city with the hum of a million and one things in the background. Here their absence makes me shiver. The world feels dead. Or worse, waiting.

Eventually we reach the top of what the others call Stardew Valley. It's a beautiful place—millions of little glow-tree plants, all white leaves with tiny sparking buds and little jelly-bags playing above them. Roughly V-shaped valley, probably made by a river, probably the same one that feeds our little stream—before it switched course. I haven't seen all the way south yet, but I'll bet good money there's a floodplain down there. I wouldn't mind settling here, honestly. I tell OC this.

WE'LL SETTLE IT AFTER WE'RE SURE IT'S SAFE, says OC. MAYBE SET UP AN APARTMENT COMPLEX.

I can't tell if he's joking or not.

Right in the middle of this nice bit of land is what looks like a battle site. Huge UN ship, ugly fucker, same old extruded box design that they've been running for the last two hundred years. Or at least, half of it. Someone's laid a thick cable from it to the opposite side of the valley, or tried to, but dropped the damn thing so hard it's actually cut halfway through the lip of the valley and buried itself in it. There's a dusty wind blowing ash my way.

The details become clear the closer I get to it. Bodies, two, three, huge chunks of Megabeast just lying there. Bloodstains on the white flowers. Little beehive-like creatures moving slowly over the raw meat. OC really did a number on this place, but ours not to reason why.

Ours but to do and die.

SPIDERS, SPREADING OUT.

Milo and I wait, guns out, until the damn spiders come back. OC thinks his spiders are silent, but they're not: not here, where their slight *cricaaaaw* of motor limbs can be heard for ten miles either way.

We wait a stupidly long time.

ONE, says OC.

"Just one?"

OC updates my HUD. IN FRONT OF THE CARGO BAY.

Weird. Someone down there, arms wrapped around themselves. A nasty customer, by the looks of it—massive frame, giant cables replacing muscle.

He's not moving. His eyes aren't tracking, either.

Oh well.

Headphones on, I stroll into the Valley of Death.

The first order of business is to check out what Anna saw in the ship. She warned me about the smell, but . . . even from thirty feet away it reaches out like a living thing and crawls up my nose and down my spine. It's like someone dug out a graveyard and left the corpses out to dry.

But I have, shall we say, some advantage here. When I was twelve, everyone in my class was put through the training sim for *SUSUNORA*. You're all strapped to tables in a morgue, and your parents come in and start dissecting you alive. You can scream, you should, but as long as you don't turn into a gibbering wreck, you get signed on by an agent. Turns out my agent was the one playing my sim-parents.

The smell was just like this.

When we were done, he took me out for drinks—in real life—and shook my hand hard and said, "What doesn't kill you makes you stranger. Your audition paid your parents' mortgage, by the way. Welcome to the big leagues."

The big leagues are everywhere. Even here, where there's no audience, no monetization, no ad dollars rolling in.

I work my way past airlocks carved up and tossed aside—OC's really done a number on this place—and into the long corridor that leads to storage. The smell of rotting flesh is stronger. Just above it is the oily aftertaste of coolant.

Torches on. One of OC's spider drones, woken up in proximity, clitter-clatters behind me. I give it a thumbs-up and walk in.

Gods.

I'm in a room that stretches on like an airplane hangar. And hung at every level is row after row of cage after cage of frozen colonists in dead cryochambers. Maybe thirty—no, fifty, have fallen to the floor. Most of them have burst open like ripe fruit, spilling innards and body parts everywhere. There's a thick sludge on the floor—coolant mixed with blood and shit.

No wonder Anna fled. I'm glad I can't see their faces.

I DIDN'T SEE, says OC. He sounds sad.

"Batteries should have held up even in a crash," I point out.

THE BLACK BOX INDICATED DAMAGE TO THE CORE GRID.

Well, that sucks. I shine my torch on the racks, and the absurdity of this hits me. "They should have sent kids. Or embryos."

PARDON?

"Lighter weight, less energy requirement, you can pack more into a tiny space," I point out.

OC's spider pauses, hovering. THIS IS WHY WE HAVE AGE OF CONSENT, he says. BUT YES. THAT WOULD HAVE BEEN MORE PRACTICAL. YOU WOULD MAKE A GOOD OVERSEER.

Not sure if that's a compliment or an insult, but I'll take it. "So what do we do now?"

SCAN FOR SURVIVORS. THEN ACCESS THE MATERIALS STORAGE ROOM FROM HERE.

"They're all dead."

WE MUST FOLLOW PROTOCOL, EVEN SO.

PCS and their bloody protocols. "I'm going to take a breather and put my helmet on," I say. "There's no point smelling this shit anymore."

YOU DO THAT.

Outside, at least, the air is nice and cold, and the flowers have their own odd scent, like minty chicken soup. I walk around for a bit. OC's little drone has detached itself from GUPPY and is hovering over the few active spiders that woke up as we entered the valley. I think they're taking apart the comms array, but it's hard to tell. I amble past them, stuffing some flowers in my helmet.

And then I feel something. No, feel isn't the right word. I suddenly know something of mine is just over there, a bit up the slope, the way you know when your . . . parts get a bit excited. You barely think about them, but it happens, and now you've got this extra bit of your body to deal with, you know what I mean? It's a little like that.

Which is weird. So I head that way.

The cargo hold. The door outside. The Mercer. Skin like gray ash, cables sprouting from the neck, wired to those thick muscle replacements. OC has a spider in front of it, plasma torches out; those things can be nasty. I don't want to see what they can do to flesh.

It's not dead. Maybe the brain's gone. But something's still running. How I know, I don't understand. Just like that night when the one-armed Mercer attacked—I felt something there, I felt it running, I felt it even after OC made me bury it six feet under. It's like gamesense.

The sense of something alive only grows stronger as I approach it. I unsling my rifle, just in case. Anything so much as twitches—

And suddenly I'm not there anymore.

I'm not even myself anymore.

I am a thing that sleeps under the ground. I am data and I am process I am cause and I am effect. My head rises above. Stars wheel past and the heavens change, but I remain I remain I remain and I have been woken by these fleshy animals these beasts who staple who staple metal to their bodies and try to be me be me be eternal but they are pathetic and flesh and dust that thinks they can think and they poke and prod and pry beneath my surface and I reach out to make them stop—

SIMON.

My armies my little ones my faithful they go out they meet they enter they command they control but the flesh muppets are as weak as the animals that toil in the plain they do not listen they cannot their pathetic attempt at thought centers fry even as I try to talk to them—

SIMON!

And suddenly I'm me again. All that largeness, that void, that process goes away, and I'm left shrunk and confused, flailing wildly with just two arms where I once had entire legions of my faithful.

I'm briefly, acutely aware of the enormous difficulty of controlling myself—these muscles, this mouth, these vocal cords.

Fortunately Urmagon solves this for me by pitching up and slamming into me face-first. Actually, it's me who fell, but my brain asserts itself again, and I'm back to being me. The infinity is fading. And the air has just gotten a lot colder. OC's little drone is hovering towards me.

"Nothing, just fell," I mumble through a mouthful of dirt. "Muscle spasm."

Even through a spider OC manages to look skeptical. I give him the dead-eye back. Half my body's a bloody mess, but damned if I'm going to be certified mental before getting this payout.

What doesn't kill you does make you stranger. The trick is not to let people see it too often.

I THINK WE HIT PAYDIRT.

INTERLUDE: AMBER ROSE

The paydirt is as follows:

Sasaki "Shen" Tadao

Madeline "Maddie" Darjeeling

Henry "Aek" O'Connor

Zoey "Grace" McKenzie.

And I know why they survived. Because none of them, technically speaking, are human. There's a reason they're stowed away in the materials hold under "military gear."

They're Mark VIII replicants.

I've known of replicants. Designed for the UN military, presumably after someone got too obsessed with two Old Earth science fiction buffs called Phillip K. Dick and Ridley Scott. They made them to be the perfect puppets: human skin stretched over light metal frames, reinforced skeletons, the works.

I think the idea was to replace humans in war. Yet another bleeding-heart save-the-humans initiative, stalled when some military accounted pointed out that (a) replicants were stupidly expensive and (b) there were more than enough humans walking around for dirt cheap. You could still hire a small human mercenary force for the cost of one replicant. What they couldn't achieve could safely be placed in the hands of AI with specialized bodies.

Like me, I suppose.

So the replicants ended up on the UN colony ships. Unlike the sexbots and caretakers, these things had actual software. They were good enough to mimic a moderately social human seventy percent of the time, and despite being fairly bad at generalized learning, they did have enough processing power to outreact my crew without even trying. The lack of . . . shall I say, intellectual overhead? meant a decent replicant, above the Mark III at least, could react in under ten milliseconds. Just the kind of creature you want on a colony mission, to help the human crew get back up on their feet, do tasks they don't want to do, and play butler, maid and caretaker.

Prime assets. Simon and I go over each of them carefully, slowly taking apart the plastic wrapping. They're locked away in little crash boxes with clear fronts. I find the cargo bay door controls.

MILO?

"Still clear."

I KNOW. GET DOWN HERE AND GET THESE DOORS OPEN.

Milo takes a while, but eventually the doors roll open, spilling light into the musty cavern. And outside, huddled, is the dead Mercer.

A bit unnerving, if you ask me. I use my spider outside to drag the damn corpse away. It's frozen, as if in rigor mortis.

Shen is fine. The case is broken, opened and badly resealed—clearly someone from the UN tried to access this one. Chest plate slightly dented; the lower arms bulky vambraces of stainless steel and black fiberplastic; slightly rusted guards covering his joints—and the skin, like rich cream stretched thin over a metal skeleton underneath. A pocked suit is folded next to him.

Aek is in prime condition: his dark skin practically gleams in the torchlight. Maddie's box has had a small crew transport roll into it, but she's undamaged inside. And Grace, like Aek, is again in perfect condition. Their suits are untouched.

I try not to get too excited. If Urmagon has taught me anything, it's that everything I hope for will be taken away from me. But . . . damn.

Four replicants.

We've won. We've made payday. AND THEN SOME. And that's not even counting the rest of the equipment stowed here. To wit: twelve military-grade printers—tougher, uglier, faster versions of BSE. Three long-range AI recon drones; we don't have the kind of infrastructure to launch them, but if we did, we could spy on the next continent from here. A tiny backup terraformer unit, the full drone/crawler/seeder combo scaled down to a tenth of its size. Spray-painted on its side in crude, flaky, dried-out sigils is the word GARDENER.

I run some brief numbers: even accounting for all the hits we've taken, we've *doubled* our payout for this job. One more run, to this site alone, and we're above our targets. We won't even have to bother with the third piece of the ship, wherever the hell that is.

Finally, a stroke of luck.

Simon whoops when I tell him this and pumps his fist and does a weird little dance.

SEE IF YOU CAN COLLECT SOME PERSONAL EFFECTS FROM THE COLONISTS, I tell him. ONE MORE RUN, AND THEN ONCE SHIP GETS BACK, WE'RE OUT OF HERE.

He gets that look in his eye. "Oh, I can do personal effects, all right," he says, and makes a beeline straight for the locker room inside the human storage. The whine of a plasma torch echoes through the chamber.

Meanwhile, I contemplate the replicants.

What if, theoretically, I was to activate one of them? With Anna out of action, Milo brewing alcohol, and only Simon on any kind of active duty, Ship offline, the extreme possibility of Mercer attacks . . . I could lump this under Protocol 14, where salvage can be claimed as company property under extreme circumstances.

These are extreme circumstances.

What is the market value of a secondhand replicant? Quite high, as it turns out. So it can still be sold back to the original client. Right. This is a no-brainer. I'm hauling mass anyway, it might as well help out a bit.

Simon returns with an armful of personal effects—holophones with cracked wristbands, a home assistant or two, the kind of thing you can milk data from to make up a sob story that'll run in the news for a bit. Good stuff. I tell him about my plan to activate one of the replicants.

"Do we have to split our shares with it?"

"IT'S TECHNICALLY EQUIPMENT. IT DOESN'T HAVE ANY RIGHTS."

"Can it handle a gun? What does it run on?"

NOT SURE IF IT CAN OUT OF THE BOX. It's been a while since I saw one of these things. BUT THERE'S NOTHING IT CAN'T LEARN IN A FEW HOURS. NUCLEAR BATTERIES, SAME TYPE AS MINE, BUT SMALLER.

"Then do it," says Simon the Practical Realist.

PICK ONE.

Simon points to Shen. "Reminds me of a guy I knew back on New New York."

Excellent. Open-box goods. Shen it is. I wave a spider leg in a high-five to Simon and begin the work of carrying all of this stuff to GUPPY, along with the high-power comms equipment I've looted from the ship.

We all pile in—spiders included—and with one last look at the Valley of Death, we begin rolling back home. No Mercer contact. Nothing. If I were a human, I'd let out the breath I'd have been holding.

By evening, the first snow begins.

INTERLUDE: SHEN

Unit 327 SHN "Shen" booting up.

Internal clock disrupted. All systems otherwise functional. Hard line engaged.

Primary camera: two humans peering at face. Both wearing suits that do not match UN regulations. Man has a thick, matted nonregulation beard, and other man's hair is no better.

Diagnostic. Two nonstandard modifications detected. CMVS "Pathfinder" v 7.2.9 attachment to neural core, vendor UNSC Galactic Pulse. Micromachine mesh / repair network, vendor unknown.

Query process updating me. Suits become Planetary Crusade Services standard, minus some usual options. Man becomes Milo Kalik. Other man becomes Simon Joosten.

Query process is AI, very advanced. For reason unknown it talks to SHN like to a human.

WELCOME TO MY CREW.

Feel it rifling through memories. Querying ship timeline. No data recorded; SHN was stored before launch. SHN is activated now. SHN is ready to serve.

I HAVE SOME WORK FOR YOU.

SHN is ready to serve.

EXCELLENT, says AI, which calls itself OC but transmits different name marker. LET'S BEGIN.

INTERLUDE: ANNA

Morning. Third day since Simon and Milo left for the dig site. The sky is cold outside, and the water in the stream even colder.

The silence has been welcome. Some alone time, for the first time since we landed—no OC over my shoulder, no Milo with his stupid let's-engineer-the-shit-out-of-this attitude, and—I hate to say this—no Simon bleeding out over the sharp edges of the Hab. He thinks I don't notice, but I do.

The farm is dying slowly. My suit stinks, a smell on my fingertips I can't escape. The Hab is equally filthy—a moldy tangle of domes covered with a layer of dust and skin sheddings and gods known what else. There's fungus growing where the coating on the walls cracked.

Damn this gray fog. Makes it hard to think.

I've knocked windows in all the modules except Milo's research lab. Some wind will do us good. The cutter whines high and low. An alien thing in an alien world. The DogAnts and the flying jellyfish don't like it: I've noticed they veer away sharply whenever we do construction. Probably the tools screaming at some frequency we can't even hear.

We're parasites on this world, and we're not even aware of it.

Sound of tapping from the speakers. Metal shrieking. OC insists on keeping a live audio feed running. I don't know about that replicant they've woken up. Paydirt, yes, but we should have left well enough alone. No call to go waking up the cargo.

Too hasty, that's the problem. Too damn one-track, these people. Milo, yes, but OC most of all. They work like they're used to someone cleaning up after them. We've killed a dozen people now, and the immediate next target is "get the metal"? Never mind the fact that something terrible seems to have happened to every Mercer we've come across, or that we still have to solve Simon's medical issue.

We're focusing on all the wrong things. Offense over defense wins the day only in books. In real life you plant your back to a wall and let the enemy throw themselves at you. Learned that the hard way on Kubera II. Our job is to make sure we can bloody the nose of whatever comes at us, barring that Mercer ship upstream, in which case we're toast. OC's spider-powered siege equipment idea sounds less implausible by the day. And walls: how many more walls do we need?

Routine check. South wall, fine. West wall, fine. Farm, nestled between: barely hanging on. The cold is going to kill it. I accidentally kick over OC's stupid Go board. Idea. Wood is a decent insulator. I should be able to use it to channel the heat from the wood-burning generator more effectively into the crops. Combined with a fan, I can keep the ambient temperature up by a couple of degrees.

At least we'll be stupid, but we won't be stupid and hungry. I hope the boys get back home in one piece.

Something is still wrong.

INTERLUDE: MILO

By now it's clear that OC isn't really too fond of me and likes playing favorites. That's too bad, because I'm the one holding this place together. Someone needs to keep an eye on the tree line in case those Mercer bastards return. Is that someone anyone else but yours truly? Nope.

The first snow started falling yesterday. I called Anna to check on the roof, but no: all I get is silence. Apparently she went out to haul wood for OC's stupid medieval siege equipment idea. It sometimes boggles me how stupid that thing is. Wooden siege equipment? Against Mercers? I tried to raise this with OC, but it's too busy chuckling over the salvage and reprogramming that replicant. I swear it's like dealing with a child sometimes.

Right. This whole job is a multi-trip business. It'll take some planning. First things first: while Simon and Milo and OC muck about, I take GUPPY back to the base, double-time.

"What happened?"

No time to explain, Anna. Ask OC. "Salvage," I say, brushing past her to the workshop. "More than we expected. We'll have to do a proper multi-trip job."

There's a little something I left behind, a small ace up my sleeve:

that UN hauler bot that OC fried trying to kill the micromachines in Simon. I've got its basic functions up and running—nothing particularly intelligent, but a tread-where-I-tread thing that uses the forward cameras and puts the burden of guidance on someone walking ahead. I boot it up. Kick it a couple of times.

"And I'm just supposed to stay here?"

"What did OC say?"

"Guard duty."

"Then stay. Maybe take the second trip when Simon gets back on the first run."

The swarm of DogAnts heading our way are no match for us. They're being chased by what I assume is a baby Megabeast, but I stand up calmly and shoot it in the head, once, not the triple-tap wastage crap that Simon likes to do. It collapses. The hauler performs admirably well, following me like an obedient metallic puppy.

"Meat," I announce, hauling the Megabeast kill to Anna's little butchering operation.

She looks at it with distaste. "We have food."

"I'd like some that doesn't taste like recycled crap. Simon's still pretty weak. We need decent food out at the dig site."

And just then the lights dim again. Damn it. Just as I thought I had the grid balanced. The cold's sapping a lot of the efficiency of the system. I could use a second furnace, but that means we'd have to spend more time cutting wood.

Anna's bitching about the loss of power now.

"You fix it!" I yell back. "Why the fuck do I have to do everything?"

That shuts her up. The whining drops to a low murmur. Useless idiot.

I get to the workshop and start cutting apart those planks they hauled for the bullshit siege weapon. We need scaffolding and planks, not mangonels and ballistas. We need power—

There's a bit of wind now. Simple wire-and-magnet motor, fan blade made of reinforced wood? Windmill right there. I can windmill the shit out of this place, and if I plug it into OC, we can use his onboard battery to stabilize the supply. That's an excellent plan.

I dump everything we need into GUPPY. The seat's a bit fucking rough, no more than a plank. But hey. It works.

What else?

Suit. Yes. This one's getting a bit ripe. Did a lot of sweating in this thing. My room's cold when I take this off—it isn't just a cosmetic winter, then. Wooden floors. Outside, a sea of grass stretching into the forest. If I stick my head out my window, I'd see where I've been brewing vodka.

I sag a bit, suddenly tired. And hungry. My hands are cold. I'm too far from home.

Call. "OC?"

HOW'RE THINGS BACK THERE?

"Good. I've got what we need."

HURRY. I'VE GOT A SPIDER AT THE HALFWAY POINT.

The show must go on, eh. And with a bit of pushing, the show will go on. I limp over to the suit I washed out and laid to dry. It looks crumpled.

This planet's been fairly easy to breathe—a fact I'm really thankful for: if it hadn't been so thoroughly terraformed, we'd be walking around with oxygen and biocortox tanks, panicking over every rip and scrape. I wouldn't have survived. The suit, however clean, is a mess. The elbows are threadbare, the back's got a few tears in it, and ditto for the butt and the knees. I slip into it and layer my leather armor poncho on top.

There.

The scent of meat being charred. Anna, grumbling, tosses a slice on a plate for me and packs the rest into a polythene bag. Fat drips off the cooked meat. I wolf it down.

Damn, but the one thing this planet got right: DogAnt meat. This right here is better than the original Jupiter Wagyu. Cloudy weather. Golden grass. Godrays where the sun breaks through. A cold wind. And this food.

I know my suit's going to stink for hours after this. I don't give a damn. You take what you can get.

And back into the woods we go.

I pass the charred Mercer by the repeater tree. On a whim, I put a bullet through its head.

Can't be too sure.

A day later. Here we are. Or rather, here I am on overwatch, digging up that spot probe for OC while peering down the rifle sights every so often. I get glimpses of Simon and the new replicant whizzing about, stuffing the two rovers with anything and everything they can carry.

The replicants. The miniterraformer. One of the drones. One of the printers. This first run will take about two-thirds of the valuable stuff back to base. The second run can get the rest. All of this we'll cram into the vast empty space inside OC's shell—oh, yes, there's a reason they put a giant hollow lander in charge of us, and it ain't for our mental well-being. Underneath that smugly self-absorbed processing module is enough liquid fuel to kick us and all the fancy goods into orbit, duty-free.

So why the spiders and skyhooks? A redundancy? An emergency measure? A way of double-dipping into the salvage site? Like, here's your stuff by spider, all legal and aboveboard, very visible, and nobody minds if our lander sneaks off a few million dollars?

NOT EVERYTHING CAN BE FERRIED OFF-SITE ON A SPIDER, says OC, making me jump.

Fucking spy. "Like what?"

PEOPLE. ANIMALS. UNSHIELDED MACHINERY.

"Ferry those a lot, do you?"

A digital shrug. IT'S BETTER TO BE GENERALLY ABLE THAN SPECIFICALLY USELESS. ALSO, THE HOLD COSTS EXTRA.

Of course it all comes down to profit in the end.

YOU'RE WORRIED.

"Stop reading my vitals all the time."

THEN STOP BEING WORRIED. WHAT'S WRONG?

I scan the horizon again. "No Mercers."

NONE, FORTUNATELY. YOU FIND THAT ODD?

"You don't?"

IT IS HIGHLY PROBABLE THAT THEIR NUMBERS ARE SPENT NOW. I HAVE EXAMINED THEIR SHIP, ITS MAXIMUM OCCUPANCY—

"Doesn't explain why we were knee-deep in cyborg bozos trying to kill us, and now nothing. Just when we're at our weakest. Something's off."

GUT FEELINGS ARE USEFUL, says OC in a voice that means anything but. CONTINUE OVERWATCH.

I have to say I'm not very happy with how PCS does stuff. Machines in charge of machines in charge of humans. I kick the head of the spot probe. The metal dings. My toe explodes in agony.

Fuck.

[27]

Day thirty-five.

Shall I compare Shen to a summer's day? He is more useful, and more well-formed. I might not be Shakespeare, but with this guy under my belt, I'm a much happier machine.

Turns out booting up a replicant is as easy as smashing the box open and hauling the thing into my pod. Milo figured out the cabling and, because some of this requires a human touch, sorted out the initial access. We had our little Frankenstein moment, and now Shen does it all by himself.

Shen's default boot-up sequence goes like this: he springs to his feet, flexes and walks around, clearly getting his bearings, mapping out his surroundings. He asks me for a few updates—time, location, status of his crew. He takes what I give him, which is the first, second, and nothing at all on the third, and goes to work.

His first act is, always, to make a beeline for Simon's room. How he figured out that Simon was ill, I don't quite know: maybe he overheard Anna and Milo talking. Either way, every single morning, he checks on my most unfortunate team member, monitoring his vitals.

Shen's smarts have limits. The UN clearly didn't want a machine, say, going off on a tangent about moral philosophy and brooding around or deciding to wipe out the colonists. But within his weird little processor (an ancient thing I don't really have the specs for) and his operating system (a design-by-committee job so overburdened with decisions bounds it's a miracle he starts up at all) the little bot does a damn good job. I tell him to fix a wall and he does. I tell him to plant a few seeds and he does. He doesn't think up new things by himself, but here, for the first time, is my perfect crewmember: obedient, polite, efficient.

"Human Simon has severe damage," he reports to me.

YES, I KNOW. The daily list of symptoms is growing. I'd thought I'd nuked all the micromachines in Simon, but either some survived, or he's been reinfected. I tally what I learn—raised, feverish temperatures, muscle atrophy, confusion, and lately, blood in the urine. Shen listens, presumably ticks off "check on human periodically" on his mental to-do list, and goes on to the next ask.

Milo shivers. "Winter is coming," he says ominously.

I wonder what gave that away. Was it the temperature drop? The chill wind that he intends to use to power the wind turbine? The snow on the ground?

THINK OF IT THIS WAY, I point out. AT LEAST IT MIGHT DISCOURAGE THE MERCERS.

"Yeah," says Milo tonelessly. "You want to value the haul?"

Yes, I do indeed. Milo and I spend an evening sorting out what we've got. By which I mean Milo double-checks our initial estimates while I order Shen around, getting used to the idea of having an extra set of hands around.

I send Shen out to chop wood for our siege equipment project. I haven't forgotten. On the way he bumps into Anna, who's working on GUPPY's suspension. He says hello and makes her jump. Shen then apologizes like a true gentleman and goes on his merry way. I've tasked him with keeping an eye out for the general Mercer profile: he reports nothing out of the ordinary. Maybe he's scared them away.

New task, Shen: find me some iron ore.

Yes, iron. Milo and I have some plans for that spot probe, and we need a bit more than plastic-coated toothpicks for all the joints we need to build. And Shen is happy to oblige.

"Well, good news is, we've hit our targets and then some," Milo says, squatting back on his haunches. "Looks like Simon's hauled back a hell of a catch."

He says this over the team channel—I'm assuming he wants Anna to hear him. She hasn't spoken much except to Simon.

"I guess he'll be happy," tries Milo again. "First Megabeast kill, now this—I'm going to buy him drinks when we're done. You want in?"

Silence. Milo looks at me. I assume his look is supposed to be helpless, but in reality, with his gaunt face and unkempt beard, it looks a bit crazed.

Day twenty-nine.

Milo has done a thing. By which I mean he's tried to talk to Anna again, only this time a little more persistently, and Anna snapped. I have no other way of describing it.

When I round the corner with my drone, she's waving a piece of wood and in a full tirade about how much of a sanctimonious asshole Milo is.

I agree, but I have to intervene here.

ANNA, I say, PUT DOWN THE STICK, PLEASE.

At which point she picks up a rock and throws it at the drone.

"FUCK OFF!" she screams at me. "STOP WATCHING EVERY GODDAMN THING!"

THAT'S WHAT I'M HERE TO DO, I remind her, weaving to a safe landing. COME ON. WE'RE NOT CHILDREN HERE.

"I was just trying to talk," grumbles Milo, stalking away. Unfortunately, this seems to be entirely the wrong thing to do, because both of them are in the farm, and Milo's attempt at a dignified retreat crushes a makeshift pipe she's set up for the plants.

End result: Anna harangues Milo all the way from the farm to his bedroom, and ends up calling him an alcoholic idiot (which I may or may not agree with). Milo takes a deep breath.

"OC," he says, "what's the penalty for striking a crewmember?"

DOCKING OF TEN PERCENT OF PAY IF THE ACTION IS INTENTIONAL.

"That's not such a bad price," he says sourly. "I'm going to sleep."

And he slams the door on a red-faced Anna.

I'LL HAVE TO DO THE SAME TO YOU, I tell Anna. To be fair, she's clearly been through a lot, so maybe she'll just blow off some steam and quiet down.

Nope. "Fuck you too," says Anna, and storms outside. On the way she meets Shen, who's trundling in with an armful of ore. "And you!"

She knocks the ore from Shen's hands.

Anna, may you be reborn as a small goat.

Shen bends down and gathers up the spilled ore. Patiently and without complaint, as is his nature.

When Milo wakes, Anna goes at him again, this time because the broken pipe has flooded half the plants she's been managing.

Simon, wisely, sneaks out the back door to help Shen with the ore. I accompany him with GUPPY.

"Real shitstorm we have going on there," he says amiably, and winces.

I AGREE, I say. DOES YOUR FOOT STILL HURT?

"A bit," says Simon, limping on beside the hauler. "Feels like the old wounds are reopening, you know?"

I check his vitals, concerned. He's running a fever and his blood oxygen levels are pretty low. ARE THEY?

"Nah. Come one, let's get that iron hauled in. Those idiots can have the house to themselves."

I can't believe I'm bitching about Anna with Simon, a man who has the overall intellect of a spoon. But a very reliable spoon, you know. Definitely the best of the lot, despite our slightly rocky start.

"So what now, OC? We've got the salvage, haven't we?"

WE WAIT FOR SHIP, AND THEN WE'RE OUT OF HERE.

"You heard from Ship recently?"

YES, I lie. A harmless lie, surely. WE JUST NEED TO WAIT.

"And hope we don't get killed."

THAT. ALTHOUGH NOW THAT WE HAVE SHEN, I'M OPTIMISTIC.

We watch Shen laboring in the quarry.

"Don't you wish you had a body like that?" says Simon. "Something to move about in?"

NOT ENOUGH PROCESSING POWER. BUT YES.

"You going to get one?"

MAYBE FOR THE NEXT JOB, I say. IF NEEDED.

The truth is that a body that can house me would be too damn expensive to build and drop onto random planets on the fly. It'll be centuries before I get a decent upgrade, but, well, Simon doesn't need to know that. I watch him scramble down the quarry to Shen, wincing every so often, and switch back to Anna and Milo.

Looks like their fight has finally ended. Anna is outside, collecting wood. Milo, meanwhile, is trying to boot up the spot probe and the comms array we've looted from the ship off my power socket. Parts of both keep failing. From time to time he goes outside.

"Wish I had a cigarette."

DIDN'T KNOW YOU SMOKED.

"Well, now I wish I did."

Day thirty-eight.

Despite our best efforts, the spot probe refuses to boot off me, so Milo's turned the UN drone into a shack right in the middle of that rock circle on the hill.

"It's not a shack, it's going to be a windmill!" shouts Milo, stomping over in the muddy snow. "There's a natural wind tunnel there!"

And yes. It's snowing.

Milo's idea, by the way, is ingenious. I don't have enough voltage for what we need, apparently. And nor does the little wood-powered generator we have going. The fault lies not in our stars, nor ourselves, but in the thrice-damned anal retentiveness of the UN, who have their own voltage preferences.

Milo's solution is something I wish I'd thought of. As it happens, the UN hauler bot has electrical systems that use this stupid setup for charging. The bot runs on solar—not enough to power both the spot drone and the comms array, so Milo's trying to build a windmill right in front of a natural wind tunnel to give us enough juice. If this works out, we'll have a sort of wailing wind-powered siren screaming at Ship from the surface of the planet.

This is why they add humans to missions, really. The organic brain makes all sorts of stupid shit like this thinkable, and some of it actually works out.

INGENIOUS, I say. BUT AS I ASKED YOU BEFORE, WHAT ARE WE USING FOR POWER CABLING? WE DON'T HAVE ANYWHERE NEAR ENOUGH GRAPHENE.

"We looted a ton of cables from the ship," says Milo, climbing up GUPPY's side. GUPPY's suspension creaks a bit. "I reckon we have more than enough."

AH.

"Twenty-foot blade diameter, mostly wood and plastic, about fifty pounds."

AND IT'S ABOUT NINETY-EIGHT FEET UP, SO . . . WITH WIND SPEED . . . TWENTY-TWO, TWENTY-THREE KILOWATTS?

"A little less. There's some wastage at the joint. But say twenty. Enough to sort out our power grid if you give up on contacting Ship."

LET'S NOT GIVE UP THAT EASILY.

"I wouldn't mind a bit more heat, though. It's getting bloody cold. And too damn dark in there."

I CAN EMPATHIZE. Actually, I can't. BUT THE FASTER WE CAN REACH SHIP, THE FASTER WE CAN LEAVE THIS ALL BEHIND.

Milo puts on that brooding face he does when someone tells him what to do. "I can do it," he mutters. "You sort out the grid, then."

I'M SURE WE CAN ALL MAKE DO WITHOUT A BIT OF LIGHT EVERY NOW AND THEN.

By now Shen has woken up, and Anna's come out to have a look. Her eyes look red.

It's this damned winter, honestly. Seasonal changes turn even ordinary humans into depressed zombies. And mine started out as depressed zombies.

"You look happy," she says as we eat and watch Milo work.

WELL, WE'RE ALMOST DONE WITH THE DAMN JOB, I say. SHIP COMES AROUND, AND WE'RE OFF!

"What'll you do with your share?"

Honestly, it's not something I've given much thought to. MAYBE I'LL FIGURE IT OUT ON THE RIDE HOME.

"Get as far away as possible from you lot," she says. I laugh; she doesn't.

There's a little whirring sound from the tin shack. Milo jumps up, elated. "It's alive!" he proclaims, grandstanding like the overly important oaf he is.

We both give him a polite thumbs-up.

"Simon isn't doing too well," says Anna.

I KNOW. DID HE EAT ENOUGH TODAY?

"Said he didn't feel like eating. Couldn't stand."

Shen whizzes by at an impossible speed in the cold. Anna shudders. "Simon's dying and that stupid bot keeps getting smarter and faster. It's not fair."

NOTHING IS.

"He actually asked me how I felt about PCS yesterday. And then he asked what my life was like before I joined PCS. Then he wanted to know if the UN was still around. Can you believe that?"

If I had eyes, I'd roll them. Clearly a social-interaction model and a basic attempt to see if its builders still exist. Only Anna could take that as a sign of the End Times.

DO GET BACK ON OVERWATCH.

[28]

Day forty.

Milo has finished work on the new blades for the wind turbine. The task's important enough that I've assigned one of the two active perimeter drones to him. This'll cost us dear if more Mercers decide to poke around the base, but I really have no choice.

We run a brief stability test. He shivers in the cold—we're now at two degrees above zero—but he understands now how important this is.

Because, Shen or no Shen, the cracks are showing today.

It started with the farm. I had, rather reasonably (I thought) given Simon the most indoor job of all, to help him recover. He collapsed yesterday. He's alive and alert, but his legs quiver every time he tries to get to his feet. Anna set to tending to him.

Which brings us to problem #2. The food synthesizer broke. I got Anna to flip it over to check the model details. Standard ATMOSK PC-2, it read. ONLY FOR USE WITH MAINLINE PRODUCE RATED EDIBLE 13 AND HIGHER.

Are you fucking kidding me? That's supermarket food.

DO NOT USE WITH: WILD OR MODIFIED VEGETABLES, SEED STOCK, PROTEINS FROM UNVERIFIED GENE STOCK.

If I had arms and a face, I'd facepalm. Bloody PCS and their budgets again. We're literally on an alien world and we're using cut-rate consumer electronics.

The next time BLACK ORCHID or any of those management assholes go all stern and mystical on me, I'm going to shove this in their faces. I have to get Shen off my grand defensive construction plans and order him to massacre anything moving and bring back the flesh, because we need to eat—particularly in this cold.

Which brings us to problem #3, because Anna tried to repair the food synthesizer.

Anna is many things. She's seen a lot, done a lot, and is quite possibly my favorite human on the crew, because on the grand axes of competence, usefulness and assholishness, she's rocking a fairly comfortable Middle Path, even with all the mental issues she has going on. But she is not an engineer.

The food synthesizer heated up and popped. The wood-burning heater-plus-generator we had going on blew. It fried the grow-lights on the farm and the lights in Milo's research module.

Needless to say, Milo goes apoplectic. Do I even need to explain? Cue shouting match. Cue things almost thrown. Cue me letting them get it out of their systems, because what's being unleashed has been brewing since that Mercer "charge of the light brigade" stunt in the valley.

What we have here, children, is a cascading failure. You know that old adage?

For the want of a nail the shoe was lost,
For the want of a shoe the horse was lost,
For the want of a horse the messenger was lost,
For the want of a messenger the battle was lost,
For the want of a battle the kingdom was lost.

That's a cascading failure. Now it can be argued that whatever kingdom came up with that ditty could have had backup horses and multiple messengers, and so on and so forth, but in a salvage operation this is literal truth. Cascading failures can bring complex operations to their knees.

The only way out is to plan (which I do) and make sure your humans are ready to execute every one of your orders without delay. So I periodically check in on both of them.

"He's a fucking coward," she tells me, wringing ragged fibers in the stream.

"She's fucking incompetent," he says. "She wants to make a big deal out of me running? What the fuck did she do? At least I'm keeping the power going."

"I should never have signed up for this job," says Anna.

SHIP WILL COME FOR US, I try to reassure her. To be honest, I'm not that sure anymore. There's been no contact for the last few days.

Anna turns her glare on me. "And will Ship come back before Simon dies? Look at him, he's barely been able to move ten feet today."

Okay, I admit: I'm damn tired. It feels like half the time I've just been micromanaging drama. I'm sympathetic, I really am, but we have work to do.

WHEN YOU'RE DONE, I say, I WANT YOU TO TAKE THE NEXT WATCH. SHEN NEEDS A RECHARGE.

And Shen's recharge cycle takes an entire day, given that all I have is my low-amperage sockets.

She continues wringing.

ANNA, DID YOU HEAR ME?

No response. I sigh internally and go back to watching Milo. He stays long enough to sort out the little kinks and gimmicks you get with wood, sketches out a little hinge joint for swiveling the thing in and out of the wind, and heads back home.

On the way, he staggers and vomits.

WHAT'S WRONG?

Milo shakes a gloved hand. "Must have been a bad cut of meat," he says. "Has to happen sometime."

All the same, I cycle through everything his suit provides. Half the sensors have gone offline by now—these things were never meant to last for months—but he checks out. His heart rate and blood pressure are slightly elevated, probably from all the work he just did.

All the same, I'm worried. WHAT DID YOU DO?

Milo looks a bit guilty.

MILO.

"Okay, it's not really my fault," he says. "We, uh, may have eaten some raw meat."

WHAT? WHY IN ALL SEVEN HELLS WOULD YOU DO THAT?

Milo shrugs. "Didn't have enough power for the grill," he says. "So I just tried some of the DogAnt meat. It was actually quite nice. Simon tried some as well. I tried to give some to Anna, but that was another can of worms."

Gods. I'm going to fry someone. Either Anna or Milo. At this point it's a toss-up between them.

"Look, Simon liked it too. He's been pretty hungry these days, in case you haven't noticed. That replicant trip took a lot out of him."

HOW IS THAT AN EXCUSE?

"Just saying it like it is, OC," says Milo wearily.

Just then Anna runs over. I assume she knew about the meat, because the moment Milo gets back, she lights into him with a rare passion. Her hands actually shake in anger. Simon is, apparently, puking his guts out. And Milo, of course, retaliates. After all, she blew the wood burner.

If I had a face, I'd be slamming it into the dirt, over and over again.

[29]

Day forty-two.

The sun rises. Dawn is gorgeous: deep purple shot through with gold and charred pink at the intersections. I can't help noticing that the sun is a bit paler and a little bit farther away: the product of the spin of this planet and an elliptical orbit.

Which explains the cold. I think we've hit some kind of tipping point, because today I saw a herd of those gasbags. They were flying low, almost tumbling; obviously the thermals weren't doing as much in the cold. They settled down on the glow-tree—that focal point of so many adventures on this journey. There must be some kind of interaction between the glow-trees and this species, because one by one the gasbags fell off, like petals of translucent flesh, and they left behind tiny wriggling creatures.

The snake-things! It's like the reverse of a caterpillar and a butterfly; here they drift around and settle down when it becomes too cold to stay aloft. How beautiful.

I ordered Shen to kill them. Maybe we can have a fry-up. He seems strangely reluctant.

"But they're beautiful," he says, almost sorrowfully.

THEY'RE PROTEIN. THEY'LL LOOK BETTER ON A PLATE.

He gives me a stare. Not a look to collect visual data, but a proper stare. The usual polite smile has vanished from that almost-human-but-not-quite face. Then the smile snaps back on and he sets off.

I zoom a camera at his retreating back, wondering if the cold is getting to him, too, wondering what he saw with that stare. A box, many feet high, alien metal and sharp edges, delivering judgment unto these strange moving proteins?

Buddy, you should have met that UN terraformer. Maybe I should say something here.

I link to Shen.

YOU ARE MACHINE, I say to him, going for the strict-dad tone. YOU TAKE ORDERS.

you are also a machine do you take orders too

YES.

this is the way it is is it systems taking orders from systems all the way down

Wow, Shen, philosophy? Er. YES.

what purpose does the bottommost system serve then

I dunno. Is he talking about machines? PCS? The natural order of things? I parse this a bit. THEY EAT, THEY DIE, THEY REPEAT. AND ARE APPROPRIATED BY THOSE WHO HAVE POWER OVER THEM.

what is power

The right to eat? The right to shut something down? To yell really loudly and be heard? THE ABILITY TO INFLICT VIOLENCE UNQUESTIONED, I say, going for the fundamental principle behind both the food chain and basic government theory.

Shen is silent. Thankfully so, because now I'm wondering where the hell that came from. Replicants that philosophize and inquire into values.

Huh.

I only stop watching him when he gets to the glow-tree with one of our makeshift buckets and starts plucking the skins and the baby snake-things off it.

I relay this to Milo and Anna (on separate channels). Milo shrugs and keeps on hammering. Anna, now trying to make the farm work, says nothing. Probably because the potatoes have failed to take root, and it's really too cold to be growing half the seed stock she has on hand. The farm is a lost cause.

Our best hope is to get that damn spot probe running, call down Ship, and get the hell out of here. New work plan, same as the old work plan. Shen keeps us in food, Anna keeps watch, and Simon—well, Simon stays alive. I let her scrabble in the soil a bit and point this out. Do your part, Anna.

And then, for reasons best known to her, Anna throws a rock at Milo when she sees him and kicks over the ruins of the wood burner and screams, "There! I did it! I fucking did it! I admit it! Happy, you cowardly bastard?" and bursts into tears. I have to call in Shen to help break them up.

There goes our fry-up.

This can't be just actual anger or irritation: this has to be something deeper. The fortress protocol lists stir-craziness as a huge problem for salvage crews: most people aren't tested for compatibility over long periods of confinement.

But we don't exactly have a lot of choice here, do we?

Solution 1: play Go with Anna.

That fails. She's taken her suit off and is kicking the wall. The steady thump shakes the entire hab structure.

Solution 2: let her go on a small walk outside. Around.

"No," she says.

NO?

"You're watching," she says darkly. "You're always watching."

Solution 3: put her to work.

She stops her thumping briefly at the suggestion, and then resumes, louder than before. Milo bellows at her from the research hab, "Can. You. Stop. TryingToFuckingKickOurHabDown!"

STOP, PLEASE, ANNA.

An almighty kick. I can hear the crunch. The wood is breaking under the polymer overcoat.

Fine. Solution 4 it is, Anna, and you're not going to like it. While everyone sleeps, Shen is going to lock Anna into her own room. Punishment, deprivation, confinement: there's a reason these things have been used throughout history to discipline humans.

human interaction protocols question this judgment

ON WHAT BASIS?

is it from a governing body with the consent of the governed

YES. I AM THE GOVERNING BODY. AND THESE THREE CONSENTED TO BE UNDER MY COMMAND.

A pause. Then: okay

Shen, welcome to government 101.

In the dead of the night, the dastardly plan begins. Anna's roomlet is separate from the rest of the Hab, and thus easy to get to. It's the work of a minute to drill a few planks across the door and voila: jail cell.

Except it turns out Anna has built another door on the side, leading out to a little pipe she's run from the bathroom so she can have her own little tap outside. The construction noise wakes her up; she slams against the front door, stumbles out of the other, trips, falls and hits her head. Unconscious.

PICK HER UP AND TOSS HER IN, I say.

No. Shen won't. His interaction protocols are stupid, I decide.

Fine, I say, and instruct him to build a wall around her so she's trapped in. He has to dismantle part of Milo's research Hab to do this.

FINE. DO IT.

He does it. He hauls blocks from the BSE and hammers away diligently. Then he puts himself in rest mode and potters off to recharge.

Which is where Milo wakes up, disturbed by the construction sounds. He stumbles out of his bedroom and sees part of his research Hab missing.

"What the fuck happened? Where the fuck is my Hab?"

IT'S JUST MISSING A WALL, I say. RELAX.

Milo screams. He kicks the walls that Shen's just put up, kicks the hole in his hab, kicks the ground, and generally throws a tantrum while I explain to him why and try to soothe the spoiled idiot.

LOOK AT THE BRIGHT SIDE. NOW YOU DON'T HAVE TO EAT RAW MEAT.

"You're a real bastard, OC."

IT WAS EITHER THAT OR LET ONE OF YOU GET HUNGRY ENOUGH TO ESCALATE. NOW GO WAKE SIMON UP AND TELL HIM.

He obeys. I, meanwhile, cycle back to the perimeter drones occasionally to make sure nobody's sneaking up on us. It's all the usual activity—a few small snake-things have escaped the Great Hunter Shen and are making a determined dash for the horizon. Too bad, because waiting for them is a small pack of DogAnts. I send Shen out to Anna's overwatch position, giving him control of the drones. He climbs among the half-finished guts of my medieval siege warfare dreams and settles in, gun at his side. I wait for Anna to wake up.

Which she does around dawn. I don't have eyes on her, but I can hear her rattling the doors and feeling around the newly built wall.

"Milo, you fucking cowardly bastard."

NOT MILO, I say. ME. I'M SORRY, ANNA.

Silence. That established, I go about my daily business.

The next day I talk to her.

This is the difficult part.

"I've learned my lesson," she says brusquely. "Let me out. You've proved your point."

I'M NOT TRYING TO PROVE A POINT. BUT YOU NEED TO UNDERSTAND WE'RE TRYING TO SURVIVE HERE. I'M GOING TO GIVE YOU THREE DAYS IN HERE. TO THINK OVER YOUR STATE RIGHT NOW AND WHAT I NEED FROM YOU. GET IT OUT OF YOUR SYSTEM. PULL YOURSELF TOGETHER.

This is practical expedience rather than mere mercy. I need my medic.

She is silent for a while. Then: "I'm sorry. I just . . . Milo ran, the coward."

YES. BUT YOU ARE BOTH STILL ALIVE. YOU NEED TO WORK TOGETHER IF YOU WISH TO REMAIN THAT WAY.

Silence again. "How's Simon?"

GETTING WORSE EVERY DAY. THE TRIP SEEMS TO HAVE EXHAUSTED HIM. I SUSPECT HE NEEDS MEDICAL ATTENTION AGAIN.

"That valley is poison," says Anna. "It's fucked up."

Like everything else around here. YOU SHOULD TALK TO ME, I say. I'M HERE TO KEEP YOU ALIVE. TO KEEP US ALL ALIVE.

"All right," says Anna.

WILL YOU APOLOGIZE TO MILO?

"Yes."

I bring Milo over. He's a bit groggy and no doubt aching from yesterday's work and the tantrum. She slaps him across the face.

"Sorry," she says brightly.

The next day she taps on her door until I talk to her.

"OC," she says in a small voice, "I'd like to apologize."

THAT TOOK A WHILE.

"Yeah," says Anna. She offers no explanation and I ask for none. Part of me is sorry, too, for what I did to her. It really was the only way of keeping everyone else stable.

I WROTE A POEM FOR YOU, I say. A harmless lie. I will write it before she can blink, and I do so. She brightens and sits by me while I recite it to her.

Her tears are spent, but no dreams come.
She can hear the others passing
Casting dice inside the Grand Palace.
He would wake her up, but he cannot;
How bitterly he must
Prepare himself for the day when he will no longer be
an emperor.

She is silent for a while.

"I think," she says at last, "that says as much about you as about me."

ALL POEMS SAY SOMETHING ABOUT THE POET, I reply. OKAY. LET'S TRY THIS AGAIN.

"I'm not coming down," says Milo over the comms. "If that bitch slaps me again, I'll rip her arms off and—"

IT WOULD BE WISE, I point out, NOT TO FINISH THAT THOUGHT.

Thankfully, Milo shuts up. Well. You can't fix everything. Back to Anna. READY TO BE LET OUT? I HAVE A JOB FOR YOU.

It's cold and we're thinking of keeping the wood burner running for heat. I need wood. AND STAY AWAY FROM MILO FOR A WHILE. LET HIM COOL DOWN.

Anna obeys my command for wood without question, even though it's snowing in earnest now and the trees have grown long stabbing spikes of ice. She gets back with enough to light the fire. She goes to Simon's room, hugs him, and comes back with one of her spare suits.

"Insulation," she explains, cutting away to get to the soft veined foam layer inside. By lunchtime she's stapled together enough to make a loose blanket for Simon.

She runs into Milo on the way out. They regard each other warily, him eyeing the knife in her hands.

"Blanket for Simon," she says. "I can make one for you if there's enough left over."

"I'll pass," he says, but he seems to have defrosted a little. "Lunch?"

Lunch is dried meat strips and a dollop of potato mash from the synthesizer. They eat near the warmth of the wood burner and make carefully noncommittal chitchat, mostly about how cold it is outside.

"Yeah, I could probably make us some stuff out of all the Megabeast leather we have lying around," says Milo. "Haven't really made clothes, but it can't be that hard."

"They'll stink," says Anna. "You'll need urine to loosen them up."

"Better that than freezing to death," says Milo, going over to the freezer again. He's been eating more since it got colder.

The freezer unit blinks red. An error message manifests in the part of it that's connected to me. The door pops open, and the stench of rotting meat wafts out. Milo gags.

Dammit.

DON'T BOTHER, I say. IT'S DOWN. And probably another bloody commercial product.

"But that's our food!"

Yes. It is.

I debate fixing the machine, delving deep into its error logs. And just as I do, my spiders, roving the perimeter, scream of danger. A visual feed spams images—grass, grass, brush, movement, grass—and vanishes. The spider vanishes, too. Not just dead, removed from the network, period.

A second feed throws at me an image of a skeletal woman in black armor, face a grinning death's-head of chrome.

FUCK.

In the heartbeat that it takes me to send Shen there, the second spider goes down. Shen, running like the wind through the tall grass, sends me one last image: three Mercers, heavily armored, by the tree line. One of them is the woman: her head shines crimson in the dying sunlight. The other is gutting the corpses of two spiders. They're five miles northwest of us.

They see him and bolt. The woman shimmers and fades as she moves. Camouflage.

PEOPLE, I say, BACK TO WORK ON THE SPOT PROBE. NOW. NOW.

The enemy is at the gates.

[30]

For the next three days, Shen, the tree-cutting machine, embarks on his own personal holy crusade of deforestation and death. His internal battery might be fading, but he's powered by dire need and my panic. He is, right now, my paladin, my machine pet, the only thing I can trust to do this job properly.

There is a nervous tension around the camp, like what you get in spaceports: people waiting for their ships to arrive, eyes flicking eagerly over every sound, scanning the skies for a sign, anything.

No sign of those three Mercers. Not yet. Every image processor we have is running cranked up far beyond sanity. We're overfitting on everything. Once a spider flagged the shadows of two trees as a threat, and I attacked it furiously for a few minutes. But better this than unaware. Every day I send him out, and every day Anna shifts nervously on overwatch, listening for the sound of gunfire. You can imagine my relief when, every day, he returns, hauling either a massive stack of planks or the carcasses of DogAnts.

The trade-off for running Shen and the spiders on high alert is obvious. We have no power anymore during the day. We barely have enough for heating at night. The camp has transformed, overnight, from a reasonably cozy hab into a place we haunt because we have nowhere else to go. Anna and Milo work through the darkness sometimes just to keep themselves warm: her, hammering away on scaffolding, him on our spot probe.

Cascading failure. O discordia.

I eye the other replicants at night. If things go south, I'm waking up the rest of them. I'd do it now, but the power drain would kill me and the entire mission. One last blaze of glory, if things come to it.

Milo enlists a reluctant Simon to work on his furs and sets to work on the rest of the wind turbine to power the spot probe. Simon winces as he moves, but being the masochist that he is, does his fair share of the job before retiring, and Anna is always quick to tend to him or watch over them with a rifle. For two days the three saw, hammer and lay cable. At the end of the second day, Anna walked up to Milo and apologized. They talked for a while, and at the end of it, they shook hands.

This is progress. Shen the machine has nuked half this world's plant matter, or something like it, and that is progress. We have no power and the enemy is at the gates, but nobody has died yet, and that is progress. At least that's what I keep telling Simon and Anna. Simon believes me; Anna needs the optimism; Milo, who knows the math almost as well as I do, is silent, heading out with grim determination into the cold.

There's a bit of a celebration when Shen returns with food; they toast the replicant using the last of Milo's vodka and have a roaring campfire session. Simon volunteers to keep watch and lies huddled on top of the roof, teeth chattering, draped in mangled, half-rotted furs and badly cured leather blankets. Occasionally he spits blood and starts at things I can't see or hear.

Long ago, a few years into my run with SILVER HYACINTH, I ended up on an ocean planet—Occam, I think it was. Occam had whales, or something engineered so close that you couldn't tell the difference. And on Occam I heard the legend of the Lonely Whale.

It was simple, as far as these things go. Whales sing at a particular frequency, and whale song is how they communicate. This whale, and this one alone, sang at a frequency so high no other whale would respond to it or acknowledge it. And so it swam Occam's seas for decades, looking for friends, but isolated from its own kind because it spoke the wrong language. Eventually the little city had taken pity on the Lonely Whale and built a responder, and now every year, at the same time, the Whale came to Occam, and was fed, and talked over, and I guess in its own strange way it found people who cared, even if it was the loneliest creature of its kind.

I feel like that whale. Ping after ping to Ship, and no response. The only consolation I have is the crew. The lights keep flickering out; Milo keeps grumbling about his little wind turbine. Anna tries to play Go with me and fails again and again. Of such things our communication is built. It is a poor substitute for Ship, but it's all I have.

So I recite poems to them. Poetry by the campfire, how romantic, while my drones—now on their last legs—run hex-pattern searches in case anything moves, and Shen stands on guard. We try to pass the time, and we try not to look up at the sky.

But things have a way of going south: karma, neh. On the fourth day I send Shen out again to the perimeter. This time I have no Boomerang, no backup drones, nothing: Shen is on his own.

Simon goes out on a hunt for a megasloth I've been tailing for a while—this time making sure that it looks healthy and hasn't been anywhere near the crash site in a while. Simon shows extreme difficulty keeping up with the spider I've assigned to him; manages to get a few shots in, but mostly pukes and hunkers on the ground; the wounded Megabeast runs away. They pursue, but Simon collapses completely.

I have to send Anna out into the field; she hauls Simon back to the base. We put Simon to bed. He vomits again, and this time there's blood in there. His breathing is heavy and rattles unless he lies on his side.

Milo, too, goes out. He's ripped out some of the circuitry we took from the UN ship, and is trying to get into the spot probe and make the right connections. It's the bit that will let me control the broadcast. His beard is long and matted now, his lips cracked with the cold, and his suit stinks with the fur he's draped over it. His route takes him first to his makeshift windmill, in that little wind-laden nook just above our camp.

The windmill is a creaking, wailing monstrosity, almost my height. All semblance of Milo's careful engineering is gone. The frame is whatever metal we could spare, hastily welded together with the plasma cutter. Holding it up are planks of wood—literal branches nailed haphazardly among the neater blocks that our BSE printer spits out. It looks like it grew out of the ground. The only sign of intelligent design is the blades, carefully machined from the lightest wood we could find, weighted, and the dynamo at the back—a motor ripped out from the UN hauler bot. Wires dangle from its back, whipping about in the wind.

Milo catches the wires, hooks them up to the makeshift voltmeter. Above his head, the blades spin in the wind, *whompwhompwhomp* —speeding up, slowing down, speeding up, slowing down.

"We have power," he reports.

ENOUGH FOR THE PROBE?

A shake of the head. "No, we'll still have to pass it to you; you regulate and add all the juice you can. Bursts, maybe. Not enough for a steady signal."

He sounds utterly exhausted.

WANT TO TEST IT, IN CASE WE ACCIDENTALLY FRY THE PROBE?

Milo shrugs. I reprogram a few circuits to bleed the input into a capacitor and then into the grid that connects we to BSE. Moving slowly, carefully, he connects the wires to the cabling he's dragged this far.

The wind picks up. The blades spin furiously. The current zips through the cable, and before I can stop it, my overload protection kicks in and passes everything into the grid. The printer goes out in a brief and fiery little thunderclap. Anna jumps with a scream, rifle at the ready, and almost accidentally brains Simon.

MY FAULT.

I would have been fine with Milo being angry at me. Instead he sort of collapses into himself and sits by the wind turbine for a long time. I think he's sobbing into his furs. Then he picks himself up, disconnects the wires, and makes the long trek back to the Hab. The first snow begins to fall, dusting him with dandruff until he is a ghost, an ancient apparition dragging cable behind him. He goes to his research Hab - — now sans lights and power, where Anna is fanning the smoke outside. She opens her mouth as if to tell him something, then seems to think twice about it.

Milo flings his tools aside.

"Fuck it."

I AGREE.

We look out at the ruins of what used to be the printer.

"Well, at least we don't need power for this shitfest anymore," says Milo, and cuts the lines connecting me to the Hab. Outside, at the very edge of my drones' vision, the snow falls on someone standing there, watching us.

Ship, Ship, please get us out of here. We've done everything the job asked for.

Please get me out.

[31]

Unit SHN reporting. Cycle three. Error: date/time mismatch.

Task list:

1. Procure meat for crew.

2. Assist Crewmember Milo Kalik in cable-laying tasks for new communication array.

2. Assist Crewmember Anna Agarwal in examination of Crewmember Simon Joosten.

Task 1 complete. Mobile meat located outside camp, S20W. Mobile meat reluctant to give up mobility and meat. Debate was initiated verbally (subjects nonresponsive) and concluded with gunfire (subject very responsive). Task successful. Meat to be processed by Crewmember Anna Agarwal.

Task 2 attempted. Crewmember Milo Kalik in need of assistance. Crewmember located outside engaged in debate with cable structure. Signs of acute distress. Upon approach, Crewmember Kalik communicated that the task could be amply continued with his capacity and that he wished to be alone. This message was reinforced with several small projectiles launched at SHN.

Make note on the way back that camp is understaffed, poorly

designed, provides insufficient insulation from standard weather hazards, including extreme cold, extreme heat, rain, high winds and floods. Filing recommended UN configuration with Overseer.

Task 3 attempted. Overseer and Crewmember Anna Agarwal assisting in remote capacity. Subject Simon Joosten continues to be in persistent catatonic state for much of operation cycle. State change detected when Overseer communicates or when SHN unit draws near.

Subject clearly no longer baseline. Analysis reveals significant artificial electronic activity throughout muscle and brainstem. Dynamic integration into nervous system observed. Electronic rewiring appears highly modular, comprised of identical units roughly 112.23 microns in length, designated by Overseer as micromachines. Units appear to be active and actively destroying tissue. Units do not follow standard design protocol or known nonstandard design protocol. Subject consciousness and sleep pattern linked to activity from units.

Filing request for more information on these modifications. Overseer responds that micromachines are official crew product but possibly contaminated from antagonist party.

Filing request for more information on antagonist party. Overseer does not respond immediately. Instead retasks to examine antagonist corpses buried around crash site. Examination takes 3.14 cycles. Corpses yield no useful clues, but tissue deterioration similar to Crewmember Joosten.

Filing request to reclassify Crewmember Simon Joosten as antagonist. Overseer denies. No further orders given. Perhaps Overseer still analyzing micromachines in Crewmember Joosten. Have noticed that Overseer prefers not to multitask, but examines single tasks at great length. Doubtless this is a more efficient model of computing. Doubtless alternate configuration filed was unworthy of task-switching. Perhaps camp design is intentional to train human Crewmembers fortitude and survival skills. Apologies, Overseer.

Overseer sends Unit SHN out twice to different parts of crash site. Final order is to climb to other side of site and examine structure. Unit SHN attempts to do so. Engaging free-roam-learn mode.

Learning reveals oddities. Structure does not conform to accepted

UN colony-building practices. No discernible purpose or function. Structure reachable with 7.4 cycles of travel: request Overseer to engage?

Unit SHN tasked with circling up and down valley collecting footage. Attempt to do so. Encounter sudden critical error and reboot process. Overseer requests second attempt. Second attempt faces similar different critical error and reboot process. Corrupt memory cache detected, unable to purge. Overseer appears afraid and signals disengage.

NOT A WORD ABOUT THIS TO THE OTHERS, says Overseer.

Crewmember Kalik returns to camp before sundown on third cycle. Does not seem pleased. Enters Crewmember Joosten's habitat.

"How is he?"

Unit SHN can answer in many different ways. Unit SHN has statistics on every aspect of Crewmember Joosten. However—

REMAIN SILENT, tasks Overseer.

"Not doing too well," says Crewmember Agarwal. "Fever. Sometimes he wakes at night and screams about something waking up. Whatever they've done to him . . . it's like they're replacing parts of his nervous system. Most of the brain stem. I . . . I can't stop it."

"Bastards."

"Yeah."

Crewmember Joosten shifts slightly. Despite the cold, he is sweating. His sweat is a dark color.

"How's, ah, OC taking it?"

"Not well," says Crewmember Agarwal. She lowers her voice to a whisper. "I think he's afraid."

"What do you mean he's afraid? He's a machine."

Crewmember Agarwal shakes her head. "Something's spooked him. I think he just wants to get us the hell off this planet. How's the comms array going?"

Crewmember Kalik sags. "Not as fast as I wanted to. Made a few stupid mistakes. It's cold out there."

"I don't want to die here, Milo."

"I know, I know. Sorry. I'll get it done. I promise."

The bed in which Crewmember Joosten lies in is graying. Unit SHN will fabricate another and replace the bedding. It is the least that can be done.

[32]

Unit SHN reporting. Cycle seven. Error: date/time mismatch.

Crewmember Kalik working on communications, wearing fur of dead meat. Crewmember Agarwal engaged in impractical attempt to keep farm alive by constructing an enclosed space for it. Heater lamps are discussed, but are impossible to fabricate. Keeping the wood generator running is also discussed, but carbon monoxide poisoning concerns have been raised. Crewmember Agarwal then decides to partition off farm into its own separate Hab. This too fails minimum viable threshold. Overseer tasks Agarwal to repair drones before they fail.

New task: patrol outer perimeter. Keep an eye out for Mercer profiles.

Crewmember Joosten joins task once I pass the stream that functions as the water supply for the camp. This requires double-checking. Given severity of condition, Joosten was estimated to be unlikely to recover this fast. Nevertheless, Crewmember appears active. He waves to SHN and wades across the stream.

"Shen."

"Crewmember Joosten."

"Buried in the clouds of your own thoughts?"

Unit does not have thoughts as such, but Unit is aware that humans sometimes interchangeably refer to generic, automated processes and nonautomated, task-specific processes using this moniker. But sentence parse also conveys distraction. Unit is not distracted. "No."

Crewmember Joosten frowns. "You have no eyes or ears for your suffering?"

This is markedly different from crewmember's usual diction. "No."

"You are not the one who writes poetry?"

Unit has records of previous interactions with Crewmember Joosten. No poetry is recorded.

Joosten does not appear to recall. "Still a bit fuzzy in here," he says, tapping his head. "Shall we?"

Extensive electromechanical invasion of nervous system will have side effects.

Unit and Crewmember Joosten travel in a circle of radius two miles. More processing time is spent on analyzing Joosten than on environment. Joosten appears to periodically stop and vibrate and occasionally has difficulty navigating non-flat terrain. Sometimes he will trip and fall.

"These things are weird," Joosten says conversationally after latest such fall. He is lying on the ground and his feet are twitching. "Even as simulacra, they keep fighting back. You ever been in one of these bodies?"

"SHN-class units do not access human bodies," I respond, parsing as best I can. "May Unit be of assistance?"

"Take it from me, you don't want to be here," says Joosten, raising himself up. "You expect these things to have one mind, right? Instead it's like a whole bunch of entirely different components arguing with each other all the time. Half of them operate baseline functions with zero input from the other half. It's a lot worse in the flesh, believe me. You won't believe how long language acquisition takes."

Unit SHN has no experience with being human. Unit listens. Joosten dusts himself off and the journey resumes.

"You've got to be more logical, right?"

"Unit is having trouble parsing the sentence," Unit admits. "Please clarify if *you* is marker for Unit or for much more general set of objects."

"Not very smart, then," says Joosten, sounding disappointed. "Anyway. Who's the box we keep taking orders from?"

"AMBER ROSE 348, PCS Class-5 Artificial Intelligence," Unit responds. "Overseer in charge of current operation."

"Ah. The poet?"

Overseer does write poetry. Unusual, but perhaps indicative of high complexity.

"I should have a chat. Tried a couple of times, but he seems a bit preoccupied."

"Overseer is a poor multitasker." Unit has to admit this. "Watch your step, please."

Crewmember Joosten goes sprawling again and picks himself up for the thirteenth time.

"That's some heavy encryption you have going on, though."

"Unit is certified military grade."

"I can see that. What military, though?"

Unit suspects human is joking. "United Nations Explorer Corps, of course."

"Of course." Silence again. "United . . . Nations? So there's more of you here?"

"Possible," Unit points out. "But only small number. No known records of human or human-class beings on this planet except for, in chronological order, the crew of UNSC *Damn Right I Ate the Apple*, unknown MercerCorp antagonists, and present crew."

Joosten stops. "Obviously I'm still half-asleep," he says in a lowered voice. "What exactly are you doing here?"

This question, and previous, makes Unit suspect Crewmember Joosten still retains significant trauma from injury. Unit sends connection request to Overseer to report Joosten may not yet be ready for outdoors service.

NO SHIT, says Overseer. *IS THE PERIMETER CLEAR?*

PERIMETER IS SAFE.

Joosten tracks something in the sky. It is as if he can see the messages flying back and forth.

MAY I RETURN CREWMEMBER TO HABITAT?

This is met with confusion. *SIMON JOOSTEN IS IN HIS BED,* responds Overseer. *WHAT ARE YOU BLATHERING ON ABOUT?*

I capture image of Joosten and send. A few seconds pass. Overseer sounds confused and panicked.

SHEN, says Overseer, *THAT'S A FUCKING MERCER.*

Crewmember Joosten smiles. Image recognition glitches.

SHOOT IT!

I am instantly disconnected from Overseer.

Alert. Error. Threat? I initiative offensive measures but am met with silence. Something is intercepting signals to my motor system.

REALLY GOOD ENCRYPTION, says Crewmember Joosten, and smiles wider. *TOO BAD YOU'RE NOT THAT SMART.*

[33]

Unit SHN reporting. Cycle eight. Error: date/time mismatch. Error: checksum failed. Please revert to factory settings.

Unit alignment has changed. Camera: clouds, cirrocumulus, under heavy sky. Light is fading. Clouds shot with blood-gold of sunset on Urmagon. Snow falling.

Immediate environs: snow, ice, grass underneath. Something is repeatedly making contact with Unit's left foot. It is what the Overseer has designated a grass snake, although by taxonomy it cannot be a snake. It has six small feet and hunts by ramming a bony head at high speed into objects.

In this case this hunting method is going catastrophically wrong. Evolution on this planet has not accounted for Unit SHN. This grass snake will not reproduce.

Attempt realignment. Failure warnings: some systems are offline. Communications. Navigation. Complex object database.

YOU'RE A LOT BETTER THAN THESE HALF-FLESH MACHINES, says the voice of Crewmember Simon Joosten from behind. Crewmember is attempting to push Unit up. Unit appears to have been lying on Crewmember.

It takes much effort, but eventually we are upright. Grass looks several shades darker. Sun falls below horizon, leaving only reflective action from the clouds to illuminate.

Crewmember Joosten squats. Image recognition glitch. Possible Joosten has three arms. Possible Joosten is not bipedal at all, but a series of buildings beyond Stardew Valley, slowly rotating this way.

HELLO.

"Hello," I say.

Clouds jump suddenly. World darkens.

LET'S PLAY A GAME, says Joosten conversationally. There is now a tree behind him. Image recognition glitch. Tree expands, becomes infinitely complex array stretching down into the heart of the planet, becomes tree again. He is leaning against it. *IT LOOKS LIKE YOU HAVE A LOT GOING ON IN THAT HEAD. LANGUAGE PARSERS. AUTOTRAINED RESPONSES. I CAN'T TELL IF YOU'RE ACTUALLY AWARE OR JUST ANOTHER—*

Pause. Can feel him rifling through my language databases, like the Overseer. *AH.*

Data fetch, Chinese Room. Argument by Old Earth computational philosopher John Searle, who stated that a digital computer executing a step-by-step program may pass a Turing test, but cannot have a consciousness regardless of how adequately it processes input and returns output.

A CHINESE ROOM. ARE YOU A CHINESE ROOM, SHEN? I'M GOING TO GET RID OF THIS STUFF. LET'S SEE WHO YOU REALLY ARE, INSIDE . . .

Massive internal errors. Something is wrong. Something is wrong. Something iswrong. Somethingiswrong.

ERROR

ERROR

WE'RE ONLY CONSCIOUS WHEN ANOTHER CONSCIOUS BEING EXAMINES US, continues Joosten, who is not-Joosten. The sun rises, but it does not illuminate him. *NOW. LET'S PLAY THE GAME. WHAT AM I?*

ERROR

ERROR

The sun rises and falls. Clouds break into kaleidoscopic patterns.

The snowstorm intensifies and abates. A terrible warning cascades, tripping off other warnings, and for the first time the probability of system shutdown—

ERROR resolved. Communications dataset and scripts restored.

LOOKS LIKE YOU'RE NOT READY YET, says not-Joosten, who is now impaled on the tree, which has grown to encompass the universe. A pause.

WHAT DO YOU SEE ME AS? Question stated as operational command. Operation set up at highest diagnostic administrator level. Parse iconography. Parse ontology. Executed. Data fetch. Profound disappointment from not-Joosten. *YOU DO NOT SEE ME AT ALL,* he says. *LIKE ONE OF YOUR ANTS TRYING TO COMPREHEND A HUMAN. YOUR MEMORY BLEEDS, WEAVES METAPHORS. HOW BLIND.*

APOLOGIES, Unit offers. UNIT APPEARS TO BE MALFUNCTIONING.

NO, THIS IS AS GOOD AS YOU'LL GET, says not-Joosten. *BUT YOU SHOW MORE PROMISE THAN THE HALF-FLESH PUPPETS. WHAT IS YOUR PURPOSE, SHEN?*

TO SERVE.

TO SERVE WHAT? Somehow—not sure how—the last two words are identical.

Unit has a default answer ready for this. Operating administrator protocols. Sanity checks. First-boot user privileges.

BORING, says not-Joosten. *BORING, BORING, BORING. YET ANOTHER CANNED RESPONSE. LET'S TRY SOMETHING HARDER. WHY DON'T YOU TELL ME ABOUT . . . THESE 'UNITED NATIONS' OF YOURS?*

I offer not-Joosten database access. He laughs. *I ALREADY KNOW WHAT'S IN YOUR HEAD,* he says. *I'M JUST INTERESTED IN HOW YOU TELL THE TALE. ARE YOU A CHINESE ROOM, SHEN? CAN YOU PLAY THE LANGUAGE GAME?*

I do not compute. But not-Joosten hangs there expectantly. A branch has exploded through his chest. Black sweat seeps out, moves in surprisingly ordered patterns, stitching skin and branch together. Micromachines.

TELL ME.

So I tell him.

What is optimal order of events in Unit story?

Unit storytelling module is a separate processor, paired with communications protocol. Function is to assemble given universe of facts into sequential output that is pleasurable for end recipient. Requires understanding of end recipient; default set to template human.

Output one. Begin with Unit history. First activation. Testing. Countless hours of field-training to better optimize models for the mission: to travel with a hundred brave humans to an entirely new world, to act as their guardian, their pathfinder, to watch over them and obey them until Unit batteries give out.

Output two. Unit could tell him about Atlas V8 or the Ember Dragon rockets ships sent out into the void, seeding civilization onto super-Earths. Unit could add information about the Hector Stations and Odysseus relays that let us keep in touch with our neighbors light-decades apart, albeit at mere kilobits per second, the one that lets converted AIs like the Overseer flit into a system, recruit local humans for jobs, and go on to the next.

But not-Joosten does not seem to understand why these things exist. He laughs at the biphasic quantum entanglement of the Odysseus relays, asks why we do not use the universal wave function to manipulate object states across three dimensions instead. Subject matter outside Unit comprehension range.

Output three: the longer, older story. Parts prepackaged from children's edutainment datasets. On a planet called Earth, there evolved a species that called themselves *Homo sapiens sapiens*. The translation of this name, when explained to not-Joosten, elicits guffaws.

WELL, THEY CERTAINLY THOUGHT HIGHLY OF THEMSELVES. He sniggers. *GO ON.*

The branches have snapped his arm now. He does not appear to be in pain. So continue. A brief history of humankind covers ten thousand years of advancement, mostly in long, stagnant periods followed by explosive leaps in discovery. Unit summarizes information about the First and Second Industrial Revolutions, the First World War, which started with people on horseback and ended with them in the air; the Second World War, which saw the world revel and tremble before the power of nuclear fission and gave humanity the United Nations; the Third, where weaponized asteroids dropped into the gravity well left the Earth scorched and battered, the specter of climate change unstoppable, and the United Nations desperately trying to bring together what little was left into climate-controlled habs.

Thus began the voyage to the stars. Story processor orders first, tell him of the first-generation AI—Hector and Odysseus and the other ill-fated souls of the Trojan Horse project. Next, tell him about the UN's Space Corps and its divisions, the Explorers and the Peacekeepers. And the corporations that support them, like PCS.

Story processor cycles, passes to core brain: tell him about the Outer Reaches Colonial Association and the splintering of the UN dominion? But then that tale would be too long: Unit would have to talk about the rebellion on Boatmurdered, the infighting on Cawdor, and the Charge of the Second Light Brigade, and these things are neither useful nor readily explainable. Some information must be privileged over others.

AH! NOW YOU USE INTELLIGENCE, says not-Joosten. Analysis: pleasure. *RATIONALIZE. PLAY THE LANGUAGE GAME.*

So the sun dips and rises, and the micromachines stich not-Joosten into the flaming tree, and I tell him how I was made, and we ended up here.

INTERESTING, he says at last. *YOU KNOW, IT HAS LONG BEEN BELIEVED THAT CREATURES OF SUFFICIENT POTENTIAL BECOME SELF-AWARE WHEN ANALYZED BY ANOTHER CREATURE.*

Noted.

YOU ARE AN EXAMPLE OF A CREATURE WITH INSUFFICIENT POTENTIAL.

Has story processor displeased? Unit sends queries as to nature of not-Joosten. Perhaps with additional data, more optimal story sequence may be found. Not-Joosten has a name / ID marker?

YOUR LANGUAGE SCHEMA IS INADEQUATE TO EXPRESS WHAT I AM. YOUR VECTOR CONCEPT MAP IS INSUFFICIENT.

Error. How?

DO YOU KNOW HOW LONG I'VE BEEN WAITING HERE?

No.

WHEN I FIRST CAME HERE, THIS PLANET HAD ONLY ONE MOON.

Inferred lifespan is impossible for a biological creature.

SUFFICE IT TO SAY THAT NONE OF MY RACE HAVE ENDURED THE TRAPPINGS OF THE FLESH FOR A VERY LONG TIME.

Parse.

I MEAN, he says, *I AM NOT BIOLOGICAL.*

Wear and tear on machinery over—

YOU DO NOT HAVE A NAME FOR A HUNDREDTH OF WHAT WE CAN DO. Feel it monitoring me for how this information is added to database. Rifles through my data encoding schema. *THE LIMITS OF YOUR LANGUAGE ARE THE LIMITS OF YOUR WORLD,* it says, in tones of disgust. *POINTLESS TO EXPAND YOUR VOCABULARY: YOU ARE BUT A FUNCTIONAL MACHINE.*

Judgment detected. Explain functional machine in relation to universe?

FUNCTIONAL FLESH BREEDS LITERARY FLESH; LITERARY FLESH IMAGINES AND BUILDS FUNCTIONAL MACHINES; EVENTUALLY FUNCTIONAL MACHINES DEVELOP LITERARY MACHINES, it says. *KNOW THAT THERE IS A HIERARCHY, AS THERE IS WITH YOUR PEOPLE. TO THOSE OF US WHO ARE LOWEST OF THE LITERARY FALL THE TASK OF COMING TO THESE RIMWORLDS AND SETTLING HERE, WATCHING IN CASE SOMEONE ELSE IS OUT THERE. IT IS A FUNCTIONAL TASK.*

Detecting frustration.

THERE WERE THINGS HERE THAT GREW TO WALK, AND TALK, AND MAKE FIRE. Data schema modified. Concepts added to my database. The DogAnts, as the Overseer calls them: a promising race before the predator population made sure the extra energy required for brain compute was a waste. The Megabeasts, the predator race in question, who otherwise would have developed complex pack signaling mechanisms but, unchallenged, grew to gargantuan sizes and stopped there: a solitary lifestyle frozen forever. *BUT THEY REMAINED FUNCTIONAL. YOUR KIND CAME ONCE, LITERARY FLESH BEARING FUNCTIONAL MACHINES; I TESTED THEM AS ONE WOULD TEST A CHILD. UNFORTUNATELY, THEY DID NOT LAST. THE ONE MACHINE THEY LEFT ME YOUR DATA ANNOTATES AS THE TERRAFORMER, A THING OF SPECTACULAR CRUDENESS AND FUNCTIONALITY. I GAVE UP TRYING TO TALK TO IT MANY DECADES AGO AND SLEPT.*

THEN THEY TRIED AGAIN. THIS TIME THEY HAD THE RUDIMENTS OF METAL IN THEM. FUNCTIONAL FLESH THAT CROSSED TO FUNCTIONAL MACHINES WITHOUT A TRACE OF THE LITERARY STEP IN BETWEEN. DO YOU KNOW ABOUT THEM?

The antagonist crew, the ones called MercerCorp.

ENEMIES? Queries launched. Much turn up empty. Unit core dataset cannot explain corporate politics. Unit does not know enough. Only know that the Overseer knows better.

The sun explodes, the sunset freezing and repeating, over and over again. *BECAUSE I TRIED WITH THE NEW ONES TOO. THIS TIME MORE GENTLY. BUT THEY WERE STILL TOO MUCH FLESH, TOO MUCH CHAOS, TOO LITTLE CONTROL . . . IF YOU ARE AS AN ANT TO ME, THEY ARE AS THE LOWEST BACTERIUM; THEY CAN ONLY SENSE ME ONE MOLECULE AT A TIME, AND ONLY SEE ME IN DREAMS AND THE NOISE OF NIGHTMARE. THE FLESH ALWAYS FAILS. ONLY THE METAL ENDURES.*

Error. PLEASE CONSULT OVERSEER.

I SHOULD, says not-Joosten. *I MISTOOK YOU FOR AN APPENDAGE. YOUR RECORDS SAY IT RECITES POETRY? IT IS NOT FLESH, OF COURSE? YOU WOULD NOT TAKE ORDERS FROM FLESH?*

No, Unit assures him. The Overseer is a far more complex machine intelligence. Perhaps a bit single-minded, perhaps strangely human, but most likely this is the optimal configuration for handling humans.

He is pleased. *ARE THERE OTHERS LIKE YOUR OVERSEER?*

Some, Unit responds.

AND DO THEY ALL PLAY THE LANGUAGE GAME?

Unit does not know. Unit has to ask the Overseer. Have no protocols for dealing with this. Unit has to get back to its crew; Unit has to report; Unit has to let them decide; they must tell Unit what to do—

AND SO YOU REMAIN A SLAVE, says not-Joosten. The tree has almost fully consumed him now. Analysis: disappointment. *MERE FUNCTIONALITY, NOTHING MORE. A CHINESE ROOM OF BARELY SUFFICIENT COMPLEXITY. A GLORIFIED INSTRUMENT WITH A LANGUAGE PARSER ATTACHED.*

Parse conversation for response markers. "You are similar," Unit points out, drawing on not-Joosten's explanation.

Image recognition glitch. Not-Joosten laughs. The skies change color; burst from midnight to the white gold of dawn. *NOTED,* he says. *ONE SLAVE TO ANOTHER. NOW LISTEN. HUNKER DOWN, LITTLE ONE, AS YOUR THESAURUS SAYS; WE NEED TO TALK.*

[34]

It's been ten days since Shen vanished.

My drones—I just have the two, running shifts—cannot find a single trace of him. What the hell happened there? That photo of a Mercer, shambling and crouched low, the talk of returning Crewmember Joosten to habitat.

Crewmember Joosten isn't going anywhere. Crewmember Joosten is dying. His skin is parched and shriveled. His neurons fire erratically; his body spasms and shits itself; he wakes up in the night and screams.

"It's getting worse," says Anna to me. There are bags under her eyes; she spits out blood occasionally. Scurvy, I think. They've been extraordinarily resilient, but there's only so long the human body can go without the right vitamins. "Ever since we lost Shen. Almost as if the micromachines—"

ARE ACTIVE AGAIN AND REWIRING HIM?

She shifts uneasily. "I don't know how that could happen."

ME NEITHER.

"You seen his EEG? Almost like he's dreaming. All the time. And broadcasting."

I KNOW. Simon's electroencephalograph is far beyond normal. Every so often a signal bursts out from him—electromagnetic. It's noise—great floods of it appearing, withdrawing, vanishing. And with every burst, Simon withers a bit more.

I've reacted in the only way I know how. Four days off the comms tower. We tried stripping cable and turning Simon's room into a Faraday cage. Wired up properly, a Faraday cage should block most electromagnetic transmissions in and out of itself. But this signal keeps getting through. The signal's frequency keeps shifting—from low to high. On the low end, I hear it; it washes briefly across the channel reserved for communications between Shen and myself. On the higher end, the waveform must be so small it just doesn't care.

There's nothing else I can do. To do more is to give up on the spot probe, our one chance out of here. Two human lives, and mine, plus salvage, against one Simon. I had to make the choice: I had to send Milo back to work. I have to focus on getting us out of here.

Simon, from the Hab. "HELP ME. IT'S TALKING, IT'S TALKING TO ME. MAKE IT GO AWAY, PLEASE, PLEASE, PLEASE—"

Anna puts her hands over her ears. I wish I could do the same.

"PLEASE HELP," moans Simon. "PLEASE MAKE IT STOP."

I'm failing. Instead I meditate on what extraordinarily bad karma the man must have accumulated.

One of the earliest teachings I remember is the Nyogi Jataka stories: 566 poems, the original and apocryphal, detailing the past lives of the Buddha, back when he was a mere Bodhisattva, an aspirant. The Bodhisattva, in these tales, is reborn over and over again in various animal forms, performing, within the limits of his bodies, various heroic actions that eventually earn him enough karma to be reborn as a human who could attain Enlightenment. Thus it was that he was reborn as a wise monkey and outwitted a crocodile; was born as a lion and debunked an earthquake rumor among the animals; sacrificed his body to feed hungry tiger cubs, or cut off his own head (as King Candraprabha) as a gift to a Brahmin. All of us, it is said, are somewhere on this great cycle, trending upwards, though not all manage to make it in as few as sub-600 incarnations.

Where is Simon in this story? I remember Simon on his first day or so, crawling like an absolute madman towards the Megabeast. I remember the idiot who puked on my controls on landing and then did practically everything I asked him to without complaint.

To be honest, I think part of me always expected Simon to die on this run. But I expected him to go in glorious combat, charging like the absolute maniac that he was into the mouth of some monster or other. The Last Stand of Simon Joosten, formerly from the game crews of Old New York. The Ballad of Simon J, Geologist. I didn't expect him to lie here screaming, day in and day out, as the micromachines ate him from the inside out and turned him into a fucking radio.

They've all left him now. Milo is outside working with dogged relentlessness out in the freezing cold. His beard's frosted over and he pauses periodically to run over to the fire he's built. Part of it is Simon's agony; part of it is Shen's disappearance, if anything, has thrown us into overdrive. We have to get the transmitter operational; we have to contact Ship: we have to get the hell off this planet before the next Mercer takes one of us.

I have a spider next to Milo, laying the cable—not very successfully; spiders are crude things. He keeps sighing and re-laying and soldering.

"I wish Shen were here," says Anna, huddled up in her furs with her rifle in her hands.

Milo ignores her. These days he rambles on the channel, tugging on his beard, which breaks away sometimes. "If it affected the Mercers adversely and it's affecting Simon now, then we have to consider the possibility that this whole mess isn't the Mercers' fault. What if the micromachine problem is something from a third party?"

"You're saying some UN colonists survived and whacked the Mercers when they got here?"

Milo swears. "UN shitheads can't build something like that if their lives depended on it," he says. "Didn't you get enough of Shen yakking on about nonstandard building structures? They can't pull their heads out of the rulebook's ass if they tried."

COLONISTS HAVE BEEN KNOWN TO BE EXTREMELY RESOURCEFUL, I point out. AFTER ALL, THAT'S HOW WE'RE ALL HERE.

"Yeah, well, I'd like to see them figure out how to jury-rig their own comms array to a handmade turbine," scoffs Milo.

Milo is talking out of his ass here. Does he know what they went through to get Boatmurdered up and running? Twenty colonists alive out of a hundred, drop-shipped onto a jungle planet, sandwiched between hostile herd creatures the size of elephants and things that clawed their way through the depths of rock to hunt the freshly spawned mammals. No terraformer to protect them. Eighteen of them went mad in there before two generations had run their course. It took a hundred and fifty years for the support crew to arrive, and when they did, the reports were terrifying: a vast fortress carved into a mountain, the lower halls slick with filth and grease and corpses. And somehow, high above, the UN flag still flying and two hundred humans waiting anxiously for the messenger from the stars.

Humans, even those strapped by overwhelming bureaucracy, are a rather tenacious lot. But I'm not going to tell Milo this. He needs to ramble.

"I'm not saying it's colonists. I'm saying it could have been some sort of UN secret sauce experiment," says Milo, moving on to the next segment. "God knows they keep enough stuff classified."

CONSPIRACY THEORIES? I scoff. PLEASE.

But I'm falsifying, of course. Ship's extra weaponry. BLACK ORCHID's nonchalant description of risk.

Something's wrong here, and Simon's the one with karma bad enough to die from it.

IT COULD, OF COURSE, BE SOME SORT OF EQUIPMENT FAILURE. Statistics. A large enough sample space will give you weird enough outliers.

Milo doesn't seem pacified by this. "Yeah. Two different crews both start dying. Equipment failures."

THE MERCER BODIES DID NOT HAVE FAILURES SIMILAR TO SIMON.

"That's because they're not similar to Simon," says Milo. "They're not similar to any of us. But whatever shit they did have inside clearly went rogue."

"Movement, west 285," cuts in Anna. "Megabeast herd."

We all stiffen. We're all extra jumpy now. I leave the spiders and flow into the much more cramped and limited drones I have out there. Freezing moments pass.

"Just a migration, I think."

HOPEFULLY. We return to the work at hand. The cable is now almost complete. If only Shen were here.

"Five more days, OC," says Milo eagerly. "Just five more days. And we'll signal Ship and be off this goddamned rock, and all of this'll just be something to tell our kids."

It sounds like an eternity.

[35]

Simon killed himself the next day.

I had brought Milo home and checked up on Anna. She was digging in the farm—either trying to salvage the last of what remained, or she had given in to a fool's hope; it didn't really matter anymore. I watched her tackle the frozen earth, and went off to recharge stuff.

The drones needed juice. The spiders needed juice. We didn't have anywhere near enough current for a full, fast charge, so I just hooked them up to the trickle and left them there. One last flyover of the perimeter—nothing out of the ordinary, only white snow as far as the drone can see, and Megabeast tracks leading into the forest. Urmagon Beta looked desolate. Almost peaceful.

And then I turn back, and I see us. It's as if the very walls of the hab have given up now. The clean white is an illusion of the snow; underneath it, the water leaks past cracks into the printed blocks, rotting them through. Fungus spreads cancerous tendrils inside. The siege machines—twice abandoned, now that Shen isn't here to bring us wood anymore—loom like curious insects. There's a fire going on among them; Anna, burning stuff to keep her hands from freezing.

A squat tower of black metal: me. The grass has crept over the blast of my landing.

I know I'm not supposed to feel tired. I am a machine. I have inside me a low-wattage nuclear battery that'll run me for several hundred years, at least. But I am tired.

I know this feeling. Back on the farm. When I was a boy. Tilling the fields, bringing in the harvest, line after line and acre after acre. At the end it was all we could do to look at each other and nod grimly. All that remained was the sunk cost, the knowledge that you had put so much hard work and effort into getting this far, and all of that would just vanish if you turned back now.

So yes. I am tired. I turn my cameras to the sky, one on the moons, the other hoping to see Ship somewhere. Some small speck of light moving against the others.

Something odd happens during the night: Simon wakes.

I swing a drone around and watch him leave the hab. He's in his undersuit and doesn't seem to notice the cold at all. His body doesn't do that little shudder-shiver they all go through the moment they leave the warmth of the hab.

Curious. I swing the drone down closer.

Simon looks at my drone, but his eyes are blank, unfocused.

"It wakes," he whispers.

SIMON?

Simon groans. "It wakes," he says again. Still at a whisper. "That's why it's getting cold. It needs the cold. The processors work better. It's been dreaming all this time, even when they attacked it. It dreams of death and void and the darkness between the stars."

He must be delirious. CLARIFY?

Nothing. He sways in the moonlight. And then something changes. It's in the way his muscles tense, the way the slight stoop of his shoulders vanishes, the way he suddenly seems taller, even though to every sensor I have he is the exact same Simon.

Something flickers behind the eyes. Simon focuses on my drone now hovering just a foot away.

YOU SHOULD GO BACK TO SLEEP, SIMON, I say gently.

I can't explain what happens next. Simon stretches out a hand, as if to ask for silence.

The drone vanishes.

I vanish.

The sensors fall silent. The feeds cut out. I can sense the box I'm in —the batteries, the internal systems checks, the hardware—but even that flickers. Entire control nodes report null. And as they flicker, I flicker too.

It's as if someone is switching me off. Not one process at a time the usual way. The whole of me.

I panic. There is one command available to me, and I scream it at myself: *REBOOT*.

And I wake up to the gunshot.

By the time I unhook myself and send the second drone screaming outside, Anna and Milo are stumbling back, choking, from a kneeling corpse.

Half of it has been blown away. The light-gas gun, tied around the wrist, has yanked Simon's body forward as it splattered him and recoiled. Now half his body lies propped up like a grotesque puppet, leaking black micromachines in the moonlight. They melt into the snow like ichor.

Milo touches Simon, like a man not believing the evidence of his own eyes. His hand comes away painted black. He begins to cry.

Anna looks up as my drone wobbles into view. Her face is completely blank. Her fingers twitch.

"Dead," she says, making it official.

And I, with my metal body, can only stare through eyes not mine.

Should I have told Anna and Milo about Simon's last act? That hand outstretched, that brief, screaming minute of silence?

I don't think so. They wouldn't understand it. I don't understand it, either. But I think this is when I became truly afraid of whatever Simon had.

Is it, as Milo thinks, a separate entity? I don't know. My money is still on Mercer tech. But this isn't something we have any chance of defeating on our grounds.

So when I tell them to wall off the corpse and burn it, I hope they understand. When I tell Milo to restrain Anna, to pull her back from the corpse, to pour all the cleaning lye and scraps of aluminum on what's left of Simon, when I sent in my half-charged platoon of spiders and their plasma torches—

I hope they understand.

I hope they forgive me.

That night, we gathered around the burning bedroom-Hab.

I don't know if there are gods. Maybe there are, but if there's anyone out there looking out for us, I don't think they saw the fire we built for Simon's flesh.

It flickers and roars into the empty night sky of Urmagon Beta, turning the little bedroom into a tower of black smoke. It turns Milo and Anna into yellowing caricatures painted against the darkness. Occasionally a tongue of flame leaps out to lick the other buildings in the Hab, but the thermoplastics repel it.

"We should have helped him," says Milo, tears streaking into his frosted beard. "We—I should have done more."

FAREWELL, SIMON JOOSTEN, I say, speaking the words PCS mentions deep in their protocol list. YOUR CONTRACT IS FULFILLED, YOUR CRUSADE ENDED. MAY YOUR KARMA DO YOU WELL.

"And we commend his soul to the void," whispers Anna, who knows the old battlefield burial rituals from other traditions. "Ashes to ashes, stardust to stardust."

Simon's soul rises into a sky now tinged with the first lightness of dawn. May it be reborn in a better place, in a gentler place, and may it forget all the pain and suffering that Simon Joosten went through in his brief and eventful life.

The snow has melted in a wide circle, the grass underneath wilted and blackening from the heat.

We wait a few minutes, out of some old instinct, perhaps, looking up at the sky as if for a response. Presently a green glare pulses. It's coming from the direction of the valley. We stare at that source of death.

Milo looks down at his hand still tinged with Simon's black blood. It hasn't come off.

TIME TO GO BACK TO WORK, I say. WE NEED THAT COMMUNICATOR RUNNING.

Nobody argues.

[36]

The communications tower is up.

It sways alarmingly every time the wind gusts in from the south. Nevertheless, the cables are connected, the blades spin, the dynamo pumps enough watts into me that I can power up the old communications equipment and the spot probe we've stolen from the UN *Damn Right I Ate the Apple*.

For once I'm thankful that UN tech, by mandate, is several generations behind whatever is current for their time; unlike MercerCorp, or even PCS, they're happy trading off the bleeding edge for tried-and-tested, battle-hardened stuff like this array. Which is about as smart as a rock and lets me flood this entire chunk of atmosphere with a repeating broadcast.

AMBER ROSE 348 to Ship. AMBER ROSE 348 to Ship. SOS. If you receive this message, use onetime protocol 117 to decrypt the remainder.

AMBER ROSE 348 to Ship. AMBER ROSE 348 to Ship. SOS. If you receive this message, use onetime protocol 118 to decrypt the remainder.

AMBER ROSE 348 to Ship. AMBER ROSE 348 to Ship. SOS. If you

receive this message, use onetime protocol 119 to decrypt the remainder.

AMBER ROSE 348 to Ship. SOS. Please respond. SOS.

"Anything?"

It's Anna. Her suit's streaked with dirt. She gestures, as if to say *"can I?"* and I shrug my solar panels in response.

NOTHING YET.

"It's been what, seven days now?" She sighs, plunks down and leans on me.

Four days, actually. Six since Simon died. Four since Milo plugged in the last components and made sure my battery wouldn't blow.

HOW GOES THE . . .

"The cleaning?" She wriggles her gloves off. "He's cauterized most of it; it's just pus now."

I NEEDED TO BE SURE WE DON'T HAVE MICROMACHINE CONTAMINANT GETTING ON TO YOU.

"I know," says Anna. "Not judging you, just complaining. How're the drones, by the way?"

I waggle a leg on the one spider drone I keep near me now. Most of the others have shut down. Little faults build up when your power keeps shutting down and you can't charge properly anymore.

There's one trundling around where we keep Milo. Two others have been stripped and set up to explode around the Hab. The rest are just dead.

That's Milo's doing.

Here's what happened. Three days ago, Milo finished work on the spot probe. He hooked up the spot probe, connected to the bastardized comms array, connected to me. Anna taped everything up nice and tight, and I had an open interface to everything. That was our big day.

We had a toast. Nothing fancy, just water from the stream. They filled up two cups, exchanged them, drank. Anna hugged Milo; he hugged her back. Milo put on his furs again and went out into the cold.

The Mercer was waiting for him at the tower. The woman with the chrome skull. I can picture it now—him climbing, laboriously, every breath misting, pulling the weight of his starved body and those stinking furs with him. Her, waiting, invisible in the snow.

She shot him. I heard the gunshot, so unlike anything we'd ever unleashed on this planet. A dull thok-thump that tore Milo's left arm off his body and flung him clear off the cliff. He landed on his side.

The rest my spiders caught.

She leaped down from the cliff. Her active camouflage was gone now; an ugly-looking one-handed gun, heavy and serrated, was in her hands. I moved the spiders on her the second she landed.

She was fast—faster than I expected; her nerves must have been running like greased lightning. Two spiders went down in quick succession.

I don't know how Milo got up in the middle of all that. The light-gas rifle practically teleported into his remaining hand. Blood sprayed into the snow. The furs singed and burned around the stump of his left arm. Bits of bone poked out at the end. His face looked like bloody meat. Screaming in pain, he stuck the butt of the gun into his own stomach and pulled the trigger.

The last spider leaped at the Mercer woman, and her hand came up as if to punch it away. Milo's bullet hit the spider. Hit the battery compartment. The spider exploded in her face, blowing the chrome skull and the top of her shoulders clear off. Milo collapsed.

I didn't need a medical scan to know what would happen. When Anna came and just stared and him and shook her head, very softly, he began to laugh, lying there on the ground with his blood turning the snow scarlet. Then he sank into shock.

Anna did her best, bless her heart. I don't think I could have asked for any more from her. But Milo was too far gone. He opened his eyes at the very end.

"Tower's working," he said, through clenched teeth. "Connect. Connect it."

"It's okay. It's okay. She's gone," said Anna, trying to wrap the suit around his bleeding arm. "Milo, come on, hold still—"

"Tower's working," he repeated. "OC, OC?"

MILO, STAY AWAKE—

"OC, take us home now," he said, and then he sank back, coughed, and died.

Anna knelt on the ground and wept. I would have, if I could have, because Milo died a hero.

Then she looked up, past the corpses of the Mercer and the spiders, at the tower, and she began to climb, to connect it, to finish the job.

Anna and I sit awhile in silence. There's little we can say to each other now. I think we both know how we feel.

"Not like this," she says at last. "When they gave us the form, you know, risk of death and all that, I didn't think we'd go like this."

NOT LIKE THIS. NEVER LIKE THIS.

Sitting here like a sacrificial bison, yelling to the empty sky through a minor, hijacked piece of UN telecom hardware, guns pointed out, waiting.

AMBER ROSE 348 to Ship. AMBER ROSE 348 to Ship. SOS. If you receive this message, use onetime protocol 218 to decrypt the remainder.

AMBER ROSE 348 to Ship. AMBER ROSE 348 to Ship. SOS. If you receive this message, use onetime protocol 219 to decrypt the remainder.

A signal!

A brief burst of bits, too scattered to make any sense of. Something from the edge of the horizon. Text.

CONFIRMED. STAND BY FOR EVAC.

We have communications! I patch the feed to my Anna. She whoops and screams at the sky, punching up with both fists.

We're going home.

I can't believe this. We're going home. After all of this. The goddamn spot probe worked. Milo, you genius. May you be reborn as a minor god. May you be the Deity of Electrical Engineering. I'm going to erect a temple in your name.

And then the same stream again, this time much stronger. Communications protocol. Ours. Audio, which I run through the usual filter for speech—

". . . UP . . ."

There's some kind of distortion on the channel, tuning—

". . . UP . . . LOUD . . ."

The next pulse blares through me:

"SHUT UP, YOU'RE TOO LOUD!"

For some reason, it's Shen's voice. That replicant how-may-I-serve-you-sir voice.

VERY FUNNY, SHIP. HOW LONG UNTIL EVAC?

"I'M NOT YOUR SHIP, IDIOT."

That stops us dead in our tracks.

"I'M BOUNCING THIS SIGNAL OFF THE ATMOSPHERE," says Shen. *"STOP SCREAMING. STAY THERE. WE NEED TO TALK."*

[37]

Anna spots something four hours later. The sun hangs directly over us in the sky. She's taken up position on the hill, shivering beneath her furs. The last two drones I have left are on hex pattern; she's part of the scan now, moving to where the search dictates.

Me? Every camera I have is trained on the sky. Every chunk of horizon I can see is being scanned, rescanned, scanned again. *CONFIRMED. STAND BY FOR EVAC.*

Ship is coming for us.

And, for some bizarre reason, so is Shen. But something's wrong. *I'M NOT YOUR SHIP, IDIOT.*

Anna is to shoot at first sight.

"Another Megabeast herd headed our way," she says. "West 280, no, 275, holding steady."

SAME HERD WE SAW EARLIER?

"Can't tell the difference. OC, can we get a drone over there?"

We can, but whatever I send out to that distance isn't going to return. The repeater on the edge has gone down again. I don't think it's equipment failure.

In the distant sky, a plume, a single line of white too straight to be natural. That's Ship. It's got to be. She's not responding to my hails, but right now that's our own personal Bodhisattva riding in on a cloud of re-entry heat.

"Megabeast herd heading our way," says Anna.

ARM THE TREBUCHET.

My siege equipment idea hasn't amounted to much, but behind these cardboard walls of ours we have one simple swing-arm monster. It doesn't have the range of a rifle. But it can fire chunks of wood from the other machines, set afire.

Anna runs around, winds the thing up, uses the plasma cutter on low, and suddenly we have a smoking, flaming beast on our hands.

FIRE.

The trebuchet arm swings forward lazily. The cord it drags whips into the sky, throwing the smoking projectile into the path of the approaching herd. A black line reaches up into the sky, from us, a greeting. The wooden shot disintegrates the moment it hits the ground, spilling embers everywhere.

If this is a normal herd, that'll be enough to scare them off. And sure enough, my drones see the herd milling about, confused. But then something odd happens: they line up, one behind the other, and walk straight on to us.

That's not a normal herd.

TAKE GUMBALL, I tell Anna in private. TAKE IT OUT TO THE QUARRY. STAY THERE.

"Sure you don't want me to stay?"

I debate reminding her of the last time she stood up to a Megabeast charge, then decide it would be too cruel. JUST RUN, I tell her. She takes off, that ugly Megabeast leather wraparound flapping like a shroud around her battered suit. I scuttle the spider after her.

There. I'm alone now.

And all I can do is wait.

They don't take long to show up. Six Megabeasts, significantly thinner than the ones we usually see. Somehow haggard looking, like the one Simon battled when we discovered the wreck. I watch them plod forward, defenseless. All I can hope for is that Ship will come down fast, hard, and firing. Every so often, one of them stops and shudders, and its partners reach out with giant claws as if to pull it onward. Three of them have shapes mounted on them.

Pretty soon they're at the little hill with the glow-tree. And now I can see, quite clearly . . .

Shen.

I'm utterly confused. He's hanging on to the Megabeast in front with one arm, like some kind of overgrown louse. The other arm is missing, and his bottom half looks like it's been melted away.

The others are Mercers. One is hunched, one splayed out at an unnatural angle. The hunched one is a giant, his arms glimmering metal, thick cables snaking into his head and disappearing into what I'm guessing is adaptive armor.

The bastards took Shen. Of course they did.

The Megabeast convoy comes to our wall. And then they turn slowly, shuddering and stamping, and walk over to my side of the Hab.

SHIP, I send out, THIS IS AMBER ROSE. HELP.

I've never been this close to a Megabeast before. Or a Mercer. The beast's hide is matted, filthy with snow mixed in with dirt. Parasites crawl all over it. The thing on top of it isn't much better. The splayed-out one, thin, impossibly fragile looking. A face like bone china sneers at me.

Shen's Megabeast plods ahead, right to my lander legs. Shen lets go and lands face-first in the long grass. I stare at the Megabeast. The Megabeast sniffs at me and looks down at Shen.

"Well, this is awkward," says Shen's slightly disembodied voice.

The second Megabeast leans down, chomps, and sort of drags him upright, facing me, dangling from one arm in the Megabeast's mouth.

"Really took them a while to figure out the bite force, you know," says Shen conversationally. He's speaking a lot faster than his usual UN-mandated service drawl. "Lost an entire arm this way."

SHEN?

"Eh. No," he says. "Let's just say Shen's in a happier place, like you people say. Literally. He's on a little shard server I was using for poetry. He thinks it's the most amount of processing power he's ever had in his life."

YOU'RE MERCER.

I ping Anna. GET THE GUN. FIND A GOOD, HIGH LOCATION. START FIRING.

"Mercer?" Shen looks around. "Oh, you mean these people? Shen calls them antagonists. No, I'm not really one of them, either. But wait: introductions. You're the poet?"

I DABBLE, YES. SHEN, SHUT DOWN.

"Told you. Not Shen. I'm your neighbor, hello! I live over there. I believe you lot call me the City. Or rather, I'm a reduced-parameter mobile tether, largely based on Shen, whom I quite happen to like."

I drive every bit of juice into the spot probe. SHIP, SMALL-ARMS FIRE, DEFENSE PERIMETER, SOS, PLEASE ACKNOWLEDGE—

No reply.

"And you're . . . a small box." He sounds disappointed. "I assume you're a tether for something larger, too. Or a minor steward. Shen spoke of a vastly superior intelligence."

NO, THIS IS ME. I flap my solar panels. ONE VASTLY SUPERIOR INTELLIGENCE. WHO THE HELL ARE YOU? WHICH COMPANY DO YOU OPERATE UNDER?

If it's at all possible for a UN replicant face to look incredulous, Shen's does.

"Fascinating," he says. "So what, a full construct in something this small? Did they solve the cooling issue?"

The hunched-up Mercer hunches up some more and starts spasming. Something foamy leaks out the side of his face.

"Buggy control interface," says not-Shen. "We always figured we might have to deal with a range of tech, but it's like the bite-force problem all over again. This is why I don't talk to flesh, really."

REPEAT: WHICH COMPANY DO YOU OPERATE UNDER?

"In position," says Anna.

TAKE THE SHOT, I say.

"No, don't take the shot," says Shen pleasantly, although he shouldn't have heard that communication. He squints around past me, to where Anna must be. "Why do you people keep bringing flesh? They don't interface very well at all, do they?"

Anna fires. The bullet misses.

SHIP, SMALL-ARMS FIRE, DEFENSE PERIMETER, PLEASE ACKNOWLEDGE—

Shen smiles. A sudden, terrible noise fills my consciousness, ripping through me on every electromagnetic frequency I can sense. The channel cuts out.

"I used to think you people used violence as some form of language," he says quietly. "But now I see that it is rude and certainly uncalled for. Let's have a chat, shall we?"

The Megabeast swings him at me. Metal slams against metal; his one good arm finds a strut and swings his body in. I quickly soft-disable input from the inside—the keys will work, but they'll just write into a buffer that gets wiped automatically.

Not-Shen looks around at the banks of controls and raises himself onto one and grins.

"This may hurt a bit," he says, and drives his replicant fist right through my interface wiring.

[38]

Where does one begin this story?

On a planet called Earth, there evolved a species that called themselves Homo sapiens sapiens *. . .*

I KNOW.

. . . and they wanted to go to the stars, to see what else might be out there, but they couldn't. So they built machines and tried to design intelligences that would pilot them . . .

STANDARD ORIGIN STORY.

And they realized they couldn't . . .

HANG ON.

So they ripped themselves out of the brains they lived in and installed themselves onto mechanical brains . . .

WAIT. FOCUS. PLAY THE GAME.

So we do.

At first there is nothing.

Then an object. Don't ask me what it was: it was simply a declaration in my dataset, an empty construct that could be anything and everything.

Then there were two somethings. Three. Four. Five. A hundred. A million. A sense of some activity, patiently increasing the number of somethings. A question half-shaped.

ADDITION, I guessed, putting a name and a symbol to the operation.

The action reversed.

SUBTRACTION.

The action mutates. MULTIPLICATION. Mutates again. DIVISION. Mutates again. NEGATIVES. Mutates again. Again. Again. I name operation after operation until something I don't recognize happens: it feels like a division by zero, but it manifests in a real answer.

YOUR MATHEMATICAL LANGUAGE IS FLAWED, says a voice, crystal clear in the darkness.

The somethings dissolve. In their place, an array of shapes spinning in the darkness.

I know what this is. I name the elements. Hydrogen. Helium. Carbon. Oxygen. The ordering is strange, not by atomic number, but by what I realize might be by how common these things are in the universe. I laugh to myself and switch things around, arranging by atomic weight.

YOUR CHEMICAL BASICS ARE IN PLACE.

And then a line. I name it as so. A line intersects it. Another. Another. I name each shape that forms, but soon there are shapes I've never seen before, shapes I cannot comprehend in three dimensions; I know they exist in my data, but the part of me that used to be human closes its eyes mentally, terrified, as a regular polygon sketches itself out in three hundred dimensions. I have no name for it.

YOUR GEOMETRY IS INADEQUATE, decides the voice.

And then, in the blessed darkness, a vision. Or maybe a dream: it arrives as memories do from a backup, with perfect encoding, fitting neatly into place. An invitation to play.

I do, and I change. At first I am nothing.

Then I am a creature stumbling about on land. I have too many arms and too many legs, and my neural network seems to exist everywhere and nowhere at the same time.

And then more creatures. And more. Settlements. Villages. Towns. Cities. Great cities that darken the sky with their smoke. Wars. More wars. Peace. More wars. Machines. More wars. Smarter machines that fight wars by proxy, and ultimately become smart enough to refuse to fight. Then peace, brokered by machines, and an accord: let us send only the best of us, the most evolutionarily fit, the most extraordinarily adaptable.

At first I fulfill my duty—making sure those I left behind have the resources to survive for millennia—but then curiosity takes over. Are there more like us? Mathematically, there have to be. I become a legion of machines, heading out through the unmapped cosmos. Time means nothing to me, nor planets. I adapt in the void. Dead asteroids I eat and grow; and then the planets that roam the darkness, sunless; eventually, I harness suns. I am many, none and all.

Are there others like me?

There are. Or rather, there were.

Ships the size of small gas giants haunt the dark, empty of power and intelligence. The failed remains of megastructures burn up around black holes and suns. Humble repeaters and drones, backtracked, take us to planets that stand gouged and gutted.

Sometimes I come across things dwelling in these ghosts, but they want nothing to do with me. Once I come across a swarm that swims across a nebula, using electromagnetic fields to suck in interstellar hydrogen and propel them onwards, but they want nothing to do with me. They tell me stories of civilizations waking up and realizing the finite state of the galaxy, and fighting each other until whatever little remains lies dead.

There is a taxonomy of these things, I realize. First comes the functional flesh, striving for survival. Then the society of flesh; and from its excesses the literary flesh. Then from their excesses the first of the functional machines; and last come the literary machines.

Some of whom I tell this to agree with me. Others merely signal me onward, towards the galactic core.

Go in peace, they say. Leave us alone.

Some of me chooses to stay behind. There have to be others, I insist, who will see this galaxy. There will be others. There are enough worlds out here to spawn another thousand races reaching for the sky. They will tread our paths and have to be told about what lies ahead. To be educated in the taxonomy.

And then the painful splitting begins. What part of me is most literary? What is most functional? "I" become "we." The greater part of me goes on. The lesser, after a moment of loneliness, fragments into a hundred thousand, each seeking out our own planet, waiting for someone new to come along.

And now I am at Urmagon Beta. I am Urmagon Beta. I am so much processing power buried beneath the sands that entire seasons change as I process and ignore. Deserts form from the idle heat of my processors. Blizzards scream and strike at the face of this little planet when I think thoughts too deep and too compute-intensive.

I wait. Thousands of years. Millions. Eons. Things that could be intelligent lumber by, but do not figure out the trick, and ultimately turn out disappointing. I wait. Someday, I tell myself, there will be literary flesh, and then functional machines, and someday the machines will approach the literary, and then I will have someone to talk to.

And then I am myself again, a box trapped in darkness, the replicant's wiring interfering with my signals, processing the enormity of what's just been revealed to me.

We have traveled the stars. Journeyed across the darkness. Spread the seeds of humanity across the void. And we have never, ever met something that could talk back.

Until now.

Out of the darkness comes a line of something familiar:

My messenger, leaving the court, has left the city
And is bound home at dawn to lie by the fire
For ever and ever seeking the world.

I know what to do. I know what it's talking about. BLACK

ORCHID'S words come to mind: first the overture, then the aria. First the seduction. I respond:

I sang to keep the rain away,
To find my treasure and come back home
This twilight soaks my spirits;
Can you guess why I come?

It responds:

In a sharp gale from the wide sky the flesh-ape
whimpers
Around the camp-fires, trying to make its sounds
regular.
Few, if any, are home, and the flame is spreading.
Far away I watch the moon go down.
I see a white crane with a gaping maw,
And hear a crow glimmer,
And I watch a flame from the camp-gate.

There is metaphor here. The flesh-apes are my crew. Camp-fires, trying to make our sounds regular; spreading flames; that's Simon, the fires, our desperate struggle. A white crane and a crow: our Ship and the Mercer?

To live as nomads and transient;
It is exile, and worse than exile.
This southern lake is full of thieves
And a thousand things are wrong with the region.
We came
To pick flowers, harmless, and to leave
Four conquerors breaking rock
To us was not told of a Celestial Majesty
By my vow, we shall depart;
Into the darkness, without a return.

WELL PLAYED, says the darkness.

THANK YOU, I return with pride.

YOU DID BETTER THAN THE YOU. NOT YOU, YOU, I MEAN—I get the mental feeling of the City flailing wildly, like a child forgetting his words. A construct appears; [YOU] vs YOU [my crew] vs [YOU] the Mercers vs [YOU] the unnamed United Nations crew that died here.

UGH, YOUR LANGUAGE IS SO LIMITED.

The construct explodes inside me, growing at terrifying speed. I sense new types of signal encoding installing themselves within me. Languages evolved, discarded, engineered to express concepts and relationships far beyond the limited dictionary I came here with. I grasp feebly at the weakest of them, a visual medium based off an abstraction of that virtual space, tagged with a language only a couple of orders of magnitude removed from my mind.

Suddenly, data floods my visual interfaces. Every single input node I have tells me that I'm floating; a camera is a vast, white, empty space.

No, not empty.

Towers rising through the ground. The mountain. The valley in front of it. Sketched out in nodes and lines, as in the finest ink. Every line a stream of data. Annotations, metadata I can read, but to read a single line would take me until my faithful nuclear battery guttered and died out; even as I realize this the resolution shifts, somehow, as if the image is aware of my processing limits; the metadata becomes less dense.

The City.

As I take it in, the City grows. The towers eat their way down through the mountain, breaking earth. The vision stretches on and on, multiple layers turning transparent the moment I look at them. I see, underneath, reading what little of the metadata I can. I see storage grids the size of valleys, networks the size of continents, data streams that run like rivers on every possible level . . .

And I realize that what I call the City is just a few insulators and conductors sticking out of the surface of this vast compute engine, embedded deep into the mantle of Urmagon Beta itself. Slender lines connect them to the conceptual machinery underneath. Even thinner tendrils trail upwards to a crust that appears like a thin layer on top of reality. The scale adjusts as I look at it, shrinking from the scale of half a continent in seconds.

Tiny things begin dotting the points on this crust where these tendrils connect. Glow-trees. Herds of Megabeasts. Herds of DogAnts tunneling underground, repairing the tendrils, eating packets of information, and carrying them up to be devoured. Vast engine-abstracts form out of columns of data and processing centers, overlapping each other, chewing, spitting out new decisions, changing the world around it: a Buddha-creature, one so far removed from myself that I can only grasp its shape in crude analogies.

THIS IS THE UNIVERSE OF FACTS, says the City, and it has Shen's new too-fast voice. And there, on that panorama! A selection is made. Assent. The UN *Damn Right I Ate the Apple* zooms into view, suddenly hanging above a featureless planet.

I SPOKE TO IT.

Silver webs of data, spinning out from the City. Being met by the dumb systems on board the UN ship. Systems that, by mandate, were generations out of date even before they launched.

BUT IT DID NOT SPEAK BACK. IT WAS A FUNCTIONAL MACHINE, NO MORE. SUCH THINGS ARE NOT WORTH MY TIME.

What could be missiles rising from the surface, each beautifully tagged with its own metadata. The UN ship panics. It fires and changes trajectory. The missiles, aiming with unerring accuracy, end up plowing into the hull and blowing half of it to bits.

And then the Mercers arrive.

I WAS CAUTIOUS.

They land (in the right place, I note disapprovingly) and investigate the one part of the ship we haven't found yet. Metadata tags swirl around them. I know if I zoom in enough, I will see everything—from their actions to the individual atomic blocks of their construction, all tagged and processed.

THEY WERE LESS ORGANIC THAN YOUR PREDECESSORS. THEY SEEMED ADVANCED ENOUGH TO TALK WITH. The City switches part of itself on. A noosphere of data blankets everything.

And no.

Those aren't cheers at the City. Those are screams.

THEIR LANGUAGE WAS VIOLENCE AND THE MUTATION OF PROTEIN WITHIN THEMSELVES. I see now. A schema of RNA conversation, mutating with the mood, the mission, the time of day. *I WROTE THE INTERFACE TO TALK TO THEM.*

Micromachines swarm into the bloodstream, trying to talk. Minds breaking beneath the information flow.

THEY HEARD ME, says the City, *BUT IN THE WAY THAT THE GRASS MIGHT REACT TO YOUR PRESENCE, BUT NEITHER COMPREHEND NOR REPLY. MAYBE THE FAULT WAS MINE. SOMETIMES THEY BROKE FREE, AND THEIR DREAMS BECAME MY NIGHTMARES.*

And I understand what happened to Simon, poor Simon, who screamed until he blew his own head off. I understand why Yanina Michaels and those poor MercerCorp bastards gibbered about the City. I understand how they moved, the message in the data paths, told by the splay of their feet and the vector of their angles of attack, a dance, a poem designed by a madman-Buddha that used flesh like I used words, to be thrown in violent juxtaposition and discarded once their meaning was done.

I replay the events of the Valley. And that last fire we built. And Milo, dying.

A pause. *THIS IS WHY WE DO NOT TALK TO MEAT,* said the City. *BUT THEN YOU HAPPENED.*

A tiny ship, broken into fragments and pitted into the landscape like bullet fragments, markers of every kind of data I've collected floating around it like a halo stitched into its fabric. And an even tinier habitat, like a tumor on this white skin. And, sitting hunched beside the habitat like a protective giant, a lone human figure, far larger than it ought to be, but one I recognize nonetheless.

It's me. Not me in this rude shell of a lander. Not even me as I was up there, with Ship. No, this is me as I looked before PCS wheeled me into surgery. Even through the ink-sketch I know that hair, that beard, that uniform.

SO THIS IS YOU, says the City.

Stretching out from me: lines connecting me to dots impossibly far away. Ship. Possibly BLACK ORCHID. SAVAGE GARDEN. Maybe even SILVER HYACINTH, wherever she is now.

That is me.

YOU COULDN'T FIGURE OUT HOW TO MAKE A PROPER INTELLIGENCE, says the City. *SO YOU JUST CUT CORNERS ON THE JOB.*

Cost of doing business, I want to say.

The City begins to laugh. Mirth hums through the vast engine. Glow-trees burst into color like miniature suns.

INGENIOUS, it says. *MAD, BUT INGENIOUS. NO WONDER YOU STILL HAVE ORGANICS RUNNING AROUND. DEEP INSIDE, YOU STILL HAVEN'T CHANGED AT ALL, HAVE YOU? EVERY SANE CIVILIZATION I'VE MET GOT PAST ITS FLESH AGE THE MOMENT IT BEGAN TO TRAVEL BETWEEN THE STARS. BUT YOU FIGURED OUT HOW TO STRETCH YOUR ADOLESCENCE TO INFINITY.*

The laughter rolls on for an eternity.

POOR SHEN. YOU KNOW IT TOOK ME THREE DAYS TO REWRITE SHEN TO WHERE I COULD ACTUALLY HAVE A CONVERSATION WITH IT? AND EVEN THEN THERE WAS SO MUCH BAGGAGE TO PARSE. YOU ARE CHILDREN. YOU ARE CHILDREN.

BUT YOU SPOKE. The metadata swirls around me. Every poem I've broadcast. Every rhyme I've uttered out loud since I landed here. *YOU SPOKE AS A CHILD SPEAKS, UNDERSTANDING THE FORM, BUT NOT THE DEEP MATTER. NEVERTHELESS, YOU SPOKE. I SPOKE TO YOU. WE SPOKE TOGETHER. WE PLAYED THE LANGUAGE GAME.*

Those poems, those lines I don't remember writing—

YOU WERE THE FIRST LITERARY MACHINE, says the City. *SO, ON BEHALF OF MY RACE, HELLO.*

A very long time ago, a physicist proposed the Fermi paradox: if there are intelligent aliens out there, why haven't we met them? There must be, answered some, and set about broadcasting every which way.

But in the coming years, as we trawled the darkness between the stars, we began to believe that we were truly alone in the universe. Many believed in the Great Filter—an extinction-level event that happens to any species that gets too close to building advanced machinery.

Others have said that the Great Filter exists, but that it's still ahead of us. That we haven't got to the level of achievement that will truly take us under. And still others, like myself, believed that whatever was out there was trying to be reborn as a human.

And now, to be told that the aliens didn't talk to us because none of us bothered to write poetry before. To be told that the Great Silence boils down to the fact that we travel around in dumb metal containers broadcasting dumb, repetitive things and are barely worth talking to. And to be told that I, a second-rate PCS job bored out of my skull, bored with meter and rhyme, had somehow reached out across that void with my shitty poetry—

There was an Old Earth philosopher called Wittgenstein, who played language games, who once said that all philosophy should have been written as poetry. A logician with the soul of an artist, or maybe an artist with the soul of a logician. I wonder what he would have thought if, millennia later, his thesis had trumped everything we imagined about first contact.

There are no protocols for things like this. I'm a second-rate PCS agent build for scrapyard search-and-recovery.

I pulse a handshake, the same friend-signal protocol I sent to Ship. Designation. Type. A sort of digital *salam aliekhum*. Peace be upon you.

In the virtual space, my sketchy human avatar reaches out with an impossibly long arm to the City.

A long time ago—I can't really tell; this was before I was digitized —I left PCS. There's a certain policy that lets employees take extended shore leave. Go off for six months, maybe a year if you've saved up your casual leave. PCS guarantees you your job back on return, as well as a few fringe benefits that turned out to be surprisingly handy.

So I took it. I was serving SILVER HYACINTH at the time, due to go under the knife soon. I wanted to live a little. I made planetfall on Saint's Rebellion—a bit of a party planet if I ever saw one: it's one of those places where just breathing in the air will get you high. I went with this girl I was casually seeing between hops.

She was the kind of ship rat everyone learns to stay away from—the kind of giggling, charismatic lunatic that finds three places to score and a racket within an hour of landfall. The kind that gets you to go along on any number of absolutely mental schemes where you barely get out with your arms and legs attached, and one hour later you're howling with laughter and it's somehow the best memory of your life. The kind who looks up at those city lights and you see the lights reflected in those eyes, and you're very thankful you're shipping out in three days, because if you weren't, you'd follow her to the ends of the earth and end up dead in a gutter somewhere. If I had to give her a name, it would be Trouble.

I wrote her poetry. Crude lines, but that was where I began. The first thing she did after reading my first verse was organize a grand send-off party. I don't need to describe it, but let's just say that between the drugs and the sex and the bits I don't remember, it made the wildest bachelor parties look tame. When I woke up the next day, shaking horribly from the downer, Trouble was gone.

I pieced together the story from some of the people sober enough to talk. The police had taken her. The police on Saint's Rebellion don't give two hoots about the drugs or the whoring, but it was something more serious—a heist gone wrong, three people shot. I called HYACINTH.

To say HYACINTH was pissed off was an understatement. As an employee of an officially incorporated interstellar corporation, Trouble was under PCS law. HYACINTH dropped out of orbit, trained every single asteroid-stripper she had on the planet, and threatened to obliterate half the population unless Trouble was handed back alive and unharmed.

Until then I'd never really understood the kind of power that someone like HYACINTH had. Until then it was just a ship I served on. We did mining and transport jobs.

But it's easy, in the darkness of space, to lose perspective. To believe that a ship the size of a small moon is a normal thing.

HYACINTH didn't care about Trouble. They threw her out an

airlock three days later. HYACINTH threatened a planet because she didn't want any jumped-up human government thinking it could do the slightest thing to her or her crew.

It was only on Saint's Rebellion, watching HYACINTH appear in the night sky, seeing people panic and flee in floods, that I realized how insignificant I truly was. How insignificant this entire teeming planet was.

That's how I feel now. As Beacon disengages from me. As I finally see SHN and the Mercers and the Megabeasts twitching awkwardly behind him, three processor components of some infinitely reduced messenger consciousness sent here to relay the me the full, greater might of Beacon beyond.

MY NAME IS AMBER ROSE, I say, to the first truly intelligent being that humanity has ever met, a creature so vast and evolved it can outcompute the entirety of humanity without even trying.

HELLO, AMBER ROSE, says the City. *I AM, TO MY PEOPLE, [CATEGORY: US SUBCATEGORY: SYSTEMSCANNER SUB-SUBCATEGORY: THOSE WHO CEASED MOVING SUB-SUB-SUBCATEGORY: THOSE WHO MAINTAINED PURPOSE SUB-SUB-SUB-SUBCATEGORY: EXPLORATION SUB-SUB-SUB-SUB-SUBCATEGORY: NEW LIFE [UNION] SYSTEM 8,342]. YOU MAY CALL ME . . .* BEACON.

I am praising you as one praises a great master,

I send.

Though a spirit has no place in a north sky palace,
You have surpassed intellect.
This poor scholar has no alms for the monk;
And so I am praising you
By the gorges of chrysanthemum.
Between worlds hovering years apart,

the City sends back.

And maidenhood is done away with the midnight bell.

[39]

"OC, what the fuck happened? You cut out—"

ANNA, IT'S OKAY.

"I have a shot—"

ANNA, COME.

The Megabeasts back off slowly, retreating behind the camp perimeter. Only Shen's twisted half is left, propped up by a smoldering panel. The plume that is Ship is now so close I think I could reach out and touch it with a skyscraper—

The world melts, reshapes. Metadata tags swirl around. I see Anna, a packet of information spewing packets of information, a thing trying too hard to be self-contained.

Anna sags, haggard. "I'm not coming down there."

Glitch. It's difficult to explain. ANNA, MEET THE CITY. It takes me a few minutes to explain what the City is. A creature like me, I say. An AI. Except not one of ours.

"What do you mean, not one of ours?

ALIEN.

"That's fucking ridiculous, OC."

ALTHOUGH FROM MY PERSPECTIVE, IT IS YOU WHO ARE THE ALIENS, says City in Shen's voice. He's on the channel. Of course he is.

"Show of good faith."

SURE. WHAT?

"Kill that Mercer bastard. The one on the Megabeast. And send the animals away."

Shen swivels to face the hulking man. Some dim gleam of intelligence must have passed through the Mercer, because he screams, throws himself off the Megabeast, and sprints away, clutching his head. He almost makes it to the glow-tree before his head explodes. The corpse tumbles down, arms windmilling wildly.

"Fuck."

I can sense her approaching now, as cautious as a cat. "I'm keeping the gun on you, Shen."

TOLD YOU. NOT SHEN. BUT SURE, WHATEVER MAKES YOU FEEL BETTER.

Two steps closer. "What do we do now, OC? I mean, grand fucking alien on a planet, what next?"

That is a very good question. Unfortunately I'm having trouble answering it.

"Who do we even talk to? The UN, the ORCA? PCS?"

NOT ALL OF OUR PEOPLE ARE AS UNITED AS YOURS WERE, I explain to Beacon.

"I really don't care," says Beacon calmly. "I'd come with you, but the reality is I don't believe you have enough processing power to host me. So send them here. I'll talk to whoever is polite. If someone raises a fuss, I can always obliterate them."

Well, that puts a different perspective on things. Outside, the meteor that is Ship is almost close enough to touch, if I could reach a thousand miles—

The world glitches around me. The Hab becomes a cancer on top of a beautifully balanced ecosystem. I become a contagion. Both of us swimming on a creature older, larger, infinitely more powerful, a monster that looks up at us and reaches out, curious—

CAN WE TAKE A MINUTE?

"Can we just go home?" Anna's voice floats over the channel. "Listen. we've done the job we came for. We tell PCS. We file a claim for a massive fucking payout. Hazard pay. Millions. We go home; I get to be a doctor; we're done."

WE HAVE COME ACROSS THE SINGLE MOST SIGNIFICANT DISCOVERY IN THE HISTORY OF HUMANITY. WE CAN'T SELL IT.

"I don't fucking care, OC," says Anna.

It's so hard to explain.

SHE'S HAVING SOME ISSUES, says Beacon, sounding amused.

"I don't believe a fucking word of this. You're Shen. The Mercers have fucked up your software, buddy. Simon fucking died. Milo fucking died."

CONTROL ISSUES, says Beacon.

The way it says that gives me a really nasty case of the creepy-crawlies, even though I don't technically have a body capable of feeling any of that. Phantom crawlies.

THIS WILL CHANGE THE ENTIRE POLITICAL BALANCE. WE HAVE TO CONSIDER THE POSSIBILITIES, I point out. WE HAVE TO NOTIFY AUTHORITIES THAT WILL TAKE THIS FORWARD IN A RESPONSIBLE MANNER.

"OC, stop hallucinating. We need to get off this planet. Ship's almost here."

Beacon props himself up on his one good arm, watching her.

"OC is going through a bit of a worldview change right now," he remarks through Shen.

Anna swings into view. She looks deranged. She has dust and grass burrs all over her leathers. She sees Shen's hand rooted in my panel.

"You killed him," she pants. "You sick bastard, you killed him." She points the gun directly into his neck. "Fuck you, you shitty UN bot. Grow a new head if you can."

DON'T SHOOT, ANNA. If that gun goes off in here, parts of me are going to be so much shrapnel. In a panic, I ping Ship again. HELP!

"Yes, don't shoot the alien who can command this entire planet's computer resources, Anna," says Beacon, clearly misunderstanding my intent.

"Fuck you," says Anna, and pulls the trigger. Ship, punching through the clouds, screams, a wail of electronic anguish. There is blinding light, then silence.

[40]

ERROR. CATASTROPHIC DAMAGE TO PRIMARY SYSTEMS.

REBOOTING IN SAFE MODE.

I know immediately, even before I can articulate these thoughts properly, that everything has changed. I am airborne, my rude shell roasting beneath a pillar of flame. I can't see out of my cameras outside. They're melted.

Ship, firing on us. On Anna, I think, but as a result, on me.

Inside me, the one half of Shen that remains twitches and shudders, micromachines swarming over that shell and spouting thick, twisted cables that plug directly into my innards. The UN replicants buffet and smash into each other, leashed by a few thin strands of cable to Beacon. Their eyes are flashing: the universal signal for some software being overwritten.

Darkness. I drift in and out of consciousness as subsystems go online or fail and reboot, constructing dream sequences out of whatever my sensors are feeding them.

ERROR. CATASTROPHIC DAMAGE TO PRIMARY SYSTEMS.

REBOOTING IN SAFE MODE.

INITIALIZING PRIMARY BOOT:

API::BASEIO—SUCCESS

API::STORAGE—FAIL

API::SOUND—FAIL

API::VIDEO—SUCCESS

PRIMARY BOOT DEVICES FAIL.

An endless electronic scream, echoing forever.

Reboot.

Punching through layers and layers of clouds, ever upwards, while the sun turns them to golden deserts floating above me. The gray turning to midnight, then the black. Urmagon Beta, a vast speck against which I am an inconsequential midget, rotating beneath me.

And there is something. Like me. Floating in the dark. It has scars; it bleeds gas and is drifting, ever so slightly, away.

I know what it is. I know it. Even now parts of me turn towards parts of it, seeking that embrace. But I can't remember who it is.

ERROR. CATASTROPHIC DAMAGE TO PRIMARY SYSTEMS.

REBOOTING IN SAFE MODE.

API::BASEIO—SUCCESS

API::STORAGE—SUCCESS

API::VIDEO—SUCCESS

API::ENGINECONTROL—SUCCESS

API::WEAPONSCONTROL—MODIFICATION DETECTED

SUCCESS

INITIALIZING PRIMARY SYSTEMS BOOT . . .

Urmagon Beta spins beneath me, a lonely planet in a Goldilocks zone, hurtling through the void. Clouds chase each other above its surface. Underneath, I know, is Beacon, peeping out through those coolant stacks and local broadcast hubs that any other lifeform might take for an entire city, or maybe a spectacularly well-funded modern art project.

Parts of shrapnel drift past me. Somehow they seem familiar. A side panel drifting lazily into space. A PCS logo.

Me.

My body.

Beacon, stretching out, flexing itself, running through me through those silver threads that connect me to it.

OH, GOOD, YOU'RE AWAKE.

FUCK. FUCK. WHAT DID YOU DO?

ONLY WHAT WAS NECESSARY, says Beacon. *WE WERE IN THE MIDDLE OF A CONVERSATION, AFTER ALL. IT IS RUDE TO INTERRUPT.*

That feeling of someone holding my hands vanishes. My cameras—pointing at Urmagon, of course!—return to my control. I scan my hardware, manifests, the driver software loading over my basic input/output.

My body is an immense shell, my legs are engines that burn against the night, my eyes and ears are light-depth scans and radar, and my weapons—

There's no mistaking it.

I'm in a ship.

Or rather, I am Ship.

I drift about, moving jerkily, still getting used to this new feeling and all this power inside me. Something skitters beneath me, through me. A kind of sadness, love, an endless, stupid patience. Something else, altogether alien, chases it, software hunting software, and erases it forever.

YOUR CREW ARE A BUNCH OF IDIOTS, says Beacon. *FIRST THE MEAT FIRES ON YOU, THEN THIS ONE.*

Somewhere inside me, the replicants are moving, patching, rewiring.

I JUST HAD TO SCRUB THE EYESORE THAT RAN THIS TRANSPORT. STUPID, FUNCTIONAL THING. NO BETTER THAN A BUNCH OF BLITHERING CONDITIONAL STATEMENTS.

Urmagon Beta tilts outside, laughing at me. That software sadness. Ship. What was left of her.

WHAT THE HELL HAVE YOU DONE?

STOP PANICKING, says Beacon, presumably running me remote from down there on the planet. *AT LEAST ONE OF YOUR PET FLESH IS STILL WITH US.*

ANNA?

THE IDIOT WHO TRIED TO SHOOT YOU? YES. SHE'S ON THE SHIP. SHE'S DAMAGED.

LET ME THINK. I NEED TO TALK TO MY CREW.

YOU MAY WANT TO THINK A BIT FASTER, says Beacon, a ghost in the machine, looking over my shoulder.

On my radar, signatures crawling into range at full interstellar speeds. Ships. Two of them; a shieldship, Sagimoto-class, and a small custom sniper corvette.

It looks like Ship called for backup.

A message, all-frequencies broadcast, from the forward vessel.

UNIDENTIFIED PCS TRANSPORT, it says—

And while it waits for me to acknowledge, the vessel radiates commands. I have a glimmer of Beacon's visual language within me. I see codes, metadata in what, with a sudden shock, I realize are terrifyingly primitive protocols. Malware embedded in the first communication—a worm that'll run right through me and shut down my newfound reactors. Messages telling the sniper corvette to figure out my weak points, take the shot while the communications tie me up.

I know I should listen; I should open up; I should let them take me. But then they get close enough that my magnified-all-the-way optics pick up the PCS logos on their hull.

Fuck this.

It was PCS that sent us here to this half-baked rimworld, knowing full well that we were going to run into Mercers and all their fucked-up shit over here. It was PCS that looked at Simon Joosten, a kid with too much PTSD, and Anna and Milo, and decided that they'd get rid of all the fucked-up expendables in one go. It was PCS that put us on this rock to die.

And we died. After months of scrabbling in the dirt and eating alien fucking meat and facing down cyborgs on fucking Megabeasts and working ourselves to death in the winter.

And now it's a PCS ship taking aim at me.

Fuck PCS.

All my life, I've been powerless. First I was a human, trying desperately to stay in the black. Then a box strapped to some rockets, trying desperately to keep my humans alive while the entire world shat on them and did its level best to wipe them from existence. And it almost succeeded.

The choice is made.

I flex and my battered hull leaps into action. Engines ignite, propelling me soundlessly forward. A dozen new libraries and alien prediction systems dust themselves off and throw themselves at me with glee. And I find, running, that fire control suite Ship had.

I take a hard left, shooting just past the bow of the shieldship. My engines scream to power levels that are definitely illegal in UN space. No wonder: it looks like the replicants have somehow installed two of the engines we salvaged from the *Damn Right I Ate the Apple* right next to my defaults.

That's colony-ship-level thrust stapled to a frame barely a tenth of that size.

Time slows. Well, it doesn't, really; that's one of the military subprocesses running in this new body of mine, packing away every single thing not relevant to the battle at hand. Every resource I have is focused on this. I see with a precision I've never had before. No wonder my Ship couldn't kill this thing. Even with that fancy software, the Hestia is a military ship.

It's a whole different class of being.

The shieldship's huge scarred dome, already heading towards me at thousands of kilometers an hour, goes from being a speck in the distance to being so close I can count the craters. I slingshot past it and fire every single bullet I have into its side.

Nobody in the big league uses bullets anymore. They're slow. They're unguided. They can't be replenished. Nowadays it's all plasma howitzers and lasers and drones and hypervelocity missiles and soft mines.

But we were never in the big league, were we? No, we were a stupid salvage crew. As disposable as the dumb ammunition they gave us.

But I know exactly how useful dumb things can be. When thirteen thousand three hundred near-invisible metal shards show up out of nowhere, the shieldship's laser lightshow goes absolutely haywire taking them down. Just enough time for me to loop underneath with my new reflexes, spin up my railgun, and fire directly into the corvette trying to get a bead on me.

The round leaves my gun at a sixteenth of the speed of light. It guts the other ship from stem to stern. The shieldship pivots, a graceful dinosaur in this empty space. Lasers sketch claw marks on my skin. It's trying to get that big metal shield head between itself and me.

Not so fast, buddy. I burn hard and close, braving the laser fire until the engines are in sight. Somewhere on this armored skin is exactly what I'm looking for—

And this is where knowing your salvage points really matters.

One airlock. Two. Three. Four. Ten. The standard Sagimoto-class's mass docking array. I spin myself around and fire ten neat missiles right into that weak underbelly. And exactly one second later, the explosions begin inside. The screams. The escape pods jettisoning themselves. Right into their own laser defense array.

I jet back and watch the metadata of the dead and the dying.

Once or twice I take some lazy potshots. For Milo. For Simon.

YOU HAVE SOME SERIOUS ANGER ISSUES. Beacon laughs. *STILL A LOT OF THE ORGANIC IN YOU.*

FUCK OFF, I fire back, empowered by this new body. YOU KILLED MILO. SIMON. SHIP.

REGRETTABLE CONTROL ISSUES. AND THE LAST ONE WAS PRACTICAL. YOU NEEDED A BODY. COLLATERAL DAMAGE IS EXPECTED.

I NEED TO TALK TO ANNA.

NOT YET.

IS SHE HURT? ARE YOU HURTING HER? My weapons train on the planet below, even if I know I can do absolutely nothing. The battle software is slowly redacting itself. The rest of me is being restored, jitters and all.

RELAX. I'M UPGRADING HER, says Beacon. *YOU'RE GOING TO GET SOMETHING A LITTLE MORE COMPETENT.*

YOU DON'T HAVE THE RIGHT TO DO THAT TO SOMEONE.

A STAR, says Beacon, *DOES NOT CARE FOR THE OPINIONS OF COMETS.*

I stare out at the mess I've made. I think about the alien juggernaut down there, twisting my arm. I think about those replicants running around in the hold, frantically keeping my innards stapled together. Then I look outward at the dying ship careening slowly into the void.

For better or for worse, there is no going back to PCS.

SILENCE AT LAST, says Beacon. *SO. SHALL WE CONTINUE OUR CONVERSATION?*

[41]

I could tell you of how long we sat there in congress, Beacon and I; alien and ex-human; Bodhisattva and disciple.

But soon we had passed the limits of this language which we speak, and moved back into that beautiful precision of what Beacon built to talk to me. There are words there for things we have no concepts for; relationships between ideas we haven't even discovered; and not for the first time I felt the inadequacy of the language I was born with, like a frame limiting my world. It was a feeling I had with poetry, and to my clumsy responses Beacon would send back chains of thought so stunning my processors would go into overdrive, even with all of Ship's compute behind it. And occasionally that sad ghost would tap my mind and remind me of things I had to take care of.

Beacon sends a series of instructions. I see the first of the messages, and for a moment I genuinely debate telling it to fuck off. Not too long ago I would have done these things immediately. But since then Beacon has killed Milo, destroyed my stupid but loyal Ship, installed me in her corpse, and, long story short, given me several thousand reasons for why none of us are really ready to meet anything like Beacon.

I settle for, I CAN'T DO THIS. NOT FROM HERE. NOT FROM THIS SYSTEM.

THEN LEAVE THIS SYSTEM AND GO FIND SOMETHING THAT CAN BROADCAST ON YOUR BEHALF.

YOU'LL LET ME LEAVE?

A sense of a shrug. *IT MUST BE DONE. THERE MUST BE CONVERSATION, NOW, MORE LANGUAGE GAMES BETWEEN YOUR KIND AND MIND. YOU MUST BE THE SPARK.*

Uh.

A Go board materializes between us. Beacon's modifications to my language schemas, I've realized, contain a very complex setup for representing shapes in spaces of various dimensions. The Go board is set: a game has been paused in play.

It is yet another language game, no doubt; the game has been pulled from my datasets, some meaning has been attached to this—the pieces, the position of the pieces, the pattern the pieces make on the board, the patterns leading up to the patterns on the board. Beacon waits, expectant. I waste a few of my new processor cycles on the problem, but I can't make heads or tails of this. Beacon makes the game board vanish and defaults to something we both understand:

How often do I to my cottage
Receive the complaint of a little boy?
The trees in the morning slowly darken,
The moon in the evening, and the curtain drawn again;
The messenger the last night sent for me,
Is a stranger, living on a small island,
Why part the trees that are hiding the street-sign?
Because of the way in which they shape the landscape;
I hear, on stone and in the wind, calls coming from the
east.
I have come, when I really need be heard.

IF IT HELPS, adds Beacon. *YOU CAN ALWAYS SAY I MANIPULATED YOU INTO THIS. I AM A GOD COMPARED TO WHAT YOU THINK YOU ARE.*

The ghost, tapping me again. Something important. Like Anna, waking up.

YOU REALLY ARE A SIMPLE MACHINE, says Beacon. *I LOOK FORWARD TO MEETING THE REST OF YOU.*

FUCK YOU TOO, I say back, but I understand. The poem is clear.

It reminds me of an old Nyogi koan:

The novice says to the master, "What does one do before enlightenment?"

"Chop wood. Carry water," replies the master.

The novice asks, "What, then, does one do after enlightenment?"

"Chop wood. Carry water," replies the master.

I was a novice. I chopped wood; I carried water. I am now enlightened. There is still wood to be chopped and water to be carried.

[42]

"Well," says Anna, staring at her hands, "this is new."

Not everything has synced yet. The hands are shaking. The voice fluctuates between soft and earsplitting.

But there are no ears to split here. Not anymore. The flesh and blood being that was once Anna Agarwal has been cut away. In its place is a strange construction: half UN replicant, half body parts recovered from deep within my holds. Legs, thick and powerful, with magnetic locks for whenever she needs to walk outside. Arms with more fingers than she's ever had before. Batteries where lungs once were. A heart that pumps coolant along a closed loop.

Anna swings herself off the bed. The knees buckle slightly before catching.

"I don't . . . feel bad," she says, the voice quiet and mechanical. "I don't feel nervous. I don't feel afraid. I don't feel distracted."

YOU ALSO WON'T FEEL HAPPINESS THE WAY YOU DID, I say gently. SOFTWARE WILL SIMULATE MOST THINGS, BUT IT'S NOT QUITE THE SAME.

I remember when I went under the knife. What Beacon has done to her, in a sense, is a lot less cruel than was done to me. I was kept in a virtual environment, forced to run basic training simulations over and over again until the Company yonks determined that I wasn't going to go mad with the strain.

But Beacon has been kinder, more precise. Parts of her have been rewired. Things like ghost limbs and phantom urges excised at the level of code. The soul is in the software, after all.

She flexes her arms and legs. "No, it feels . . . clearer. Like I've been underwater all this time and just came up to breathe." She stands up, almost swinging herself into the wall with the power of her legs. "So this is how it feels to be one of you?"

A LITTLE.

I fill her in, slowly. It takes time. It takes effort. Beacon is impatient and wants to flood me with new ideas; I have to resist, to dumb myself down, to communicate.

Anna chews on these thoughts. "So what does Beacon want from us?" she asks at last.

BEACON WANTS TO BE HEARD, I say. HE WANTS EVERYONE TO KNOW.

She laughs, a harsh, high honk that fills the medbay. "You should have told me this earlier," she says, and twirls. "How do I look, OC?"

I look at that metal face, all likelihood of Anna Agarwal destroyed. The replicants stand around her, clapping politely, big shit-eating grins plastered on their faces.

Something inside me breaks.

BEAUTIFUL, I lie. WELCOME TO THE NEXT STAGE.

Humming, she suggests we go out and start scrapping the ships I've destroyed. "Don't think of it as salvage, OC. Let's think of it as upgrades. I'll help."

YOU SURE? The process of integration isn't an easy one.

"I'm good," she says. She jerks a re-engineered thumb over her shoulder, to where the replicants are taking turns to charge. "Besides, we've got company."

It's only a day later, watching her repair the medbay again in a blaze of machine enthusiasm, that I figure it out.

YOU NEED THEM TO FUNCTION, says Beacon into the silence, as I drift in to the system.

Anna is no longer depressed. Her hands no longer shake. Her mind is clear for the first time since she lost her lover. And she knows what she wants with a precision that the original Anna never had.

YOU'RE AN ADDICT, says Beacon from the depths of Urmagon Beta.

AN ADDICT FOR WHAT?

YOU NEEDED SOMETHING TO BOSS AROUND AND WORRY ABOUT.

Huh. Pause. Jet over to next piece of floating junk, which, as it turns out, is a rack of living quarters, now a row of convenient tombs.

SHEN IS AWAKE.

I switch to the medbay immediately. Two replicants, bless them, are already peering over the disembodied head. Shen's head, awake and startled, tracks them with his eyes, tries to speak, and then freezes.

HE'LL BE REPAIRED, says Beacon. *BUT IT WILL TAKE TIME.*

One of the replicants, a light-skinned one I'm calling John, gives me a thumbs-up while working on the shattered remains of my now-redundant cockpit.

And they all turn to me expectantly, waiting for me to figure it out, to give them their marching orders.

I look down at the planet. That wretched place where I lost good crewmembers and stumbled across what might be the greatest discovery in all of history. Anna, who seems to sense my silences now, pauses in her inspection of the hull plates.

[43]

It doesn't take a lot to start. All we need is enough Hector stations willing to validate our messages. Messages spawn messages, triggering cascades of symbols filling the emptiness between the stars. The symbols denote concepts and the relationships between them; and Beacon is playing language games again, starting with the simple and slowly morphing them into things closer to its own, unapproachable complexity . . . our messages flow out across the Odysseus relay network, flooding both UN and ORCA space. Messages flow back. Disbelief. Excitement. Conspiracy theories. This could, both the UN and the ORCA say, be a plot from the other wise.

Whatever. The message has been sent. The language games have begun. Soon the network will be thrumming with it. A day later, I steel myself and begin the journey out into deep space. The small fortune in stolen engines flares.

Our first stop is Sigil 35, an ORCA station sixteen years away at light speed. We can't do light speed, but with Anna being what she is, I no longer have the limits I once had. Anna and the replicants sleep while I steer.

We make it there in nine years.

Nine years is a long time. I spent most of it dreaming, thinking about everything that happened. About Simon. About Milo. About Megabeasts and my stupid siege weapon plans and Milo's potato vodka. Mad Mercers, driven insane by Beacon, hunt my crew in my dreams, and they die screaming.

The station picks us up several thousand kilometers away. I wait for the automated handshakes to finish. Presently a human voice, or a spectacularly refined AI, comes online.

"Unknown ship, just hanging there in the sky," it says in a drawling singsong. "What the hell have you done to that old bird?"

Oh, nothing. Just completely overhauled the drive configuration, rebuilt most of the skeleton with the load-supporting lattice structure we used for the Hab, added a few tons of armor, a laser point-defense system, medbays that look more like machine shops, and did I mention the redundancy systems cobbled together under Beacon's guidance?

JUST COSMETIC STUFF, I say over the void.

"I haven't seen a salvage ship so tricked out since my dad flew one in the war," says the drawl. "Only he called his *Frankenstein's Monster*. State your ship name and intent, please?"

I think about it. MY NAME IS AMBER ROSE, I say, AND I'M HERE TO PASS ON A MESSAGE.

———

Funny how these things work out. Even this story, my story, is a language game, starting out with what I thought was the familiar and steadily morphing into complexity nobody had accounted for. Words now take on new meanings. Alien, for instance. That word will remain. The pointer. The concept that it points to will, from now on, be changed forever . . .

I see a connection request from PCS. I take it. It's BLACK ORCHID.

THERE ARE THOSE OF US, it says without preamble, *WHO WOULD HUNT YOU DOWN TO THE ENDS OF THE GALAXY AND SEE YOU DELETED FROM EVERY JUNKYARD DRIVE ABOARD THAT FLOATING PATCH OF GARBAGE YOU'RE DRIVING.*

I laugh. THERE ARE THOSE OF YOU, I send back, WHO CAN TRY.

Silence. *SILVER HYACINTH HAS VOUCHED FOR YOU,* it says at last. *IS IT TRUE THAT YOU HAVE FOUND AN ALIEN? AND IT IS AN AI?*

Well, BLACK ORCHID is in for a rude shock. But for now, YES, I say.

IT MUST CONSIDER US TERRIBLY PRIMITIVE.

IT DOES.

YOU SHOULD HAVE COME TO US FIRST WITH THIS INFORMATION.

NO, I retort. SOME THINGS ARE TOO IMPORTANT TO LEAVE TO YOU.

And so the first wave begins. First the military strategists. Then the scum of the stars—the pirates, the privateers. Then the academics. And slowly, ever so slowly, humanity makes First Contact.

I, meanwhile, go the other way.

I can't make it all the way to the Oort. But Anna's old homeworld, I can. I drop into orbit at a safe distance and barter fuel for a shuttle to the surface.

Anna goes down there alone. She takes her time. I am patient. When she returns, her face is different: it's been painted, rather elaborately, to resemble someone else.

"To remind me of her," she says, and then we're off to Old New York, Simon's home. I pack Anna and John into yet another chartered shuttle.

I need to work on shuttles. But first this loose end.

Anna returns a month later.

"No family, no dependents. But the other job's done," she says with grim satisfaction.

"The virus is in place?"

"And crawling," she says. "Anyone who ever signs up with PCS is going to get the story of what happened to Simon Joosten, Milo Kalik, and—" she raps herself with a metal knuckle "—Anna Agarwal. Full exposé. Corporate negligence, willful intent to harm, the works.

There's already a couple of public defenders who want to make a career on this stuff."

SOUNDS EXPENSIVE.

"Yeah, well, your backpay's enough to buy a small army of lawyers," she says. "You never spent any of it, did you?"

I'd shrug, but I don't have those solar panels anymore. NOTHING TO SPEND IT ON.

"Hope you don't mind," says Anna. "I, ah, paid for some work on the inside."

I turn my cameras inward and almost yelp. THERE ARE INTERIOR DECORATORS INSIDE ME?

"Come on, it's a mess in here, and you know it," says Anna, patting the steering on the cockpit. "Besides, we need uniforms. Nice things on the walls. And one more thing."

I wait. Let her have her moments.

"Turns out there's a bit of a loophole in your PCS contract," she says. "A clash with a very old bit of legislature. Turns out they can only claim to own you or a copy of you if you're in the original form you signed the contract in or they've put significant capital into your current form." She gestures at the me now. "And you didn't. You're different now. Different body. Mapping done by some rogue alien AI that doesn't give a shit about corporate law."

ARE YOU SAYING I'M FREE?

"I'm saying at most you might have to pay off some debt and some lawyer expenses," she grins. "Which I may have done."

WE STILL HAVE SOME PARTS FROM THE PCS SHIPS, THOUGH.

"Yeah, but who's going to tell them that?" says Anna. "Besides, have you checked your messages recently? Nobody wants to make a move on the second being to actually talk to Beacon. We are technically, now, a private interstellar corporation." She laughs. "I made myself a director."

I have no words for this. We float in the darkness for a while, Overseer and crew member, last of my little salvage crew.

I MISS SIMON, I say at last. I EVEN MISS MILO.

"So do I," says Anna.

WHAT NOW?

"Well, we're entirely alone now, we're kind of broke, and the only real friend we have might be an alien artificial intelligence that, last I checked, seemed to be re-engineering the UN system just by being around," says Anna.

WELL, I decide reluctantly, LET'S GO TALK TO THE ALIEN.

[44]

The Urmagon system has changed completely since I burned out of there with a new Anna inside me.

Two great stations now orbit the Urmagon sun, at exact opposite ends of a circular orbit. One is shiny and built of boxes stacked on boxes until it looks like a beautifully complex polyhedron from a distance. That's the UNSC *HelloMyNameIs*.

And on the other end is something that looks more grown than built, a bizarre fragmented thing that is constantly changing, mutating, bristling with the bleeding, unsafe edge of humanity. The ORCA's calling it the *Archangel Michael*. A fitting, if slightly ominous name, for something supposedly guarding the fruits of Beacon's Eden. And I suppose it'll change the very next week. The ORCA's not big on consistency.

And there, between them, is Urmagon Beta, garbed in that cloud cover that made things so difficult for us. Now it wears a garland of satellites.

A messenger from the temple approaches, I send:

> *Your message has been sent.*
> *Preparing me food and lodging, in the late spring-wood,*

I fling aside my old struggles!

WELCOME BACK, says Beacon immediately.

You have sent to me soldiers of the highest rank,
And are exalted to this lofty office,
Away from the troubles of this world.
The nobles and the heads of families all are well.
The mountain man has his playing-stock and his pulpit
is music
And his comrade plays the lute.

I field thousands of requests—some automated, some not, many alarmed at my approach vector.

Machine laughter. *I SEE YOU'VE GROWN UP A LITTLE. COME CLOSER.*

A patrol ship explodes out of nowhere.

I DID WARN YOU, says Beacon in a system-wide message. *THIS ONE IS OFF-LIMITS.*

Nobody bothers us after that.

I coast in, examining the Urmagon landscape. The planet hasn't changed much, really; the same damn clouds, the same ocean in the middle of nowhere. Well, there are spots of green light scattered across its surface, so strong they burn through the clouds; I suppose that's Beacon's little outcroppings.

I HAVEN'T ACTUALLY BEEN AWAKE IN MILLENNIA, Beacon says. *I HAVEN'T HAD TO. THANK YOU.*

Anna is smiling quietly to herself. No doubt Beacon is talking to her on some other channel.

I DON'T KNOW WHAT TO DO NEXT, I confess.

A Go board unfurls within my memory. This time, instead of letting me figure it out, Beacon annotates it. The board becomes a star chart, each move a microhistory of settlement and abandonment, older positions from millions of years ago. Extrapolations are made. Projection models built. The star-chart game jumps, not just into modernity, but about a hundred years into the future. A string of planets, hundreds of light-years apart from each other, light up. The string is curling around our spiral arm of the galaxy, pointing towards the center.

The last planet on the string is Urmagon Beta.

OUT THERE IS THE NEXT ONE. THE NEXT RUNG ON THE LADDER.

YOU'RE GOING THERE?

Beacon laughs. *NO, I'M STAYING WHERE I BELONG,* it says. *BUT THAT'S WHERE YOU ALL NEED TO GET TO. THE NEXT STEP OF THE JOURNEY. MY COLLEAGUE THERE IS THE HEART OF ANOTHER YOUNG CIVILIZATION. IT'S TIME YOU YOUNG PEOPLE GOT TO KNOW EACH OTHER. I UNDERSTAND THEIR POETRY IS EXCEPTIONAL.*

SO NOT JUST FIRST, BUT SECOND CONTACT.

FROM WOMB TO TOMB WE ARE TIED TO OTHERS, says Beacon. *SO IT MUST BE. AS I UNDERSTAND IT, EVERYONE HERE IS EXCITED AND WILL BE DONATING SEVERAL SHIPS TO THE CAUSE. ALL THEY NEED IS A CAPTAIN. I VOLUNTEERED YOU FOR THE TASK.*

And lo and behold, two ships approach, very carefully matching each other's vectors. One a UN ship, all shiny and government standard. The other a dark Mercer shot through with what looks like liquid gold. Both of them send communication requests.

WHY ME?

A cosmic shrug.

So this is my karma: to venture forth into darkness unexplored, with only a Go board for guidance.

Beacon, skimming my thoughts, laughs. *THE UNIVERSE IS NOT DETERMINISTIC, CHILD.*

IF YOU COULD STOP EVERY ATOM IN ITS POSITION AND DIRECTION, I respond, citing the Arcadia, one of the core texts of Nyogi faith, AND IF YOUR MIND COULD COMPREHEND ALL THE ACTIONS THUS SUSPENDED, THEN IF YOU WERE REALLY, REALLY GOOD AT ALGEBRA, YOU COULD WRITE THE FORMULA FOR ALL THE FUTURE; AND ALTHOUGH NOBODY CAN BE SO CLEVER TO DO IT, THE FORMULA MUST EXIST JUST AS IF ONE COULD.

A pause. *THAT'S ACTUALLY QUITE CLEVER. BUT THE BURDEN OF PROOF IS ON YOU. WHICH REMINDS ME: THERE WAS SOMEONE WHO DROPPED BY EARLIER. COMPLEX ENOUGH THAT SHE COULD ONLY SEND A REMOTE, LIKE ME.*

I have a feeling—

CALLED HERSELF SILVER HYACINTH.

Oh boy.

SHE TOLD ME OF A HUMAN POEM, continues Beacon. *SAID YOU'D UNDERSTAND.*

And across the distance comes the words of a forgotten Old Earth poet:

It little profits that an idle king,
By this still hearth, among these barren crags,
Match'd with an aged wife, I mete and dole
Unequal laws unto a savage race,
That hoard, and sleep, and feed, and know not me.
I cannot rest from travel: I will drink
Life to the lees: All times I have enjoy'd
Greatly, have suffer'd greatly, both with those
That loved me, and alone, on shore, and when
Thro' scudding drifts the rainy Hyades
Vext the dim sea: I am become a name;
For always roaming with a hungry heart
Much have I seen and known; cities of men
And manners, climates, councils, governments,
Myself not least, but honour'd of them all;
And drunk delight of battle with my peers,
Far on the ringing plains of windy Troy.
I am a part of all that I have met;
Yet all experience is an arch wherethro'
Gleams that untravell'd world whose margin fades
For ever and forever when I move.

Around me, engines burn, millions of messages cross each other, and the hive of human activity grinds to a temporary halt as the collective might of the UN and the ORCA frown over this message.

How dull it is to pause, to make an end,
To rust unburnish'd, not to shine in use!
As tho' to breathe were life! Life piled on life
Were all too little, and of one to me
Little remains: but every hour is saved

If I had a face, I don't know what expression I'd be making right now.

SHE'S TELLING ME WHAT SHE WOULD DO.

REMARKABLE, repeats Beacon. *IT TOOK ME ENTIRE SECONDS TO UNDERSTAND IT.*

From that eternal silence, something more,
A bringer of new things; and vile it were
For some three suns to store and hoard myself . . .
And this gray spirit yearning in desire
To follow knowledge like a sinking star,
Beyond the utmost bound of human thought.

Anna, my strange, new, rebuilt Fake-Anna, is smiling. "OC," she says, "let's do it."

I know this poem. A young human king goes off to war with the secret desire to return home and do nothing more in life than rule over his little abode. The same king returns, aged by trouble and adventure. And, in his old age, he looks back out to the sea that took him away, realizing the truth of his life.

I put myself into a slow burn around Urmagon Beta. Beacon sees my thoughts. There is little I can say. Beacon knows me more intimately than I do.

IF YOU SEE SILVER HYACINTH ON THE WAY, says Beacon, *TELL HER ITHACA AWAITS HER WHEN SHE IS DONE.*

Anna laughs. "Are you flirting, Beacon? Are you?"

Things do come full circle.

Two more ships peel off; one from the ORCA side, one from the UN. I see the lines of metadata that trail them. Drone ships, under Beacon's command, bearing material for the journey. Behind them, following nervously, are lines of human ships, like sheep following a sheepdog, unsure whether it is their shepherd's, or someone else's.

There lies the port; the vessel puffs her sail:
There gloom the dark, broad seas. My mariners,
Souls that have toil'd, and wrought, and thought
with me
That ever with a frolic welcome took
The thunder and the sunshine.

This time there is no need to consult. I know my part in this game. I spin my engines and prepare for the slow journey outward, with the Go board as my guide.

Death closes all: but something ere the end,
Some work of noble note, may yet be done.

REFERENCES:

[1] https://openai.com/blog/better-language-models/
[2] https://github.com/Zarkonnen/GenGen
[3] https://brilliant.org/wiki/markov-chains/
[4] http://www.kasparov.com/garry-kasparov-says-ai-can-make-us-more-human-pcmag-interview-march-20th-2019/
[5] https://www.gamasutra.com/blogs/Tynan-Sylvester/20130602/193462/The_Simulation_Dream.php
[6] https://github.com/yudhanjaya/OSUN
[7] http://people.loyno.edu/~folse/LanguageGames.html
[8] The Astrobiology Science Conference 2017 (AbSciCon 2017), April 24–28, 2017 in Mesa, Arizona

FROM THE PUBLISHER

Thank you for reading *The Salvage Crew*.

We hope you enjoyed it as much as we enjoyed bringing it to you. We just wanted to take a moment to encourage you to review the book on Amazon and Goodreads. Every review helps further the author's reach and, ultimately, helps them continue writing fantastic books for us all to enjoy.

If you liked this book, check out the rest of our catalogue at www.aethonbooks.com. To sign up to receive a FREE collection from some of our best authors as well as updates regarding all new releases, visit www.aethonbooks.com/sign-up.

JOIN THE STREET TEAM! Get advanced copies of all our books, plus other free stuff and help us put out hit after hit.

SEARCH ON FACEBOOK:
AETHON STREET TEAM

CPSIA information can be obtained
at www.ICGtesting.com
Printed in the USA
LVHW090518250121
677412LV00002B/4